THE QUEEN'S BALL

THE QUEEN'S BALL

Anthea Lawson
Rebecca Connolly
Jennifer Moore

Mirror Press

Interior Design by Cora Johnson
Edited by Jennie Stevens, Kristy Stewart, Hopey Gardner, and Lisa Shepherd
Cover design by Rachael Anderson
Cover Photo Credit: Richard Jenkins Photography

Published by Mirror Press, LLC

ISBN: 978-1-947152-86-1

Timeless Victorian Collections

Summer Holiday
A Grand Tour
The Orient Express
The Queen's Ball
A Note of Change

Timeless Regency Collections

Autumn Masquerade
A Midwinter Ball
Spring in Hyde Park
Summer House Party
A Country Christmas
A Season in London
Falling for a Duke
A Night in Grosvenor Square
Road to Gretna Green
Wedding Wagers
An Evening at Almack's
A Week in Brighton
To Love a Governess
Widows of Somerset

Table of Contents

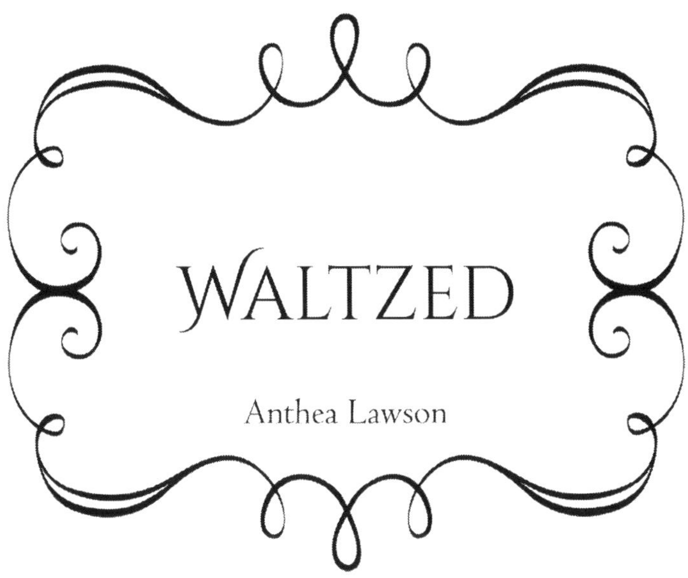

WALTZED

Anthea Lawson

Chapter 1

London, May 1851

THE SOFT GRAY DRIZZLE of an English spring coated the half-open buds of the rhododendron flowers in the garden and glazed the windows of the late Viscount Tremont's townhouse. However, his only daughter, Eleanor, was oblivious to the rain or the wet flowers or the chill in the library despite the coals on the hearth.

She had a thick woolen shawl tucked about her shoulders and was deeply engrossed in the adventures of David Copperfield. Like the hero of Dickens's latest novel, she, too, had known happiness as a child. And had subsequently been the unfortunate recipient of a stepfamily who was, as one might put it, less than kind.

"Ellie!" Her stepsister Abigail burst into the library. "Whatever are you doing in here?"

"Reading," Ellie said, marking the page number in her mind with a silent sigh. She knew from experience that she would not return to her novel any time soon.

Abigail tended to overexcitement, as redheads often did. Thankfully, she was not as spiteful as her older sister, especially when she and Ellie were alone. But whenever one of Ellie's stepsisters caught her reading, they found some reason to interrupt her—usually to put her to work.

"You must hurry up to your room," Abby said. "Your hair looks dreadful."

With some effort, Ellie kept herself from reaching to pat the bun at the back of her head. No doubt it was a bit messy, but she'd learned that any sign of weakness in front of her stepsiblings—or worse, her stepmother—would result in heapings of scorn.

"I'm not overly troubled about the state of my hair," she said. "After all, it's only me and Mr. Dickens." She lifted her book in emphasis.

Perhaps, this once, Abby would not insist that Ellie come untangle her hair ribbons or polish her jewelry or any of a thousand annoying little tasks, and Ellie might return to her novel in peace.

Abby made an exasperated noise. "But that's just it. You have a caller!"

"I what?" That was unexpected. Ellie never had callers. With a prickle of interest, she closed her book and laid it on the side table.

Was this a cruel trick or was Abby telling the truth? Her other stepsister, Delia, would certainly enjoy raising Ellie's hopes. It would be like her to send Ellie hurrying to her room to make herself presentable, then laughing when she entered the empty parlor to find no one awaiting her after all.

"I've been trying to tell you." Abby crossed her arms. "Why don't you ever listen? No wonder Mama is always displeased with you."

Privately, Ellie thought the source of that displeasure had more to do with her existence as the late viscount's only child and the discovery that Papa had apparently left a much smaller fortune than expected upon his death. Not enough to keep a viscountess and her daughters in any kind of style, as her stepmother often reminded her—as if it were Ellie's fault that her father had not, in fact, been as well-off as they had all thought.

Oh, Papa.

Tears threatened to clog her throat, and she swallowed them back.

"Hurry!" Abby said, tapping her foot. "You oughtn't keep him waiting too long."

"Who is it?"

"A gentleman—I didn't recognize him."

"And he asked for me?" Perhaps it had something to do with Papa's estate, although any solicitor would call upon her stepmother and not Ellie. And besides, all that had been settled months ago.

"I heard him ask for you specifically," Abby said, a hint of contempt in her voice. "But if you'd rather not believe me and prefer to make a fool of yourself . . ."

"Very well," Ellie said. "Tell Mr. Atkins—"

"Miss Eleanor," the butler said from the threshold, as if summoned by the mention of his name. "You have a caller. I've put him in the front parlor."

Abby shot her a scathing look. "I don't know why I even bother with you, Ellie."

With that, she tossed her head and whisked out of the room, nearly running over the portly Mr. Atkins in the process.

He hastily stood aside, then nodded at Ellie. "I'll tell Lord Newland you'll be down shortly?"

"Please do."

She'd no notion who Lord Newland might be, unless he were somehow related to the Newland family she'd known several years ago. Papa and Mr. Newland had been fast friends until the family had left for India. She'd exchanged letters with Kit, the son, for nearly two years until their correspondence trailed off into silence.

In truth, for quite a while she'd cherished notions of marrying the black-haired boy who'd been such a merry companion in her youth. Even after they'd removed to India, she spent time reading about the country and daydreaming about living in that bright and exotic land, Kit at her side.

Then Papa had remarried Lady Tremont, which had been somewhat trying. Not much later, he'd died, and nothing mattered anymore—except battling through the fog of grief surrounding her. And running to do her stepfamily's bidding, which only amplified her misery.

As soon as the butler left the library, Ellie glanced at her reflection in the mirror over the mantel. Oh dear—Abby had been correct. Her pale hair was straggling out of her bun, a hairpin hanging from one of the fine strands like some strange spider over her shoulder.

There was a smudge of soot on her cheekbone, ashy against the pallor of her complexion. She glanced down at her wrist to see a matching smear from where she must have brushed against the hearth when she'd poked up the coals. She certainly couldn't meet her mysterious caller in such a state of dishevelment.

Quietly, she peeked into the corridor. It was empty, thank goodness. Luck was with her, and she encountered no one as she hurried down to the end and nipped up the servants' staircase. She really oughtn't to use the smaller stairs, but it was a much faster—and more discreet—method of gaining her room than using the main staircase.

Far less chance of encountering her stepfamily on the way as well. Ever since Papa's death, it was easier to avoid them rather than bear their spite. The few times she'd encountered maids in the stairwell, they'd stood respectfully aside. Ellie pretended not to see the pity in their eyes or hear them whispering about how dreadful it all was.

Back in her room, she washed her face and repinned her bun, taking care to tuck away the loose strands. There was no time to change her gown—and at any rate, she had nothing but dreary mourning dresses crowding her wardrobe. Whoever was calling upon her must take her as she was.

Chapter 2

LORD CHRISTOPHER NEWLAND TUGGED up the collar of his coat and tried to ignore the clammy chill seeping into his bones. England was ridiculously cold, even in May. In Assam, it was already hot, all the winter clothing was packed away and the monsoon season was already on the horizon. He'd forgotten how chilly his homeland was. And damp. He turned to stare absently out the rain-spattered window of Viscount Tremont's parlor.

The late Viscount Tremont, that was. Christopher was sorry he'd not returned to England in time to call upon the man while he was alive. He had recollections of a rotund, jovial fellow who had always treated him kindly, even when he and the viscount's daughter, Eleanor, got into scrapes together. Which was often.

But at least he might pay his respects to Ellie. He was glad of the excuse to see her—and not only because he planned to return to India with a wife. He'd always been fond of his childhood companion and hoped she might still harbor some warmth toward him, despite the passage of time.

"Kit?"

He turned, recognizing Ellie's voice immediately, and the smile of greeting on his lips died. She looked dreadful.

Of course, it had been nearly six years since he'd seen her—but this pale young woman with bruised-looking eyes was a far cry from his memories of golden, laughing Eleanor Tremont.

He strode forward and took her hand, noting how very white her fingers were against his sun-browned skin. "Yes, it's me. It's so good to see you, Ellie, though I was sorry to hear of your father's passing. Are you well?"

Clearly, she was not, but he didn't know what else to say. Although her father had been gone for over seven months, she was still garbed in mourning. The black crepe of her dress made her pallor even more pronounced, and his heart squeezed in his chest to see the unhappiness in her eyes.

She cast her gaze to the carpet and carefully removed her hand from his.

"I am well enough, considering. Thank you." She waved to a pair of armchairs. "Would you like to sit? I can ring for tea."

"I can't stay." And honestly, he wasn't sure he wanted to. This sad young lady was not the girl he'd been hoping to see. "I just came by to offer my respects."

It had been foolish to expect to find the sunny companion of his youth, especially given the circumstances. A young woman plunged deep in mourning was hardly a suitable candidate for matrimony. With regret, he mentally crossed her name off the top of his list.

The charming, adventurous Ellie Tremont—the girl who might have accepted his suit and gladly accompanied him to India—was gone.

"Ellie!" A stern-looking woman with gray-shot dark hair stepped into the room. She, too, was dressed in mourning, but the severe black and white suited her. "Whatever are you doing, entertaining a gentleman caller alone? I thought you were better bred than that."

A flush rose in Ellie's cheeks, two spots of color that quickly faded.

"I am sorry, my lady." She bobbed an apologetic curtsy. "I was about to ring for the maid. Allow me to introduce Mr. Christopher Newland. We knew each other as children. Or, wait, is it Lord now?"

"Yes—now that my father is, rather unexpectedly, the new Marquess of Kennewick." He gave her a gentle smile.

Luckily, his older brother—who'd never liked India and preferred to remain in England—would inherit the burden of that title. Still, their father and mother would have to return to London for a time, leaving Kit in charge of their interests in Manohari.

Which was why time was of the essence. He must find an agreeable wife and make the journey back to India before the heaviest rains set in, rendering travel nigh impossible.

"A pleasure to meet you, my lord." The widow extended her hand so that Kit could bow over it. "I am Lady Tremont. I must apologize for whatever poor welcome Eleanor might have given you. This household is usually better mannered than that."

Despite his irritation at Lady Tremont's rudeness toward his old friend, Kit dipped his head. "Mourning can be a difficult time. I understand completely. It's a pleasure to meet you, Lady Tremont, and do forgive me for intruding. However, I must be off."

The viscountess gripped his hand, allowing him no retreat. "Certainly not. You must meet my daughters before you go." She turned to Ellie, her voice hardening. "Go fetch your stepsisters. At once."

As if she were nothing more than a servant, Ellie nodded and hurried from the room. Brows furrowed, Kit watched her go. Something did not seem right in the Tremont household.

Paying no attention to his reaction, Lady Tremont pulled him over to the settee and all but forced him down beside her.

"Tell me about yourself, Lord Christopher. How you are acquainted with the Tremont family?"

There was an avaricious light in her eyes, but Kit had dealt with grasping mamas before—particularly since his father had inherited the title. He explained to Lady Tremont the scholarly bond between his and Ellie's fathers and how the two families would often visit one another with their children in tow—especially after Ellie's mother died.

"Then you see her as somewhat of a sister, I imagine," Lady Tremont said, a complacent note in her voice. "How kind of you to call upon her. As you can see, her father's death has affected us all terribly. Luckily, my fortune is large enough to sustain us in comfort. Alas, poor Ellie has no dowry."

He frowned at her words, and not only because it was tasteless to bring money into a conversation with a new acquaintance. Without a marriage portion, Ellie was now doubly disqualified from his list of prospective brides. While he did not need an heiress per se, it was essential he marry a girl with a sizeable dowry.

"I'm sorry to hear that," he said.

Indeed, it was surprising news. Despite his somewhat eccentric nature, Viscount Tremont had always seemed sensible about managing his estate. It must have been a blow to Ellie to discover she had no dowry. No wonder she seemed so downcast.

Lady Tremont leaned forward. "If your families were such great friends, why have we not met you before?"

"My father accepted a position with the East India Company. When I graduated from Eton, I joined him in Assam."

And a happy change that had been. In addition to finding India quite to his tastes, Kit had discovered a talent for organization that was indispensable as he helped his father with various ventures. The most recent, a tea plantation in the fertile highlands, promised to be a rousing success once the bushes were ready for harvest.

But with his father unexpectedly inheriting a marquessate, the management of the plantation was now in Kit's hands. He took that responsibility quite seriously—and not only because it would make or break their fortunes abroad.

A commotion at the doorway served as a welcome distraction from Lady Tremont's interrogation. Kit rose as two young women—presumably the widow's daughters—entered the room. Ellie trailed behind them, a pale shadow.

"My darlings." Lady Tremont stood and held out her hands. "Come meet our distinguished guest, Lord Christopher Newland."

Her daughters joined her, one on each side. Neither of them were in mourning. In fact, they each wore bright colors that seemed to relegate Ellie to the background even more.

The girl to Lady Tremont's left sported a yellow-green gown that accentuated her red hair—natural red, not stained with henna, as Kit was used to seeing. She gave him a curious look, her brown eyes wide with interest.

The other daughter wore bright blue and was dark-haired, like her mother, with the same disdainful tilt to her nose. And the same appraising expression, as though weighing Kit's value to determine whether he might be advantageous to her in some way.

"This is my eldest, Delia," Lady Tremont said, nodding to the dark-haired girl.

Delia curtsied low, clearly deciding he was worthy of her favor. "A pleasure to meet you, my lord."

Lady Tremont indicated the redhead. "And my other daughter, Abigail."

"A tremendous honor, indeed." Abigail dropped him an

even deeper curtsy, then shot her sister a gloating look, as though it had been a contest of some kind and she'd emerged the victor.

"Charmed to meet you both," Kit said. "I hope in the future I might become better acquainted, but, regrettably, I must bid you farewell. I've an appointment with my father's solicitor."

Which was true—although the meeting wasn't for some hours yet. But this visit had taken an uncomfortable turn into marriage mart territory, and he had no intention of adding Ellie's stepsisters to his mental list of prospective brides.

"Oh, I'm so sorry to hear that, my lord." Redheaded Abigail fluttered her lashes at him.

"Indeed." Lady Tremont's tone was dry. "As you're a long-standing friend of Ellie's, we'd be delighted to further our acquaintance. When might we expect you to call again?"

He glanced at Ellie, who stood a pace behind her stepmother. While he had little interest in getting to know the other girls, his conscience gave a twinge at the obvious unhappiness in her eyes. She needed friends, and it seemed clear there was not an overabundance of warmth between her and her stepfamily.

She glanced up at him, and he thought he detected a hint of entreaty in her expression.

"The day after tomorrow?" he asked, somewhat impetuously. It was only for old time's sake, of course. One more visit, and his duty would be discharged.

"That would be lovely," the widow said. "We shall look for you in the afternoon. And would you stay to dinner?"

"Please say yes." Dark-haired Delia stepped forward. "I would simply *adore* hearing of your travels abroad."

"Indeed." Abigail nodded vigorously and moved up beside her sister. "I've no doubt they're utterly fascinating."

Behind her stepsisters' backs, Ellie's brows rose, and she gave him the slanting look he recalled from childhood—the one that meant trouble lay ahead. Her face was transformed: a twinkle of mischief in her eye, the slightest lift to her lips. It was a welcome change, and he didn't mind that it was at his expense.

"I would be delighted to dine with you," he said.

It seemed he was willing to endure what promised to be a dinner full of dreadful attempts at flirtation if it would banish the shadows from Eleanor Tremont's eyes. *Only because we are long-standing friends*, he told himself.

And while he searched for a suitable bride, he could spare an afternoon to make Ellie smile. Happily, his father and mother were in good health, but he could imagine the devastation he'd feel if one of them passed. Poor Ellie had lost not one, but both of her parents.

"Splendid," Lady Tremont said. "We shall expect you at five o'clock on Thursday."

"Thank you for visiting," Ellie said, finally moving forward to face him. "It was good to see you again."

"Of course." He smiled at her.

"We mustn't keep you, my lord," Lady Tremont said briskly. "Allow me to see you out."

She stepped in front of Ellie, took his arm, and steered him toward the door. Ah, well. Lady Tremont might be the most maneuvering mama in London, but he was in no danger of falling into her snares. There were meddlesome English mothers aplenty in India—in Calcutta, of course, but even in his home station of Manohari. He'd learned to watch his step, moving as carefully as a mongoose in a garden full of cobras.

Under the widow's watchful eye, the butler gave Kit his hat and gloves then opened the door. Kit unfurled his umbrella. The rain made a gentle, almost friendly patter over the surface.

"Good day, my lord," Lady Tremont said. "I know I speak for my daughters as well when I say we very much look forward to seeing you again."

"Of course." Kit wondered if she included Ellie in that reckoning. Probably not.

As he turned down the sidewalk, he glanced at the parlor window to see Delia and Abigail pressed close to the glass. Abigail waved furiously while her sister lifted her hand and gave him a demure waggle of her fingers.

Ellie stood off to one side. She tilted her head and shot him another pointed look, which made him grin. Plainly, there was little love lost between her and her stepsisters—and from what he'd seen, he could hardly blame her. Dinner on Thursday might be awkward, but he'd no doubt it would be equally entertaining.

Chapter 3

"DID YOU SEE THAT?" Abby clasped her hands under her chin and twirled about. "He smiled at me!"

"It wasn't at you, ninny." Delia gave her a withering glance. "Obviously he was looking at *me*."

Ellie bit her tongue and said nothing.

It was curious how quickly she'd felt the old childhood rapport with Kit rekindle, as though they'd just come in from a bit of mischief—like catching frogs to frighten the maids or sword fighting with sticks in the hayloft. They'd been a pair of rapscallions, as his mother had put it. And oh, how Ellie had missed him—missed his whole family—when they'd left for India.

But now he was back, and a lord into the bargain. She wasn't sure how she felt about that. Yes, it had been kind of him to pay a call, and even kinder to agree to come to dinner, but would his new station preclude them from becoming friends again? And even if it did not, was there any hope her stepmother would allow that to happen?

It had been marvelous to see him, though, Ellie had to admit. She felt as though a crisp wind had blown in, pushing away the haze of sorrow she'd been stumbling through. He'd nearly made her laugh, and she couldn't recall the last time she'd felt that way. Certainly not since Papa died. She was glad he was coming to dinner in two days, even if it meant he must endure the fawning attentions of her stepsisters.

"Girls," Lady Tremont said, returning to the parlor and giving her daughters a stern look. "Contain yourselves. There is nothing a gentleman finds more unbecoming than a lady who has obviously set her cap for him."

"But, Mama—" Abby began.

"You in particular, Abigail, must learn to curb your emotions. Lord Christopher is a catch, no question, but subtlety will win the day, my darling."

Ellie folded her arms, an unhappy knot forming in her stomach. Of course Lady Tremont wouldn't allow a friendship between the stepdaughter she detested and the son of a marquess. And she wouldn't rest until one of her own daughters had managed to snare him into a betrothal.

A fate Ellie wouldn't wish on *any* gentleman, let alone Kit.

The only way to save him from Lady Tremont's machinations would be to pretend she had no interest in renewing their friendship. When he came to dinner, she must be cold and distant. She must extinguish that spark of camaraderie between them.

The thought made her throat tighten with dismay, but there was no other option. Kit Newland must depart her life again, for both their sakes.

"My lady." Mr. Atkins bowed from the parlor threshold. "An invitation just arrived. I thought it advisable to inform you posthaste."

He held out a silver salver bearing a letter opener and a cream-colored envelope. The seal of Queen Victoria was prominently displayed on the creamy vellum, and Abby gasped audibly.

"A royal summons, Mama! How thrilling."

Lady Tremont took it with every evidence of calm, but her eyes gleamed with excitement. She slit the envelope and pulled out a card embossed with the royal coat of arms.

"*The Lord Chamberlain is commanded by The Queen*," she read, "*to invite Lady Tremont and her daughters to a Costume Ball evoking the reign of Charles II on Friday the thirteenth of June at half past nine o'clock. Buckingham Palace.*"

"What fun," Abby exclaimed. "I do hope Lord Christopher is invited as well."

With a pleased expression, Lady Tremont set the invitation back on the salver. "We must visit the modiste at once to have our ball gowns designed."

"I will look well in a Stuart-inspired gown," Delia said smugly.

"Does that mean we are out of mourning?" Ellie asked, glancing down at her dark skirts.

The requisite six months had come and gone, but she'd been so shrouded in despair she hadn't given any thought to putting off her blacks.

Her stepsisters, however, had only worn mourning for the first month, "to spare the expense of an entirely new wardrobe," Lady Tremont had said.

For herself, Ellie had only been allowed three new mourning gowns and then was given the cast-off clothing of her stepsisters with the expectation she would alter them to fit. Never the most skilled seamstress, she had admittedly not done her best work with the alterations. It was difficult to sew a fine seam when one's vision continually blurred with tears.

"I don't believe *you* were invited to the ball," Delia said, lifting her nose. "You're not Lady Tremont's daughter by blood."

"I am by marriage, however," Ellie retorted, her fingers

curling into her palms. "And I'm certain my godmother will support me in this, now that she's returned from the Continent."

Sadly, Baroness Merriweather was a rather absent, as well as absent-minded, woman. She had been an old family friend on Ellie's mother's side—thus her role as Ellie's godmother—but after Mama died when Ellie was young, the Baroness became more of a myth than a matronly figure in Ellie's life.

She would resurface every few years, bringing some impractical trinket from abroad and remarking on how much Ellie had grown, then disappear again without notice. But her last visit had been only a few months ago, to offer her condolences. And she *had* told Ellie to ask if she needed anything.

Whether or not she would remember that offer was another question, but it was past time for Ellie to assert herself within the Tremont family once more. She would carry the shadow of grief for Papa in her heart forever, but seeing Kit had reminded her that life continued. The sun rose, the earth spun, and it was possible to smile again.

On no account would she let her stepfamily spoil that for her or bar her from attending social events on some flimsy pretext. No matter how much Lady Tremont might try.

Her stepmother sniffed in displeasure. "No doubt Lady Merriweather has better things to do than listen to your groundless complaints, Ellie. Let me remind you that stubbornness is very unbecoming in a young lady."

"Still." Ellie lifted her chin. "I am a daughter of this household."

"True, if unfortunate," Delia said quietly.

Lady Tremont's nostrils flared. "Very well. I decree we are no longer in mourning for your dear departed father, God rest his soul. And you may attend the Queen's Ball."

"Thank you—"

"*If* you manage to procure something suitable to wear. I'm sure I needn't remind you that there is no money to furnish you with a costume. But I'm sure with your sewing skills, you'll be able to make a very fine ball gown."

Delia tittered, and Abby laughed as well, though at least she had the decency to muffle her giggle behind one hand. The remark stung, as it was meant to, and Ellie felt embarrassment warm her cheeks.

"I will be ready," she said stiffly.

Though truly, she had no notion of how she would manage to come up with an elaborate Stuart-era costume in under three weeks. Still, she refused to be daunted.

It seemed she must pay a call on Lady Merriweather and ask her to be true to her promise to help. Whether she remembered giving it or not.

Chapter 4

KIT PAUSED BEFORE THE front door of the Tremont household and glanced down at the bouquet he carried. Pink peonies and white roses. He meant it for Ellie, of course, and had been hoping to find daisies and cornflowers, having a recollection of her weaving flower crowns from the fields.

But those blooms were not yet in full season, and at any rate he suspected Lady Tremont would turn up her nose at such a common bouquet. He also suspected that the widow would dislike seeing him pay particular attention to Ellie, and much as he relished the idea of tweaking the viscountess's feathers, he worried that Ellie would suffer the consequence.

So he had settled on a lovely, impersonal posy of flowers for the entire household. With a single daisy hidden in the center, much against the wishes of the florist. Kit hoped Ellie would understand the secret reference.

"My lord." The butler opened the door. "Welcome. The ladies are expecting you in the drawing room."

Kit nodded and surrendered his hat and coat. He followed the man down the wide hall, bypassing the smaller front parlor, and was ushered into a much grander room. Tall windows let in the light, accentuating the yellow-and-white color scheme of the drawing room. A pianoforte took up one corner, and Lady Tremont and her daughters were arranged, as carefully as flowers, in the center of the room.

His gaze went to Ellie, seated off to the side. To his relief, she no longer wore stark black, but a gown of soft lavender. Still somber, of course, but the color did not highlight her pallor—though it did echo the shadows beneath her eyes.

"Good afternoon, ladies," he said with a bow, presenting his bouquet to Lady Tremont. "Your house is already filled with sweet blooms, but I hope you'll accept my humble offering."

"You are too kind." The viscountess glanced at the flowers. "Ellie, take those and fetch a vase. We can display them on the table, there."

Ellie nodded, rising, and Kit had to bite his tongue on his objections. Why was she letting her stepmother treat her like a servant? On the other hand, if she were the one to handle the flowers, perhaps she might see the daisy hidden among the blooms. He hoped it would make her smile.

"Thank you," she said to him, taking the bouquet and not meeting his eyes.

"Do hurry," the dark-haired Delia said. "We don't want them to wilt. Such a thoughtful gift from Lord Christopher should be treated with care." She gave him a coquettish smile.

"Oh, yes," Abigail added, not to be outdone. "It's a truly magnificent bouquet."

He should have brought them daisies and cornflowers after all, just to dash their expectations—although he had the unsettling notion that he could do no wrong in their eyes.

Ellie, however, was another matter. She hurried out of the room, and he resolved to find an opportunity to speak with her privately. The warmth he'd felt between them the other day seemed to be gone, and he wanted to know why.

Was she in trouble? Did her stepmother mistreat her, beyond the obvious relegation to servant status? He wasn't sure what he could do to intervene, as a single gentleman taking rooms at Claridge's, but surely there must be a way to extricate her from the situation, if it were untenable.

In India, beneath the bright blue sky, things were much simpler. In truth, he felt a little at sea, thrown into the upper strata of Society in London. He'd navigated it well enough, he thought, until now. But what did a lord do if he suspected trouble within a household that was, on the surface, none of his business?

A pity there was not enough time to post a letter to India and receive a reply in return. His mother would know what to do—but in her absence, he must muddle along as best he could. *Your heart has ever been a true compass*, she told him as he boarded the ship to England. *Steer by it.*

And so, he would do his best. Even if the currents of the *ton* were deep and treacherous.

Lady Tremont rose from her place at the center of the sofa.

"Please sit," she said, waving to the vacant spot between her daughters.

"Thank you." Kit shot a glance at the safe bulwark of the nearby armchair.

Unfortunately, it would be rude to snub the lady's daughters so openly. With an inward sigh, he settled between Delia and Abigail, then had to resist the urge to rub his nose.

Each girl wore perfume, their scents competing instead of complementing one another. Delia smelled as though she were drenched in jasmine, and a nose-stunning overabundance of violet wafted from Abigail.

"Did you receive an invitation to the Queen's Ball?" Abigail asked. She bounced up and down a bit, clearly excited at the prospect.

"I believe so," Kit said, recalling that an envelope embossed with the royal seal had arrived just that morning.

"Will you be in attendance, my lord?" Lady Tremont asked as she settled in the chair across from him, her cool tone a subtle reprimand to her daughter.

"I intend to, yes."

The ball would be an excellent opportunity to further winnow the field and settle upon the perfect candidate for a wife. He wouldn't say such a thing aloud, of course. Lady Tremont and her daughters needed no further encouragement along such matrimonial lines.

"Have you planned to come as any particular figure from the era?" Delia asked, leaning toward him. "The Duke of Richmond, perhaps? I had thought I might emulate Lady Frances Stuart. She was known as a great beauty."

If Kit recalled his history, the two had married, despite the lady in question being desired by the king.

"I'd not given it much thought," he replied. Indeed, as the invitation was yet unopened, he'd been unaware the ball had a particular theme.

"Do consider it," Delia said, looking up at him from beneath lowered eyelashes. "The duke was such a dashing figure."

"Oh, but he died tragically," Abigail said. "I think you'd be better served as a courtier."

"I'm certain Lord Christopher will take your suggestions under advisement," the viscountess said. "Ah, Ellie, there you are. My, what a long time you took to arrange the flowers."

Ellie set down the cut crystal vase of blooms, the delicate pink of the peonies echoing the color in her cheeks. Kit suspected that whatever length of time she might have taken with the flowers, her stepmother would have found equal fault.

He surveyed the bouquet, seeing no hint of daisy petals among the blooms.

"Do you like my flowers?" he asked Ellie directly.

"Of course," she said, moving to take the armchair. "It's very kind of you."

Her answer was frustratingly vague. Then again, he could scarcely expect her to have worn the daisy openly, even if she had discovered it.

"We were just discussing the Queen's costume ball," he said. "Do you have plans to attend as any particular personage?"

The color in her cheeks deepened, and Delia let out a titter.

"I'm certain Ellie will attend as someone appropriate," Lady Tremont said. "Now, Lord Christopher, how long do you intend to remain in London?"

"I plan to return to Assam by the end of June," he said. "I'll be managing my family's tea plantation there while my father comes to England to take up the duties of his new estate."

"Oh, that's a shame," Abigail said. "A month is scarcely long enough to get to know you before you leave again."

"I am of the opinion that the measure of a gentleman can be judged within a meeting or two," her mother said, arching a brow. "And I believe you, Lord Christopher, are quite worthy."

Of marrying either of her daughters—the implication was clear.

Kit swallowed. "Most kind of you, Lady Tremont."

He sent Ellie a somewhat panicked glance. A faint, mischievous smile crossed her lips, gone so quickly he suspected he was the only one who saw it.

"Tell us about your home in India," Ellie said. "I understand the climate is rather warmer than what we are accustomed to in London."

He gave a solemn nod. "It's true. Imagine the hottest summer day here in England. Now multiply that by a factor of one third, add a host of stinging insects, and a general sense of ennui that can be difficult to overcome, and you have a June day in Assam."

It was an exaggeration, of course, but he was gratified to see Delia's mouth turn down in distaste.

"It sounds a bit challenging," she said primly.

Abigail, however, was not so easily put off.

"Surely there are Englishwomen who brave the climate for the sake of their families," she said. "Your mother has lived there for years after all."

"True, but it has been difficult for her," he lied. Then he mentally shrugged and heaped more untruths upon the first. "She can scarcely wait to return to London—especially since her lady's maid was bitten by a cobra just this spring."

"How dreadful," Lady Tremont said, casting an anxious glance at her daughters.

"It's a dangerous country, between the poisonous snakes and diseases, not to mention the flooding and landslides caused by the monsoon rains each year." He shook his head. "In truth, it's a wonder so many English manage to carry on—especially in the wilds of Assam, which is where our plantation is located."

Ellie gave him a wide-eyed look. "But surely you are not so far from civilization as all that?"

"We manage to visit Calcutta a few times a year," he said truthfully, neglecting to mention that the town of Sylhet was much closer and provided all the basic amenities.

"It sounds very exciting," Abigail said, clearly undaunted. "And if one is in love, I imagine such things are no obstacle."

Her mother gave her a sour look. "Most matches are made for practical reasons, my dear. You'd do best to remember it."

"I don't care if my husband is titled or rich," the redhead said, tossing her head. "I intend to marry for love."

With those words, she leaned toward Kit, giving him a moon-eyed look that left no doubt as to the object of her affections. Unfortunately, he could not shift away from her or he'd be too close to her sister. It was a sticky situation.

"Don't be a ninny, Abby," Delia said. "Marrying for love is the outside of foolishness. I'm certain Lord Christopher would agree that practical matters such as breeding and fortune should be the foremost things to consider."

Her words hit a bit too close to the mark, and he gave her a strained smile. "I think practical romanticism is the best way forward."

At any rate, it seemed to work for his parents, whose strong affection for one another had helped them weather any number of tribulations. Of course, when they'd married, neither title nor wealth had come into play. It was only now, with the marquessate hanging over their heads that such things took on importance.

"Speaking of gentility," Lady Tremont said, "may we entertain you with some music, my lord?"

"Certainly," he said. "I don't have much opportunity to hear the pianoforte. The tropical climate is hard upon the instrument."

"Girls," the viscountess said, "do the honor of entertaining our guest, if you will." She turned to Kit with a self-serving smile. "Delia plays the pianoforte and Abigail the violin, and they both sing delightfully. My daughters are very talented."

"I don't doubt it," he said.

Ellie coughed into her hand and would not meet his eyes—a sure sign that he needed to brace himself for the concert to come.

Chapter 5

THE SISTERS ROSE, TAKING their suffocating perfumes with them, and Kit pulled in a cleansing breath. Delia seated herself upon the piano bench, while Abigail took up the violin resting in a silk-lined case.

Forewarned by Ellie's reaction, he managed not to flinch as the younger sister drew the bow across the strings, producing a sound like an ailing cow.

"You're not on pitch," Delia snapped from her place at the piano. She tapped one of the keys relentlessly. "Here's the note. No, higher than that. Wait, that's too high! Go lower."

Finally, Abigail managed to get the instrument in some semblance of tune, and they launched into their first piece. Kit guessed that Abigail did not play often, as she struggled through the music. At least the pianoforte produced a pleasant enough sound, though Delia had a tendency to hit the keys with too much force.

It was difficult to discern, but he thought they were performing a Bach minuet. Thankfully, it was a short selection, and he applauded vigorously at the end, relieved it was finished.

That turned out to be just the beginning, unfortunately.

His only consolation as the sisters warbled unsteadily through a rendition of "The Last Rose of Summer" was that

Ellie was clearly biting her cheek to keep from laughter. He shot her a pained glance, and her gaze skittered away from his.

Just as well. He knew they could easily set one another off, and no matter how untalented Delia and Abigail were, it would be too rude to dissolve into laughter during their recital.

It did not escape his notice that Ellie was not asked to contribute. If he recalled correctly, she had a clear, light soprano and an adequate mastery of the keyboard. No doubt Lady Tremont wanted no competition for her daughters' so-called talents.

Finally, the butler summoned them to dinner, and the caterwauling came to a blessed end.

"What do you think, my lord?" the viscountess asked, clearly proud of her offspring.

"That was an entirely memorable concert," he replied. "Your daughters have no equal." Though not quite in the direction she thought.

Ellie's mouth was screwed into a fierce frown—no doubt to hide her smile.

"That scowl is most unbecoming, Ellie," Lady Tremont said to her. "May I remind you that jealousy is unladylike in the extreme."

"You are correct," Ellie said, clearly attempting to master herself. "Do forgive me."

"Breeding will show," Delia said, rising from the piano bench and smoothing her skirts. "Lord Christopher, would you be so kind as to escort me in to dinner?"

Which was, Kit thought, rather an ironic breach of etiquette.

Her sister shot Delia a poisonous look, but the viscountess gave a regal nod.

"Indeed," she said. "Dinner is waiting. Please, follow me."

She led the way out of the drawing room. Kit followed with Delia clutching his arm, leaving Abigail and Ellie to bring up the rear.

At least Ellie was seated where he could see her, though with Delia on his left and Abigail directly across from him, he'd have to be mindful not to show her any particular attention. Lady Tremont presided over the head of the table, of course. She kept the conversation firmly fixed on her daughters throughout the meal, extolling their needlework, dancing, and impeccable taste in fashion.

This last was said with a sneering look at Ellie, and Kit quickly turned the topic to the food.

"This is an excellent roast," he said. "I've missed having beef as a regular part of my meals."

"Do they not have cows in India?" Abigail asked.

"Yes, but they are sacred beasts, and not for slaughter or eating," Kit said.

"How barbaric," Delia said with a patronizing sniff.

Ellie glanced at her stepsister. "I rather imagine that we are the barbaric ones in their eyes."

"Well put." Kit smiled at her—he couldn't help it.

"What else do you eat, or not eat, in India?" Abigail asked. "I never imagined foreign customs would be so fascinating."

He would wager she'd never given much thought to the world beyond London. Well, if nothing else, perhaps this conversation would broaden her mind a bit.

"Curries, of course," he said. "And there's a great deal of spice in all the food. It takes some getting used to." He did not add that, as a result, the food in England seemed quite bland.

Ellie sent him a glance, as if reading his thoughts. "It must be rather a change for you."

"I'm enjoying reacquainting myself with British cuisine," he said.

Well, perhaps *enjoying* wasn't the right word. He looked forward to returning to the pungent and flavorful meals of India.

"We have a lovely blancmange for dessert," Lady Tremont said.

"A fitting end to the meal," he said, keeping his tone serious. "White pudding. So very English."

Ellie twitched, and once again refused to meet his eyes. He smiled internally to see her reaction. At least her mood had lightened, which made him doubly glad he'd come that evening.

As the servants removed the plates, the viscountess turned to him. "When might we have the pleasure of your company again, Lord Christopher?"

A pity his harrowing tales of India had not discouraged her from foisting her daughters upon him.

"I've quite a bit of business to attend to in London," he said. "I really can't say."

"At least we'll see you at the Queen's Ball, won't we?" Abigail gave him a longing look.

"Assuredly." He glanced over at Ellie, partly to avoid giving Abigail any encouragement and partly to see Ellie's reaction.

She did not seem excited at the thought of the ball—not in the way her stepsisters were. In fact, her expression had teetered into melancholy. He was once more reminded that something was amiss in the Tremont household, and resolved to have a private word with Ellie before he left that evening.

"How unfortunate that you have no female relations to accompany to the ball," Lady Tremont said to him. "A bachelor arriving alone to such a prestigious event is always cause for comment. Queen Victoria and Prince Albert do like to see their subjects surrounded by family."

Clearly she was angling for an offer of escort, but he was not willing to go quite so far. He glanced once again at Ellie, noting the bleakness in her eyes.

"I hope you'll save me a dance," he said.

Although his words were directed at Ellie, both Delia and Abigail fastened upon them.

"Of course, my lord," the dark-haired sister said. "I would be delighted."

"May I put you down for the first waltz?" Abigail asked.

Her mother gave her a quelling look for being so forward, but Kit was amused by her lack of subtlety.

"Certainly," he said. "And a polka set for you, Miss Delia. They still dance the polka at balls in London, do they not?"

"Most assuredly," Delia said, somewhat stiffly. "I would be delighted, my lord."

The narrow-eyed glance she sent her sister made it clear she wished she'd spoken sooner and claimed the waltz instead.

"I shall mark you down for the quadrille, if I may?" Ellie said.

"Please do—though you might have to steer me through some of the moves."

Thankfully, he had a few weeks to brush up on his dancing skills before the ball. They did not, as a general rule, perform the more elaborate choreography at the informal dances held in the Manohari Assembly Rooms.

I must admit," Ellie said, her eyes holding a spark of amusement, "it has been some time since I attended a ball myself. I was hoping you might guide me."

"We shall invent our own steps, then." Kit grinned at her.

"I assume you are jesting," Lady Tremont said in a reproving tone. "I would not like to see you make a fool of yourself on the dance floor, Lord Christopher."

"Oh, he's far too graceful for that," Abigail said. "I can

hardly wait for my waltz with you. It was so kind of you to ask."

Kit's brows rose. It seemed the redhead had already come up with her own version of events.

"Shall we retire for a few hands of cards?" Lady Tremont asked, rising.

It was more a command than a question, of course. They all stood, Delia taking a possessive grip upon Kit's arm, and obediently followed the viscountess to the drawing room.

He tried to sit next to Ellie but was outmaneuvered by her stepsisters. For the rest of the evening, he found no chance to have a word alone with her. Lady Tremont was vigilant as a hawk, and her daughters were too fixed upon him for any opportunity to arise.

At last, as he was preparing to take his leave, he caught Ellie's eye.

"Do you still ride, Miss Tremont?" he asked.

"Yes," she said, fingering her skirts. "But not recently."

"Mourning does take its toll." Lady Tremont gave an unconvincing sigh. "At least we are now emerging from its pall. But I'm afraid Eleanor has far too much to do to go gallivanting about on horseback."

"A pity," he said, keeping his tone light. "I hear the weather tomorrow is clearing at about two in the afternoon. At any rate, I thank you for a most inspiring evening, Lady Tremont."

"It was entirely our pleasure," she said with a satisfied look. "Until the Queen's Ball, my lord."

"Until then." He bowed over her hand, then Delia's, then Abigail's.

When he came to Ellie, he squeezed her fingers lightly, and she returned the pressure in two quick pulses. Good—she'd understood his message.

Whether she could contrive to escape the prying eyes of her stepfamily remained to be seen. But Eleanor Tremont had ever been a resourceful girl, and he trusted her to prevail.

The thought enabled him to smile at the gathered ladies one more time before he donned his hat and stepped into the cool English night.

Chapter 6

"OH, GRACIOUS," ABBY EXCLAIMED as the door closed behind their visitor. "Just think—Lord Christopher asked me to waltz with him!"

"Ninny," Delia said. "You were the one who asked *him*. Very unladylike of you, I must say." She reached over and pinched Abby's arm.

"Ow!" Abby jerked away from her sister. "You're only jealous because he obviously prefers my spirit of adventure. Anyone could see how frightened you were when he spoke of the dangers of India."

"Why, I—"

"Girls," Lady Tremont said in a stern voice. "There is to be no more bickering over Lord Christopher. Whichever one of you he chooses, the whole family will be the better for it. The son of a marquess after all! Why don't you concentrate on *his* qualities instead of your own?"

"He has wonderful green eyes," Abby said with a sigh. "Perhaps our children will have his eyes and my hair—wouldn't that be a stunning combination?"

"You wouldn't want to curse any child with that red," Delia replied. "Dark hair is so much more becoming—which is why Lord Christopher and I would make a far better match."

She plumped her coiffure with a self-satisfied smile.

Ellie bit her tongue and tried not to think of Kit or his future; but as her stepsisters rhapsodized about his broad shoulders and ruggedly handsome face, she could not help but add her own mental comments to the list.

Kind, as he had ever been. Perhaps too kind, as his offer of dancing with them at the Queen's Ball demonstrated. Though she had to admit, it did add to her anticipation of the event.

Intelligent, with a wry humor that still matched her own. Several times during the course of the evening, she'd had to bite the inside of her cheek to keep from laughing aloud at some of his sly jokes.

Adventurous, of course. It was plain that India suited him. And she knew she shouldn't have encouraged him in his wild tales of that country, but it had been such fun seeing her stepmother's expression sour with disapproval.

It was a pity that by the end of the evening, Lady Tremont had overcome her reluctance. She seemed perfectly happy at the thought of sending either of her daughters off to face the dangers of a foreign land, as long as it would earn her the social cachet she coveted.

As if Papa's title wasn't enough!

Ellie tamped down her spark of temper at the thought. There was no use feeding her anger at her stepfamily. She knew it was a conflagration that would ultimately consume her if she let it rage forth.

But what was she to do?

Pondering that question dampened her mood completely. Now that she was emerging from mourning, it was clear there were very few options open to her.

She had no dowry and no useful connections, now that her father was gone. Perhaps someone might marry her for love, but that was a foolish notion indeed. She had no callers, except for Kit—and he was departing back to India in less than a month's time.

She was relegated to a status of unpaid servant in her own home. And although she supposed she ought to be glad to have a roof over her head and no fears about when her next meal would arrive, it was no way to exist. Especially given the spiteful natures of Lady Tremont and Delia, who were glad to belittle her at every opportunity.

Perhaps Kit would have some insight for her, provided she could slip out on the morrow. He'd been quite clever with his clues. First the daisy, which grew in a meadow in Hyde Park where their families used to picnic on warm summer days, and then his invitation to go riding and comments about the weather clearing at two o'clock. She knew precisely when and where to meet him.

Whether or not she *should* was another matter, of course—but she would bring her maid, Henderson, along. There could be no accusations of impropriety, should their meeting be discovered. Despite her resolution to keep him at arm's length, she found that the prospect of having a friend to confide in, just once, outweighed all other considerations.

Hyde Park was lovely—fresh, green, and sparkling from the morning's rain. Ellie drew in a deep breath as she walked beneath the oak trees. The little lane was peaceful, the grasses starred with tiny daisies. The air brightened ahead, the trees opening up to a clearing where she and Kit's families used to take picnics on warm summer days. She tried not to hasten as she and Henderson came closer to her destination, though her pulse began to pound.

It was good to be out, even if it wasn't simply to take a refreshing stroll between her shopping errands, as she'd told her maid. Henderson was circumspect, and as one of the household's long-standing servants, she was loyal to Ellie. She had known Kit's family, too, and had never liked the fact that Papa had remarried—though of course she would never say so.

"Is that Christopher Newland?" the older woman asked as they approached the meadow and caught sight of a figure waiting beside one of the tallest oaks.

"Yes," Ellie said. "You won't say anything, will you?"

Henderson frowned. "If it were anyone else, miss, you know I would. Don't do anything foolish now."

"I only want to talk to him." Ellie couldn't help the pleading note in her voice.

"Aye, well." Henderson's expression softened. "I expect it's no bad thing to speak with the lad. Just mind your manners."

"I shall."

They reached the edge of the trees, and Kit looked up, smiling. "There you are. I was worried you wouldn't be able to meet. Hello, Mrs. Henderson. It's good to see you. You look as well as ever."

The matronly woman bobbed her head. "May I say the same, my lord? India seems to agree with you."

It was true. Kit had seemed to grow into himself while abroad. He carried himself with an easy confidence, and though his manner was still direct, he was not as easy to goad into saying rash things as he'd used to be. Which, upon reflection, was probably a good thing, despite Ellie's attempts to provoke him at dinner last night.

"It does agree with me," he said. "I'm eager to return to Assam."

"Well, then." Henderson nodded to a plain wooden bench in the shade. "I'll just rest here while the two of you have your chat."

Suiting action to words, she marched over and settled herself on the bench, appearing completely disinterested in whatever Kit and Ellie had to say to one another.

"I'm glad she hasn't changed." Kit offered his arm. "We can stroll around the clearing—staying within eyesight, of course."

"Of course." Ellie slipped her arm through his, resting her gloved hand on his forearm.

"You've changed, though," he said, giving her a keen glance. "Is everything all right, Ellie? Beyond the obvious, I mean."

She hesitated. Despite the fact that she so badly wanted someone to confide in, was Kit Newland the right choice? Perhaps she ought to seek out someone else.

But the sad fact of the matter was, she had no one else. After Papa's remarriage, the family had begun socializing with the new Lady Tremont's set, cutting ties with former friends. And Ellie's godmother was too scattered to be any kind of confidante.

"Come now," Kit said. "There's nothing so bad that you can't tell me. Whatever it is, I'll do my best to help. Is Lady Tremont mistreating you?"

The concern in his voice brought Ellie perilously close to tears. It felt like ages since anyone had truly cared about her well-being.

She swallowed, grateful the edge of her bonnet shaded her eyes. When she'd mastered herself, she looked up at Kit.

"She doesn't beat me, if that what you mean," she said. "I'm not in any physical danger."

She paused, thinking of how to frame her words, and Kit pressed her hand, waiting. The wind ruffled the green leaves overhead, as if in reassurance.

"It's just that, with Papa gone and no money left for me, I'm relegated to a lesser standing within the household."

"I saw that." His voice hardened. "And I didn't like it one bit. They shouldn't treat you as anything less than the daughter of a viscount. You're not a servant, Ellie. You don't have to do your stepmother's bidding."

Oh, but she did, or Lady Tremont would make her life even more miserable.

"I think . . . I ought to take a position as a governess." There, she'd said it aloud, which made the possibility seem more real.

"A governess?" Kit frowned. "You can do better than that."

"Better, how?" Bitterness flared within her. As a man, he'd no notion how few options were open to her. "It's not as though I can board a ship to India to make my fortune or take a position as secretary to a lord with a promising career in politics."

"But you could marry him," Kit said, in what he no doubt thought was a sensible tone.

"I cannot. Not without a dowry."

"But surely any man can see your worth."

"That's not reasonable, Kit. You know it as well as I. Respectable gentlemen don't marry girls of good breeding without money or connections. They have so many other choices, you see." She let out a resigned breath. "Perhaps a paid companion would suit me better."

"Nonsense." He turned to face her. "You're pretty; you've a good mind and an even disposition. What man wouldn't want you?"

Their eyes caught and held, even as warmth flooded her cheeks. He thought she was pretty? The air seemed to shimmer between them, his green eyes full of promise.

Perhaps . . . perhaps there was another option.

He *had* wanted her to meet with him after all. And he'd

visited twice within the span of a week. Was it possible—could he care for her the way she always had for him?

Heart racing, she forced herself to ask the question.

"What about you? Would *you* marry me, Kit?"

His gaze slid away from hers. "I'm sorry, Ellie. You know I like you very well. But . . ."

She stepped back, her heart plummeting. Oh, she'd been an idiot to ask. She forced herself to speak through the tightness in her throat. "You see? No one will have me, despite all your fine words to the contrary. Clearly, I have little to recommend me."

"That's not so." He caught her hand. "I confess, when I first came to call upon you . . . Well, you can guess the direction of my hopes. But the sorry truth is, I must find a girl with enough money to keep the tea plantation from going under."

She blinked, trying to take in what he was saying. Had he just implied he'd been considering courting her?

"But doesn't your father's new estate have plenty of funds?" she asked.

"That's just it." Kit let out an unhappy laugh. "The marquessate is in wretched shape. The estate has been mismanaged for years, apparently, and it's going to take what's left of father's money—plus considerable loans—to make it prosperous again."

"Then why insist on this plantation? It seems clear your family can't afford both."

He shook his head, a glint of desperation in his eyes. "If only we'd known in advance. But almost all our savings is in the ground of Assam in the form of several thousand tea plants, plus the men to care for them. And the tea won't be ready to harvest for another three years. We're trapped, frankly."

Unwilling sympathy moved through her. Despite his appearance of freedom, Kit was as bound by his circumstance as she was. Oh, but life was cruel and miserable, to bring them both to this unhappy point.

"I'm sorry," she said. For everything that might have been, and could never be. "I'm sorry there's nothing we can do for one another."

"Can't we still be friends?" He searched her eyes. "I care for you, Ellie."

She knew, deep in her heart, that she and Kit would have suited one another as husband and wife. As lifelong companions. If only Papa had left her with a dowry.

It was too painful to stand with him in this clearing so full of happy memories of their youth, and see everything she'd most wished for turned to ashes.

She pulled her hand from his and turned away. "If you hear of a governess position, do let me know. At any rate, I need to return home."

He came and walked beside her. "I'll see you out of the park, at least."

"No need." She made her tone brisk. "Henderson and I can manage perfectly well on our own."

He touched her arm. "Remember to save me a dance at the Queen's Ball."

"Very well."

She would—and then she would say goodbye forever and do her best to forget that their lives had so narrowly missed being entwined.

Pretending her throat wasn't choked with misery, she bade him farewell and left him standing in the clearing, the green boughs of the oaks whispering empty promises overhead.

Chapter 7

"LADY MERRIWEATHER WILL SEE you now," the Baroness's elderly butler said, returning to the formal parlor where he'd deposited Ellie.

She gave him a stiff nod and rose, then glanced at Henderson, who remained perched on the settee.

"I'll await you here," the maid said. "You don't need an audience to meet with your godmother, after all."

"Thank you." Ellie gave her a grateful smile.

For the second time that week, Henderson had staunchly stood by Ellie on her clandestine visits. First with Kit, and now to beg for help from her godmother.

Despite Ellie's best efforts with a needle, she was no closer to having a costume for the upcoming ball, and time was quickly running out. Lady Merriweather was her last hope.

The butler showed her to a room full of exotic displays: a huge Chinese vase filled with peacock feathers, a marble statue of some Caesar or another, an ornate screen inlaid with gemstones. In the midst of it, the Baroness sat, a writing desk on her lap. She was garbed in a bright blue walking dress accented with a tasseled fringe, and her coiffure boasted ostrich plumes dyed to match. In her right hand, she held a quizzing glass. When she looked up at Ellie, her right eye was alarmingly magnified.

"Ah, Eleanor," she said, lowering the glass. "My, don't

you look peaked. Bone broth—that's just the thing." She pointed the quizzing glass at her butler. "Send up a cup of broth for our guest. And lemon tea for myself."

"Madam." The man bowed and departed the room before Ellie could protest that she had no need of cosseting.

Not to mention she despised the flavor of bone broth.

But there was no use for it now. Pulling in a breath, she went to her godmother and curtsied.

"Good afternoon, Lady Merriweather. It's kind of you to see me."

"Pish—you're family after all, even though you almost never call. Come, sit." She patted the armchair beside her own.

Ellie refrained from pointing out that the Baroness was seldom at home, let alone open to receiving visitors, and took a seat. The chair was uncomfortable, the arms carved like mermaids so that there was not a smooth surface for her elbows to rest upon. Instead, she gripped her hands together in her lap and tried to find the words to begin.

"Spit it out, girl," the Baroness said. "Clearly you've come to ask me for something, and there's no point in beating around the bush, as they say."

"I . . . yes. You offered your help after Papa died—and so I've come to ask if you might assist me with procuring a ball gown."

"A ball gown? Surely you have plenty of those, not to mention the wherewithal to procure more as you desire." The quizzing glass came up again. "Unless your dear stepmama is being troublesome about money. Ah, I see that she is."

Ellie tried not to squirm. For an absent-minded old woman, her godmother was disconcertingly observant and direct—qualities Ellie admired, when they were not fixed so keenly upon herself.

"I don't know if I told you," Ellie continued, "but Papa left me no dowry. We're living on Lady Tremont's money."

Lady Merriweather's lips tightened so much that they nearly disappeared from the force of her disapproval. "No dowry? Rather suspicious, that. Your father wasn't a fool about money. Are you certain the solicitor informed you correctly?"

"Yes."

Though in truth, Ellie's raw grief had prevented her from entirely following the details. It had been a difficult meeting, full of Lady Tremont's coldness and the solicitor's apologies.

"Hmph," the Baroness said. "Well, be that as it may. What kind of gown are you in need of?"

"A Stuart gown, for the Queen's costume ball."

Her godmother blinked. "You plan to attend that foolish fete? The *ton* prancing about, pretending to be in Charles Stuart's court. Really! He was a naughty king, you know. Not at all a fitting candidate to inspire a ball."

Heat rose in Ellie's cheeks. Even if Charles II had run an unsuitable court, one didn't speak of such things. Except, apparently, unless one were Lady Merriweather.

"It's what the Queen has chosen," Ellie said. "And our household is invited. It's the first ball I'll be allowed to attend after coming out of mourning, and I do want to go." If for no other reason than to see Kit one last time, and bid him farewell.

"And you have nothing to wear." The Baroness shook her head. "It's rather short notice to procure a costume gown, my girl. You should have planned ahead."

"I was trying to make my own," Ellie admitted.

Her godmother let out a bark of laughter. "I suppose you have as little talent with a needle as your mother. Hopeless, she was. She disguised it with the clever use of sashes and ribbons and the like, though. Made it seem as though her gowns had been completely refurbished, when in fact it was her own resourcefulness with a bit of trimmings. That was before she married your father, of course. Afterwards, she could have as many new dresses as she liked."

The story kindled a warm ember next to Ellie's heart. She had so few memories of her mother that every bit of information was a gift.

"So you'll help me?" she asked.

"I can make no promises. Ah, here's Prescott with our beverages. Set the tray down, my good man." She patted the lacquered table next to her chair.

The butler complied, then departed as quietly as he'd come. With a satisfied look, the baroness handed Ellie a heavy stoneware mug. A slightly sweet, unappetizing odor drifted up from the cloudy liquid.

"Drink up," her godmother said, lifting her own porcelain cup of tea.

Ellie could hardly refuse, as she was there begging favors. Trying not to wrinkle her nose in disgust, she forced herself to take a swallow.

The cloying taste stuck to her teeth and tongue, and she must have made a face because the Baroness let out a guffaw.

"Oh, child, it might taste dreadful, but it is very good for you. Like so much of life. You must steel yourself and pass through unpleasantness, but there's a reward at the end, I promise you."

"Yes, my lady."

There was no other response Ellie could make, though she was inclined to doubt her godmother's promises. Both of a reward at the end of unpleasantness and of a Stuart ball gown. But at least she'd tried.

Chapter 8

AS EXPECTED, THE WEEK passed, and no gown arrived for Ellie. She chastised herself for hoping and redoubled her efforts to cobble together a suitable costume. The days were slipping by at an alarming pace, and the Queen's Ball was imminent.

The closer it came, the more Ellie's stepfamily found every excuse to heap work upon her. From dawn till dusk, it seemed she was needed—to run to the milliner's, to consult with her stepsisters on their gloves, to rearrange the gowns in Lady Tremont's closet, as she refused to let the maids do it, claiming they wouldn't take proper care.

All of it was designed to keep Ellie far too busy to create her own costume. They didn't say as much, of course, but it was quite clear.

Despite the fact, they pretended to "help" with her ball gown, bestowing upon her various odds and ends, as if they would make any difference.

"Here," Delia said, handing Ellie a length of unused gold ribbon, frayed on the end. "I won't be needing this. Perhaps you could use it on your gown." Beneath her syrupy-sweet tones, there was an undercurrent of laughter in her voice.

"You may take this shawl." Abby tossed a length of scarlet fabric at her. "There's a tear on one edge, but if you wear it folded, no one will notice."

Even Lady Tremont participated, giving Ellie a pair of

embroidered dancing slippers. "These are too small for me, but I'm certain they'll fit you. You have my permission to wear them to the ball."

As it turned out, the slippers were tight on Ellie's feet as well, pinching her toes quite painfully. But her other shoes had been dyed black or given to her stepsisters when she'd gone into mourning, so the too-small slippers were all she had. Every night, she attempted to stretch them out, but they remained stubbornly petite.

The ribbon and scarf, however, she was able to put to good use. Heartened by Lady Merriweather's remembrances of her mother, Ellie switched her focus from sewing a new gown to transforming one of her mourning gowns into something worthy of the ball. She snatched bits of time to work on her costume, staying up late into the night and working by the light of a single candle.

At least the frenetic pace kept her from thinking too much about Kit. Her childish dreams had been well and truly trampled, and there was no point on dwelling on them—no matter how much her heart ached to think on what might have been. Life had turned out differently, for both of them, and she'd do well to accept that fact and move on.

They were friends. Nothing more. And perhaps even less. Ellie had worn her heart on her sleeve at their last meeting, and he hadn't even noticed the depth of her feelings.

Enough, she told herself and concentrated on tacking the gold ribbon around the neckline of her made-over gown.

As the days passed, the severe black dress transformed. She consulted the engravings in the history books in the library, doing her best to emulate the square-cut lines and full sleeves of the Stuart era. Finally, two days before the ball, Ellie felt she'd managed to produce a satisfactory costume.

It wouldn't hold a candle to her stepsister's bespoke

gowns, of course, but there was an elegant simplicity to the dress that suited her.

Finally, the day of the Queen's Ball arrived.

The last time she would ever see Kit.

For he would marry a lady with money. No doubt he was courting her even now. They would wed, and he'd take her back to India to raise a family and a crop of tea.

And that would be that.

High time Ellie turned her mind to the practicalities of becoming a governess. As soon as the endless labor of preparing for the ball was ended, she must find herself a position. Perhaps Lady Merriweather would help—though Ellie had to admit that was a bedraggled and forlorn hope. Clearly, there was to be no ball gown, and she doubted her godmother would bestir herself overmuch to help find a place for Ellie.

Then one of the maids knocked at her bedroom door to tell her she was wanted in Delia's room, and the day exploded into a whirlwind of activity.

"Which necklace should I wear?" Delia demanded, waving at the jewelry spilled across her dressing table. "You must help me decide."

It was not as simple as that, of course, because every suggestion Ellie made was countered with reasons why that particular item would not suit. There were no earbobs to match. The color would clash with Delia's underskirts. And so on, until Ellie's jaw was clenched tight with frustration.

Just as Delia finally settled on her choice, Abby dashed into the room.

"Oh, Ellie, there you are! Come tell me which combs I should put in my hair this evening." She grabbed Ellie's hand and towed her out the door.

At least Abby wasn't nearly as fussy as her ill-tempered sister. She and Ellie even laughed together as one of the feathered hair ornaments refused to stay in place.

"I don't fancy looking *quite* so much like an ostrich," Abby said, pushing the offending plume out of the way.

"More reminiscent of a cockatoo, I think," Ellie said. "Here, let's try it in this direction."

In the end, Abby abandoned feathers altogether in favor of white silk flowers that set off her auburn hair beautifully. But there was no time left for Ellie to attend her own preparations before dinner.

As the family ate, she tried not to glance too often at the clock upon the dining room mantel. The minutes ticked away; each lost moment a lead weight dropped upon Ellie's heart. Sinking. Sinking.

At last Lady Tremont set down her fork, signaling the meal was at an end.

"The carriage will be drawn up at nine," she said to her daughters. "I expect you to be ready promptly. We don't want to keep Lord Christopher waiting to claim his dances."

"But how will we find him in the crowd?" Abby asked. "Surely it will be a dreadful crush."

"I've no doubt he will locate us," her mother said. "After all, how could he not be drawn to two of the most lovely young ladies in London?"

Abby tittered, and Delia looked smug. Ellie lifted her chin and tried to pretend she hadn't been slighted once again.

"Oh, Ellie, it's too bad you aren't coming with us," Delia said, her voice sweet but her eyes sharp. "Shall I say farewell to Lord Christopher from you?"

"There's no need," Ellie replied calmly. "As it happens, I have a suitable gown."

Lady Tremont's expression hardened instantly. "I find that difficult to believe."

"Nevertheless, it's true." Ellie met her stepmother's stony gaze. "I am coming to the ball. Now, you must excuse me. There's not much time left for me to prepare."

Before her stepmother could reply, Ellie rose and hurried from the room. She ignored Lady Tremont's call for her to stop and didn't slow her pace until she'd reached the safety of her bedroom.

There, she closed the door and leaned against it a moment to let her racing pulse slow. Goodness, it had felt good to assert herself. Along with putting aside her mourning clothes, she vowed to continue pushing away the haze of sorrow that had made her so malleable to her stepfamily's demands.

Sorrow and, if she were honest, despair that Papa had left her nothing. But the fact that she had no dowry didn't mean she ought to be treated as a servant.

And . . . She drew in a wavering breath, trying to catch hold of the truth.

It also didn't mean that Papa hadn't loved her with all his heart.

Tears pricked her eyes as she realized how the notion had shadowed her ever since his death, the insidious thought that if he'd cared for her more, he wouldn't have left her in such straits.

She closed her eyes and forced herself to breathe past the tightness in her chest. Inhale, then exhale.

Papa had loved her, and wanted everything good for her. The knowledge unfurled in her heart like a flower opening to the light, and she couldn't believe she'd let herself lose sight of the fact. He had loved her. A tear slipped down one cheek, and she wiped her eyes on her sleeve.

Whatever unlucky turn his fortunes had taken, he certainly hadn't meant it to happen, and had no doubt been distraught at the fact.

But there was no changing the fact that he had left her penniless. Her task now was to go bravely into the future, not spend the rest of her life as a dejected orphan in her own home.

And the first step was to don her costume and attend the Queen's Ball, showing the world that she was out of mourning and ready to carry on.

She rang for Henderson, who was aware of Ellie's late nights working on her costume and stood at the ready to help her prepare for the ball. With the maid's help, Ellie would manage to be ready on time . . . she hoped.

Thank goodness the ball gown was simple, as was her chosen coiffure—a bun over each ear, dressed with leftover pieces of the gold ribbon.

"There you are," Henderson said, fastening a garnet choker about Ellie's neck. "You look lovely, I must say. It's good to see you in colors again."

"Thank you for all your help." Ellie turned and pressed the maid's hand. "I don't know what I'd do without you. I'll miss you when I go."

"Go?" Henderson's eyes lit up. "Have you heard from Lord Christopher, then?"

"No." Ellie swallowed, trying to ignore the spike of pain at hearing Kit's name. "I only meant when I obtain a position as a governess elsewhere."

The older woman's expression fell. "As to that, perhaps whatever household you go to would be in need of a chamber-maid too. I wouldn't want to stay here without you, Miss Ellie."

"We shall see what turns up, then." Ellie tried to give her a cheery smile. "I'd be glad of a friend, wherever I land."

It was doubtful, of course, that they could find such a situation—and even if they did, she suspected Lady Tremont would not give a good reference to any servant leaving her household. But there was no use borrowing trouble, at least not tonight. On the morrow, she would face up to the difficulties ahead.

Henderson consulted the pocket watch pinned to her bosom. “You’d best hurry. There are only five minutes to spare.”

Hastily, Ellie jammed her feet into the tight slippers and snatched up her reticule. She paused to give Henderson a quick kiss on the cheek, then, taking her skirts in both hands, hastened down the main staircase to the foyer.

The ball awaited.

Chapter 9

ELLIE'S STEPFAMILY WAS GATHERED in the foyer below, opulently dressed and coiffed for the ball. They turned to watch as she descended the stairs. The looks of surprise on Abby's face and envy on Delia's were gratifying, but the narrow-eyed stare of Lady Tremont sent a shiver down Ellie's back.

Still, her stepmother could not keep her from attending.

"What a singular costume," Delia said. "A pity it doesn't match our gowns. You'll look like a raven among peacocks, I'm afraid."

It was true that Ellie's somber colors were quite a contrast to Abby and Delia's pastel garb, but she wasn't overly concerned. The white silk overskirt she'd added to her gown—the lining taken from a moth-eaten woolen cloak—along with the gold and scarlet touches, transformed her costume from dreary black to an understated elegance.

Abby, as usual, was more effusive. "But how clever! I never would've guessed you could do it, Ellie. Look—there's bits of my scarf."

"And my ribbon." Delia gave her a dark look. "I wish I might take it back from you."

She took a menacing step forward, fingers crooked as though she were planning to rip the ribbon from Ellie's dress.

"Delia," Lady Tremont said. "No need to be so undignified. Ah, here comes the blackberry cordial I sent for. We could use a bracing sip before we go out, don't you think?"

One of the maids hurried up, a decanter of the dark liquid and four small goblets balanced on a tray. Just as she arrived, Delia stepped forward, knocking against the girl.

The maid lurched, the decanter of cordial swaying perilously. Lady Tremont snatched it up and then, looking Ellie right in the face, tipped it over onto her gown.

Ellie yelped and jump back, but it was too late. Sticky purple-black liquid splashed over the white overskirt of her costume, staining it instantly.

"What a clumsy thing you are," Lady Tremont said, turning to the maid. "Clean this mess up at once."

"Milady." The girl bobbed a frightened curtsy and scurried away, the empty goblets rattling on the tray.

"Oh no, Ellie," Abby said, genuine distress in her voice. "Your dress is ruined."

Ellie wanted to protest that it wasn't so, that she could still go to the ball, but the tight knot in her throat prevented her from saying a word. She could not deny that Abby spoke the truth.

"Unfortunate." Her stepmother's tone held an undercurrent of triumph. "It seems you won't be joining us after all. I'm afraid we can't linger, however. Girls, the carriage awaits."

Delia gave a satisfied sniff and turned to follow her mother, but Abby lingered a moment.

"I'm so sorry," she whispered. "I'll give your regards to Lord Christopher, shall I?"

Ellie, lips pressed together to keep from sobbing, managed a nod.

Then they were gone, and she was left standing in a puddle of blackberry cordial, her hopes for the evening as ruined as her permanently stained gown.

Kit arrived punctually at the Queen's Ball. That is, he *meant* to arrive on time, but he hadn't realized that the line of carriages would extend so far down The Mall. After a quarter hour where they moved forward perhaps five yards, he knocked on the window of the cab he'd hired and told the driver to let him out. It would be easier simply to walk, despite the impediment of his ornate, full-skirted coat and somewhat ridiculous bloused sleeves.

At least his hose-clad legs were unencumbered. As he strode toward the palace, overtaking several carriages, he wondered how the gentlemen of the Stuart court had kept their shins warm in winter.

It was a temperate enough evening for a stroll, however. The Mall bordered St. James's Park, which breathed green and silent in the London dusk. Kit savored it. If the carriages were any indication, Buckingham Palace would be packed tighter than the crowds haggling for bargains in the morning marketplace of Sylhet.

"Lord Christopher!" a voice called out as he passed a nondescript black coach.

He glanced at the open window framing Abigail Tremont's head. Part of him wanted to act as though he hadn't seen her and hasten his steps, but the rest of him wondered how Ellie fared. She'd been much in his thoughts since their meeting in the park, and he felt guilty at how quickly he'd brushed off her suggestion that they marry.

At the very least, he owed her an apology, even if he had very good reasons why they could never make a match.

"Hello-oo!" Abigail waved frantically at him, and he could no longer pretend he hadn't seen her.

He slowed his steps and moved closer to the carriage, trying to catch a glimpse of Ellie.

"Good evening, Miss Tremont," he said to Abigail. "Are you looking forward to the ball?"

"Oh, so much." She batted her eyelashes at him. "Our dance, most particularly."

Kit simply nodded, not wanting to encourage her. Someone inside the carriage spoke, and she turned her head a moment, nodded, then looked back out at him.

"Would you like to come up with us?" she asked.

"Is there room?" he asked doubtfully. The only thing worse than going at a snail's pace would be simultaneously enduring being smothered by four sets of voluminous skirts.

"Sadly, Ellie's not with us," Abigail said, then her voice brightened, "which means there's plenty of space for you!"

"Ellie's not here? Why didn't she come?" he asked, a pang going through him. Was she that unhappy with him, that she would forgo the event just to avoid his company?

"There was a . . . mishap with her dress," Abigail said. "But I know she's sorry to miss the ball. And seeing you, of course. Shall we stop the carriage?"

It was a moot question, for the vehicle was already at a standstill, but Kit shook his head.

"I'm enjoying my stroll, thank you. But I'll wait for you at the entrance. I look forward to our dances."

In truth, he looked forward to discharging his duty and giving Ellie's stepsisters their requisite turns about the floor. The rest of the night would be spent in trying to muster up a spark of attraction for the handful of young women he'd identified as the best candidates for his suit.

Surely, he reasoned, there must be some warmth between himself and the woman he was to marry—especially if was carting her off to India. But so far, he'd felt nothing but a resigned sense of responsibility as he sought a bride. And time was running out.

"Very well," Abigail said. "We shall see you anon, Lord Christopher."

He nodded to her, then lengthened his stride. The remainder of his walk to the palace was spent pondering whether there was any other solution besides marrying a girl with money. Alas, no other possibility presented itself.

With a heavy sigh, Kit glanced up, wishing he could see the stars. Only the faintest spatter of constellations were visible as he passed between the gas lamps, and he missed the diamond-strewn night sky of India with a sudden, fierce yearning.

Perhaps he needn't marry after all. Perhaps he ought to return to Assam and . . .

And what? Dismiss the workers, watch the tea bushes die, and return to Calcutta to beg a position as a junior officer in the Company?

Which was worse: being trapped in marriage with a wife he had no feelings for or seeing all the family's hope of a prosperous future wither away?

There was no answer, and dwelling on such grim thoughts was no way to spend the evening at a fancy dress ball. Even if Ellie Tremont wasn't going to be in attendance, he could enjoy himself—or at least try.

With a last glance up at the distant, nearly invisible stars, Kit stepped onto Buckingham Palace's porticoed entrance. At least, while he waited, he had an entertaining parade of nobility to watch.

Finally, the carriage bearing the Tremonts pulled up. He went forward to greet them, compliment them on their costumes, and offer his escort up the stairs. He could not help noticing that Lady Tremont looked entirely too self-satisfied as they ascended.

There was another wait at the door while the Lord

Steward verified the attendees and announced their arrivals, but at last their turn came.

"Lord Christopher Newland," the man bellowed. "Viscountess Tremont and the Honorable Misses Delia and Abigail Tremont."

Abigail giggled at the announcement, then turned to Kit. "Do you think our dance will be soon?"

"I most fervently hope so," he said, though not for the reasons she thought.

Unfortunately, there were any number of presentations to the Queen and Prince before the orchestra struck up. The first dance was a polka, and he dutifully took Delia out upon the floor. She alternated between flirtatious looks and an artificial-sounding laugh that soon grated against his ears, but Kit did his best to be amenable. For Ellie's sake.

His waltz with Abigail was a bit easier to bear, despite her moon-eyed gazes and heavy sighs every time he guided her into a turn.

"Will Ellie be at home tomorrow?" he asked. He could not leave London without saying goodbye.

"We all will be." She gave him a bright look. "Why, are you planning on paying us a call? How delightful."

So much for his hopes of seeing Ellie alone. Perhaps they could meet in the meadow once more instead. If he gave the butler a note, could the man be trusted to pass it to Ellie without alerting Lady Tremont?

Kit attempted to steer the conversation back toward safer ground, but it seemed Miss Abigail was determined to view everything he said as a particular flirtation toward her. Finally, he gave up and simply danced—no easy feat, considering the crowded condition of the floor.

At the conclusion of the waltz, he returned Abigail to her mother, then fled as quickly as he might. There were other young ladies in attendance he must seek out—no matter that he had little enthusiasm for the task ahead.

Indeed, there was Miss Olivia Thornton, a young heiress whom he'd met at a musicale the week before. Ignoring the heavy sensation in his chest, he went to pay his regards and ask her to dance.

He was determined to make up his mind by the end of the evening. The sooner he chose a bride, the sooner he could return to India. The rains would not hold off just because he was squeamish about doing his duty. His future—indeed, his family's fortune—depended on it.

Chapter 10

ELLIE HUDDLED BESIDE THE fire in her room, a thick shawl over her shoulders, and tried not to let misery engulf her. In the hour since her stepfamily had departed, she'd tried desperately to scrub out her gown, but it was no use.

There will be other balls, she told herself.

But none with Kit in attendance, and that was the bitterest blow of all, that she would not be able to say goodbye.

"Miss Ellie!" Henderson knocked on her door, her voice urgent. "There's a delivery for you."

"What is it?" Ellie rose, suddenly feeling the aches of all her labors echo through her bones.

"Just come—quickly."

When Ellie opened her door, Henderson took her by the elbow and towed her rapidly down the hall.

"A footman is waiting in the foyer," the maid said. "And if I'm not mistaken, he arrived in Lady Merriweather's coach. I caught a glimpse of it waiting outside. That color is quite unmistakable."

"The orange one?" Ellie caught her breath, hardly daring to hope.

"Yes, the one that all the gossips deplore."

"Is the Baroness here, too?"

Henderson shook her head. "I don't know. Perhaps she remained in the coach."

They reached the stairs, and Ellie hastened down, Henderson at her heels. As the maid had said, an elderly footman stood near the front door. The butler, Mr. Atkins, had taken up his post and was ostensibly reading the newspaper. Between the men sat an upright trunk. Ellie's heart skipped a beat.

"Miss Eleanor Tremont?" the white-haired man asked. At Ellie's nod, he gestured to the trunk. "Your ball gown has arrived, compliments of your godmother, Lady Merriweather."

"A bit late, isn't it?" Henderson said under her breath.

Ellie sent her a quelling look, then turned back to the footman. "Did she accompany you, by any chance?"

"She did not," the man said. "But she gave strict instructions to convey you to the Queen's Ball with all haste."

"You must give her time to dress," Henderson said, giving the man a cold look.

"I won't be long," Ellie promised. After all, her hair was already coiffed, and she still wore her jewelry.

"We will take as long as is necessary," Henderson said. "Bring the trunk up to my lady's dressing room now, if you please. Follow us."

The footman nodded and heaved the trunk onto one shoulder. Little caring about the etiquette, Ellie led him directly up the main staircase. When they reached her room, he set his burden down with care, then made her a half bow.

"We await you downstairs," he said. "At your convenience."

As soon as he left, Ellie unfastened the latches, her fingers clumsy with anticipation. Henderson moved to brace the upright trunk, and Ellie slowly pulled it open.

"Oh," she said softly as the ball gown inside was revealed.

The dress was stunning. The pale blue silk of the bodice

and overskirt shimmered, as though interwoven with silver threads. Rosettes of darker blue velvet lined the edges of the skirt, setting off the embroidered gold underskirt beneath. Another rosette decorated the front of the bodice, with touches of gold at the sleeves and neckline.

"My stars," Henderson said. "In that gown, you're fair to outshine the Queen."

"No one can compare to Her Majesty," Ellie replied. "But it *is* a beautiful gown."

"Then let's get you into it, posthaste." Henderson lifted the dress out and laid it across the bed. "Fortunate that your hair ribbons match the gold. Oh, and look—a lace cap to go with it. That will suit perfectly."

A blue velvet bag remained, tied to a hook inside the trunk. Ellie retrieved it and found a jewelry box tucked within. Inside the box was a set of sapphires—necklace, earbobs, and brooch—and her breath caught in a sob at the generosity of her godmother.

"Heavens." Henderson laid a hand on Ellie's shoulder. "The Baroness has outdone herself on your behalf."

There was a note tucked under the necklace. Ellie's eyes were too blurred with gratitude to read it, so she handed it to Henderson.

"*The jewels are a loan*," the maid read. "*You may return them within the week. But keep the dress—I hope it fits. Your affectionate godmother, Constance Merriweather*."

Ellie pulled in a deep breath, mastering herself with effort. There were times to dissolve into tears—but this was not one of them.

Fortunately, the dress *did* fit. A few small adjustments in the shoulders and waist, a quick pinning of the lace over her hair, the sapphires fastened on, her gloves donned, and she was ready.

"I'll accompany you in the coach," Henderson said. "We must be mindful of the proprieties, and I want to see you safely delivered to Buckingham Palace."

"Thank you." In truth, Ellie was glad of the company.

She feared her nerve would fail her, arriving so late to the Queen's Ball. But with Henderson there, she would not turn back from the intimidating thought of entering the palace alone.

True to his word, the footman waited below, with Mr. Atkins keeping a watchful eye.

"Best of luck, Miss Eleanor," the butler said. "I'm pleased you'll be able to attend the ball after all. Most unfortunate, that mishap earlier." He frowned and shook his head.

"Thank you, Mr. Atkins," she said, warmed once again by the support and kindness of the servants.

"Look after her," he said gruffly to Henderson, then opened the front door.

The footman bowed and ushered them out to where the singularly orange coach waited. Inside, it was upholstered in pumpkin-colored velvet, with candles behind glass shedding a warm illumination. Ellie climbed inside, assisted by the footman, and settled her voluminous skirts. Henderson followed, taking the seat across from her.

They did not say much during the ride. Ellie's heart hammered with fear and excitement. What would her step-mother say, to see Ellie gowned like a princess and arriving so remarkably late? Would Kit still be there? Oh, she desperately hoped so, and that she might claim one last dance with him.

Almost before she was ready, the walls of Buckingham Palace were in sight. The guards at the gate waved them through, and the coach pulled up to the Grand Entrance.

"At least there's not a crush to get in," Henderson remarked. "There's one advantage of arriving so late."

Ellie simply nodded, her throat tight with anticipation.

The footman opened the door and handed her down from the coach.

"If you find it agreeable, I shall escort you in," he said to Ellie.

"Yes. Thank you." Even an elderly footman was better than approaching that intimidating facade by herself.

"And I will find the ladies' maids and wait until the ball ends," Henderson said. "Dance well."

"I'll do my best." Ellie managed a smile.

She would not mention that her embroidered slippers still pinched her feet quite uncomfortably. A pity the baroness had not sent footwear, but, she chided herself, her godmother had been more than generous.

Luckily, the gown was a trifle long, the skirts sweeping down to trail on the ground. If Ellie removed her slippers to dance, well, no one would be the wiser.

Setting her gloved hand on the footman's arm, she entered Buckingham Palace. The red-coated guards on duty at the front door did not even glance at her as she and the footman walked between them. She supposed that was better than reproving glances on the tardiness of her arrival, though it rather did make her feel invisible.

At the long, red-carpeted sweep of the Grand Staircase, she nearly lost her nerve—but truly, she could not turn back now. Instead of focusing on her racing heartbeat, she tried to concentrate on the ornate gilded balustrade, the huge portraits of former monarchs lining the high walls.

They reached the top of the stairs, and now she could hear the crowd—a murmur like the sea, punctuated by occasional strains of music. The doors of the Green Drawing Room were open, though she could not see much of the room beyond except a few bright dresses and plumed hats. An official-looking fellow—perhaps an under steward—presided over the threshold.

"My lady," he said, stepping forward. "Have you an official invitation?"

"I was invited, yes." Ellie met his gaze. "I am Miss Eleanor Tremont, joining Lady Tremont and her daughters, who arrived earlier."

Much, much earlier. But there was nothing to do but brazen it out.

"Miss Tremont, is it?" The steward gave her a penetrating look. "I was not notified you would be coming so late. The ball is well underway."

"With all due apologies," the footman said, "she was unavoidably delayed by my mistress, the Lady Merriweather. But Miss Tremont is here now, and, as you can see, quite ready to make her entrance."

The steward raised one bushy brow. "Lady Merriweather, you say?"

"Yes," Ellie said. "She is my godmother."

The man let out a harrumph, but it seemed the baroness's reputation as an eccentric stood Ellie in good stead.

"Very well," he said. "I will announce you. Most everyone is gathered in the Throne Room, however, and will not hear you come in."

"I don't mind," she said.

"Best of luck, milady." The footman bowed over her hand.

She smiled her thanks at him, and then he was gone and the steward was announcing her name in a deep voice. It was time to step forward—in every sense of the word. Shoulders back and chin high, Ellie made her entrance to the Queen's Ball.

Chapter 11

IT WAS, ADMITTEDLY, RATHER anticlimactic. As the steward had said, most of the attendees were packed into the Throne Room, just visible through the double doors at the end of the Green Drawing Room.

Ellie walked through the high-ceilinged room, trying not to wince as her slippers pinched her toes. The chandeliers shed brightness over the figured green carpet and olive-hued walls. A half-dozing elderly gentleman in one of the scattered chairs marked her passage, as did a wilted-looking young lady and her companion, but with those two exceptions, the room was strangely empty.

Noise poured from the scarlet-draped Throne Room ahead, however—a blast of music followed by the sound of applause. She edged into the room in time to see a line of costumed dancers make their bow to the Queen and prince, who stood on a raised dais to one side of the crowded space.

Ellie noted with relief that Queen Victoria wore a magnificent ball gown. Intricate lace framed the neckline, and gold trimmings accented the white silk bodice and overskirts, while the underskirt was a rich, rose-colored brocade. The Queen made an altogether splendid picture, especially with her equally well-garbed consort at her side.

Pride filled Ellie, that she was a subject of such a regal

couple. And thank heavens she would not have to worry about outshining the monarch at her own ball.

While the dancers filed off the floor, Ellie glanced about the room, hoping to catch sight of Kit. And her stepfamily, so that she might avoid them.

She thought she glimpsed Abby's red hair in the far corner, but she couldn't be sure. Then her heart lurched as she spotted Kit making his way toward the door. He looked rather unhappy for a fellow who was attending the most celebrated ball of the Season.

"Excuse me," Ellie said, wedging herself between a woman wearing bright green skirts and a courtier in a coat that stuck out so far from his body she wondered if he'd put part of a hoop crinoline beneath.

After a brief struggle, she emerged, just in time to catch Kit's arm as he went past. He turned, and the look on his face transformed in an instant, like sunlight breaking through storm clouds. The light in his eyes made her catch her breath, and she berated herself for a fool.

Even if Kit had feelings for her, he'd made it all too clear that he would never ask for her hand.

But in that moment, with the musicians striking up a waltz and the crystal chandeliers overhead sparkling with a thousand tiny fires, she didn't care.

"Ellie," he said, the warmth in his voice unmistakable. "I thought you weren't coming."

"I was delayed," she said. "Luckily, my godmother managed to procure me a gown at the last instant."

"And a lovely one it is too. You look particularly beautiful in it."

She blushed. "You weren't leaving, were you?"

"Not any longer." He lifted his head and scanned the floor. "I know it's cramped quarters, but might I have the pleasure of this dance?"

"I'd be delighted," she said, then frowned at the thought of trying to waltz in her too-tight slippers.

"What is it? I promise not to step on your toes."

"I *am* worried about my toes," she confessed. "My dancing slippers are intolerably small."

He leaned forward. "Slip them off, then," he said in a confiding tone. "I won't tell."

"I'm scandalized," she teased. "What an improper thing to suggest."

However, she had already stepped out of the offending footwear, pushing them off each foot with her toes. The bare floor felt blessedly comfortable.

"They're already off, aren't they?" His eyes twinkled with mischief.

"Yes—except I can't bend over to pick them up." Not only was the space too crowded, she feared her skirts would fly up. She wasn't used to wearing such voluminous lengths.

"Push them to the edge of your gown, then drop your fan," he said. "I'll pick it up and collect your shoes into the bargain."

"But where can I put them? My reticule is too small."

"Leave that to me." He gave her a conspiratorial smile.

Trying not to grin too broadly in return, she let her fan fall, then scooted the slippers out from under her hem.

Kit swooped them up. Bowing, he presented her with her fan. His other hand was tucked awkwardly beneath the skirts of his coat.

"You can't simply hold them there," Ellie said. "It looks very odd."

"Take my arm, then. Your sleeves will cover them. Yes, like that."

It was ridiculous, smuggling her slippers through the crowded room, and she was on the verge of laughter as Kit maneuvered them close to one of the floor-to-ceiling windows. With one swift motion, he thrust the footwear behind the red velvet draperies, then turned to her with a triumphant look.

"Now we are free to dance."

"You're incorrigible," she said, laughing.

It felt like old times—like she had a family and friends and no worries for the future.

"And yet eminently practical." He gazed down at her with a warm smile. "You can retrieve them when you go. It's the last curtain."

"Yes, I've marked it."

"Then come—this dance won't last forever."

He deftly swung her out onto the floor, and suddenly Ellie wished it *would* last forever. She could happily spend an eternity with her hand clasped in his, his arm about her waist as they whirled in a scarlet sea beneath a thousand diamond suns.

Her pale blue skirts swung out, and anyone watching could have seen her stockinged feet—but she did not care. Nothing else mattered except this moment, waltzing with Kit—the way they used to practice in the daisy-starred meadow, when she had no cares, no sorrow chaining her to the ground.

But, as it must, the music ended, and her heart regretfully returned to earth. Kit released her, and she was conscious that her pulse was racing—partly from dancing, but mostly from being near him. The heat and jostle of the throng pressed in upon her.

"Might we step out a moment?" she asked. "I could use a bit of air."

"The Picture Gallery should be less crowded," Kit said.

"You know your way about the palace." She lifted one brow. "One might almost think you're a frequent visitor here."

He gave her an amused look. "I'm not, I assure you. I discovered the gallery as a useful retreat earlier this evening when your stepsisters were trying to cajole me into multiple dances."

"Completely understandable," she said, tucking her arm through his. "Lead on, good sir."

He wove them through the mob to the wide opening leading to the gallery. Several other guests had the same notion and were perambulating about the wide hall, but on the whole it was much less crowded.

They paused before a large painting of Queen Charlotte, and Ellie pulled in a breath. "This is much better."

"I agree—though I did enjoy our waltz very much."

"As did I." Bittersweet melancholy tugged at her heart.

She was nerving herself up to ask him when he was departing England, when an older gentleman viewing the next painting glanced over at her.

"Why, is that Miss Eleanor Tremont?" he asked, a note of pleased surprise in his voice.

"Hello, Lord Brumley." She made the earl a curtsy, recognizing him as one of Papa's old friends. "Yes, it's Eleanor."

"How good to see you, my dear—and looking well. I must say, I was sorry to hear of your father's passing."

"Thank you." And for the first time in eight months, she was able to respond without fighting back tears. "Allow me to introduce my escort, Lord Christopher Newland."

"A pleasure." Lord Brumley extended his hand. "Newland, is it? Any relation to the new marquess?"

"Yes, he's my father," Kit said.

"Will he be taking his seat in the House of Lords this fall? I understand he has connections in India. I'm rather interested in the spice trade myself."

"My father certainly intends to take up the duties of his

new title," Kit said. "He plans to arrive in England within the next two months."

"Excellent. Tell him to call upon me when he reaches London. We can trade tales of our travels abroad, compare India to Indonesia and whatnot." Lord Brumley gave him a jovial smile. "In fact, why don't you pay a visit yourself, young man? Find me at Brumley House on Grosvenor Square."

"I shall, thank you."

"Now, off with you both," the earl said, waving them away with a shooing motion. "You young folk should be dancing and enjoying yourselves."

"Yes, my lord," Ellie said. "It was nice to see you again."

With a lighter heart, she and Kit continued their stroll. His company, plus her newfound ability to bear hearing condolences on Papa's death, made her feel as though she were returning to herself. No longer the grief-stricken shadow of a girl or the pliant servant of her stepfamily, but Ellie Tremont, who would face the world on her own terms.

They reached the end of the gallery, where columns flanked a small, nearly hidden anteroom. Ellie glanced at Kit.

"Is this the last time I'll see you before you return to India?"

"I expect so." His gaze met hers, green eyes the color of shadowed oak leaves, no trace of a smile on his firm lips.

As she had feared—and expected. "Will you give me something to remember you by?"

"Of course." He pressed her hand. "Anything you ask."

Her heart thumped wildly. Oh, it was daring of her, but this was her last chance . . .

"A kiss," she said softly. "Just one."

If she were fated to life as a spinster governess, she wanted a glimpse of what it would be like to share a kiss with the man she loved. A single, perfect moment to hold next to her heart and carry with her always.

His eyes widened a fraction, but he nodded. Without a word, he pulled her into the shadows behind the columns. His head dipped to hers, and between one heartbeat and the next, their lips met.

Sensation glittered through her, as though starlight were pouring atop her head and sifting down through her body in silver waves. The place where their mouths touched tingled, and she swayed forward. He caught her against his chest, and tears pricked her closed eyes at the feeling of being pressed so close to him.

It was anchor and storm all at once, safety and tempest whirling in a delicious mix through her very being.

And then it was over.

Blinking, she stepped back. His gaze fixed on hers, Kit gave her a crooked smile that seemed equal parts tenderness and regret.

"Will that do?" he asked.

No, she wanted to say. *Never. Stay with me.*

Instead, she gave him a somewhat stiff nod and stepped back into the main gallery. None of the others in the room had seemed to notice their brief absence, although she thought she saw a flutter of pastel skirts at the entrance to the Throne Room.

After a moment, Kit joined her.

"My ship sails next week," he said, a hint of bleakness in his voice.

"And what of your quest to find a bride?" The words felt like shards of glass in her throat, but she must ask.

"I believe Miss Olivia Thornton is amenable to my suit," he said, not sounding any happier than she.

Ellie swallowed. She did not know Miss Thornton other than as a very distant acquaintance. "She seems a pleasant young lady. And well dowried, I suppose."

"Yes, that." Kit shook his head, his expression strained. "Please, can we talk of something else?"

"There she is!" Delia's shrill voice cut through the air.

Ellie glanced at the doorway to the Throne Room to see her stepfamily approaching. A sneer of triumph on her face, Delia marched in the lead, followed by Abigail and Lady Tremont. Ellie curled her hands into fists, resisting the urge to turn and flee. Cold apprehension washed through her, erasing the last echoes of Kit's kiss.

"Eleanor." Lady Tremont's voice was hard. "How very irregular. You have a great deal of explaining to do."

Ellie's throat went dry as she confronted Lady Tremont's baleful stare.

"My godmother sent me a ball gown," she said, forcing her voice to remain steady. "And Henderson accompanied me."

"You should have joined us directly," Lady Tremont said. "Instead, I discover you sneaking off with Lord Christopher—"

"I asked Ellie to dance," Kit said, stepping forward to shield her. "She'd only just arrived. And then the crush on the dance floor demanded we take a moment to catch our breaths. If you must find fault, Lady Tremont, then I ask you lay it at my feet, not hers."

Delia sniffed and gave him a pointed look. "You are not the gentleman you've led us to believe, Lord Christopher."

"I never pretended to be anything other than who I am," he replied.

"Be that as it may," the viscountess said, "you are henceforth forbidden to visit our home, sir. And speaking of which, we are headed there directly. Girls, collect your things."

Ellie wanted to protest that she'd only just arrived, but the evening was well and truly ruined in any case. She moved toward the ballroom to retrieve her slippers, but Lady Tremont took her arm in a tight grasp.

"No more sneaking away into corners," her stepmother said. "You'll wait outside with me while they bring the carriage around."

Pointedly turning her back on Kit, the viscountess stalked to the doorway leading into the Green Drawing Room, pulling Ellie along with her.

Ellie glanced over her shoulder, hoping Kit could read the apology in her eyes. It was a mortifying end to a night that had careened from bliss to humiliation, and it was certainly not the way she'd wanted to bid him farewell.

"Goodbye, Kit," she called.

His expression set, Kit made her a low bow, as if she were truly a princess. He straightened and their gazes met one last time.

Then Lady Tremont hustled her out of the room, and everything was gone. Her hopes. Her dreams. Her childhood friend.

Everything, except herself.

Ellie pulled her arm out of her stepmother's grip.

"I can navigate the stairs on my own," she said coolly.

Not to mention the rest of her life. On the morrow, she would pay a call on Lady Merriweather to return the sapphires—and secure her help in finding a governess position as quickly as possible.

Kit watched Ellie go, a hot, uncomfortable knot in his chest.

He shouldn't have kissed her—he knew better—but he'd wanted to for weeks, if not years. And she *had* asked.

Unfortunately, all he wanted to do was keep kissing her.

That, and sweep her off to India with him. She would thrive there, he suspected, once she grew accustomed to the climate and culture.

Tonight, he'd seen the old Ellie—the girl who'd challenged him to a tree-climbing contest and, when he'd lost, forced him to read books of poetry that he'd found surprisingly enjoyable. The girl who'd teased him into being a better person and awakened his sense of adventure. The girl he'd once known he'd marry—known fiercely, with the entire burning surety of his fifteen-year-old heart.

As Kit stood in the opulent gallery, the sounds of gaiety drifting from the Throne Room, the realization slowly crystallized within him. His younger self had been right.

He could not marry anyone except Eleanor Tremont.

If he did, he knew that, despite his best efforts, he would constantly compare whomever he wed with Ellie, and find her lacking. That was a sure recipe for a miserable marriage.

Ellie might have no dowry, but life with her was the only path to happiness he could see. For both of them, if he read her emotions aright.

He must find a way to save the tea plantation without marrying for money. True, he and his father had spent long nights turning the problem over and they had not seen a better way.

But he could not save the plantation at the expense of his own heart.

There had to be a solution—and he vowed he would find it.

Chapter 12

ELLIE REGARDED HER BARE wardrobe, then glanced at the partially empty trunk on her bedroom floor. Perhaps she would fill the rest of it with her favorite books. There was no guarantee her new employer would let her make free with their library, after all.

"Must you really leave?" Abby asked from her perch on Ellie's bed. "And to take a job as a governess, of all things? I'm going to miss you."

"I know." Ellie sent her a fond glance. "But I must take this position with the Granvilles, especially as Lady Merriweather arranged it on such short notice. Please, try to understand."

"Oh, I do." Abby grimaced. "As soon as I can, I'm going to find an agreeable husband and leave the house, myself."

"Don't settle for just anyone." Ellie tucked her small pouch of jewelry into one of the trunk's pockets. "You deserve someone who will treat you with consideration."

Abby heaved a sigh. "I would much prefer love—but as Lord Christopher has been banned from the house, there's no hope of that."

Not that Kit had ever intended to offer for Abby, but Ellie kept that thought to herself. There was no need for unkindness, especially during this last hour before her employer's coach came to collect her.

"Kit has left for India, in any case," Ellie said, the knowledge weighing heavily upon her heart.

She'd hoped for a note of farewell, at least, and kept a careful eye on the mail to make sure Lady Tremont didn't get her clutches on any envelopes meant for Ellie. But the days had passed, and there was nothing from Kit.

And now he was gone.

"Miss Eleanor." Mr. Atkins rapped upon her half-open door. "You have a caller."

Sir Granville must have sent his carriage early.

"I'll be down in a moment," she said.

With a sigh, she shut the lid of her trunk. As she straightened from doing up the latches, Abby flung herself off the bed to give her a tearful embrace.

"Don't go," her stepsister said with a choked sob.

"There, there." Ellie patted her back. "I'll have one day off a week, and I'll come visit. The Granvilles don't live so far away as all that."

When they were in town, that was. She didn't mention that the family was planning to repair to their country estate for the rest of the summer. Why add to Abby's unhappiness? With her mercurial nature, she'd recover as soon as Ellie stepped out the door.

Well, perhaps not that quickly, but still.

Leaving her stepsister blotting her eyes, Ellie went downstairs. She paused before the parlor door to pat her hair into place, wondering who Sir Granville had sent to escort her.

A man stood in the center of the room. Ellie froze, heart clenching as she saw it was not some unknown stranger, but Kit Newland, grinning unrepentantly at her.

"Hello, Ellie," he said. "I wasn't sure if the butler would let me in."

With a tremendous thud, her heart resumed beating.

"It's really you?" she asked, trying to balance her careening emotions. She didn't know whether to laugh or cry—or quite how to interpret his unexpected visit. "I thought you'd taken ship already."

"Not yet," he said. "I brought you something."

He stepped forward and handed her the slippers they'd hidden behind the curtains at the Queen's Ball.

"You fetched them out?" she asked, a catch in her throat.

He certainly had no obligation to do so, and his thoughtfulness nearly undid her altogether—no matter that she despised the too-small slippers.

"Of course." He raised his brows. "It wouldn't do to leave evidence of the crime behind. This way, you can dispose of them properly."

"Please don't tell me you delayed your journey simply to bring back my slippers," she said, setting them aside.

"Not entirely." His expression turned serious. "The truth is, there's something I couldn't bear to leave behind."

Her hands trembled, and she squeezed them tightly together.

"What might that be?" she asked, trying to keep her voice steady.

"Can't you guess?" He took another step and gently set his hands on her shoulders. "My heart, Ellie. Don't you know it's in your keeping?"

She shook her head. "But . . . what of Miss Thornton and her dowry?"

"After the ball, I realized you were the only one for me. Drat it, I'm not doing this properly." He released her shoulders and went down on one knee. "Miss Eleanor Tremont, would you do me the very great favor of becoming my wife?"

She wanted to say yes—oh, how she wanted to—and yet . . .

"What about your tea plantation?" She knew she must turn him down, despite the anguish burning in her chest. "I can't let you ruin your future for me, Kit."

"I wouldn't ask you to," he said solemnly. "Lord Brumley has agreed to become an investor."

Ellie drew in a disbelieving breath. "He has?"

Kit reached and took her hands, smoothing her fingers and clasping them in his. "It took some convincing—and even more time to settle the paperwork, or I would have been here days ago—but yes, the plantation is saved, whether I marry for money or not."

"And would we live in India?"

"Is that agreeable to you?" Concern shaded his eyes.

"Yes," she said fervently. "I would very much like that. And more to the point, I would very much like to marry you, Lord Christopher Newland. Someone has to keep that title from going to your head, after all."

He gave a shout of laughter and stood. Then they were in one another's arms, and Ellie's despair turned to a brilliant, shining joy.

"What's this?" Lady Tremont's voice snapped through the room. "Lord Christopher, you are not welcome beneath this roof. I require you to leave, immediately."

"He can't." Ellie faced her stepmother defiantly. "He's my betrothed."

Lady Tremont blanched, her eyes wide with shock.

"You can't marry," she said in a voice shrill with anger. "I forbid it. Forbid it! Do you understand?"

Kit stepped between them. "Too late. And now *I* require you to cease threatening my fiancée."

"Out!" Lady Tremont shrieked, pointing toward the door. "Out, the both of you."

"Gladly," Ellie said, feeling a sure calm descend over her.

"My trunk is already packed. See it delivered to Lady Merriweather's. Come, Kit."

Ignoring her stepmother's poisonous glare, she brushed past and headed for the front door, Kit at her shoulder.

Mr. Atkins held the door open, an apologetic look on his face.

"So sorry, miss," he said. "I'll send Henderson to you."

"Please do." She paused. "When we depart for India, I'll offer you a place. If that's all right, Kit?"

"Of course," her fiancé said, his hand warm at her back. "And your maid too, it goes without saying."

A loud crash from the parlor made them turn, and Mr. Atkins winced. "I'm afraid that was the Chinese urn. You'd best be going."

Ellie nodded. "Please tell whomever Sir Granville sends that I've had a change in plans."

She would have to make her apologies to that family, and to her godmother, but under the circumstances, she wagered they'd understand.

As she and Kit climbed into the cab he'd hired, another shriek of rage drifted from the house. She'd no idea why her betrothal had sent her stepmother into such a fierce tantrum, and she had no intention of returning to find out.

"Lady Merriweather's," Kit told the driver, and the man nodded.

The coach jolted into motion, and Kit took her hands once more.

"I even brought a ring," he said, a bit forlornly, "but that didn't go at all as planned."

"It was a memorable proposal, at any rate." She smiled at him, her spirits rising with every moment they traveled away from Tremont House. "May I see it?"

He drew a small velvet bag from his pocket and shook out the ring. "I had to guess on the fit."

She held her left hand out, and he slipped the ring onto her finger.

"It's perfect," she said, looking down at the yellow tourmaline surrounded by diamonds.

"The closest thing I could find to a daisy," he said with a smile.

"Absent that flower, it will have to do." Then she laughed and leaned forward to kiss him, and everything was right with the world.

It was not, of course, quite as simple as that.

Lady Merriweather required several explanations, but at last she was satisfied and agreed that Ellie might remain with her until their departure for India.

Henderson appeared in due time, along with Ellie's trunk, which proved to contain some books and Abby's second-best pelisse. The additions made Ellie's heart warm even further toward her stepsister, and she vowed to ask Kit's parents to look in upon Abby when they arrived in England.

The most surprising development, however, came three days later, when Papa's solicitor paid Ellie a call.

Her godmother gave a nod, as though she'd been expecting such a visit, and accompanied Ellie down to the yellow parlor to meet with the man—a brown-haired fellow named Mr. Tippet.

After the pleasantries had been concluded, the solicitor set his folder of papers on the table before them.

"Now that you're to be married," he said, "we have the details of your inheritance to be worked out."

"I beg your pardon?" Ellie regarded him with some confusion from her place on the sofa. "I was given to understand that Papa left me no money."

Mr. Tippet gave her a precise nod. "True, but only until your marriage. Then you are to come into the thirty thousand pounds he left you."

The breath left her in a whoosh, and she sagged back. It was a substantial sum, and suddenly Lady Tremont's rage at hearing of her betrothal made sense.

"Excellent," Lady Merriweather said, lifting her quizzing glass. "If I might take a look at those papers?"

The solicitor pushed the neat stack her way, and she made a few *hms* and *tsks* as she paged through.

"I take it my stepmother knew of this provision," Ellie asked, the first surge of anger overcoming her shock.

"Of course she did." The solicitor blinked at her in dismay. "Do you mean to say she did not inform you? She said the news would come better from her and bade me not to speak of it."

"No." Ellie's voice was hard. "She said nothing."

So much of Lady Tremont's behavior made sense now—keeping her in mourning, treating her as a servant so that she would remain downtrodden in her own home. Telling her she had no dowry! It was the outside of enough. Bitterly, Ellie wondered how many callers her stepmother had turned away for fear of Ellie catching some suitor's eye.

"I am so sorry." Mr. Tibbs sounded flustered. "I had thought . . . that is, I assumed . . ."

"Not everyone is as honorable as you are, sir," the Baroness said dryly. "However, all the paperwork appears to be in good order. Congratulations, my dear. You are an heiress."

Ellie still could not grasp it. If only she'd known! She and Kit might have married right away.

And then she would have spent the rest of their marriage wondering if he loved her more for herself, or for her money.

No. Despite the terrible enormity of Lady Tremont's lie, it had allowed Ellie and Kit to find their true way to one another, to follow the compass of their hearts without going astray.

"I imagine your young man will be glad of the news," the solicitor said. "He must think quite highly of you, if he believed, er . . ."

"That he was marrying a penniless orphan?" Ellie said tartly. "As a matter of fact, he does love me, very much. And while this is a very welcome circumstance, it will not matter to our happiness."

Lady Merriweather cleared her throat. "I assure you, it will make a difference—though I've no doubt you would have been happy either way. But it is far easier to be content in life when one has a small fortune at one's disposal. Speaking of which, I rather fancy the thought of coming to India for your wedding. Perhaps I'll be your chaperone until you're wed. What do you say to that?"

Ellie smiled at her. "I think it would suit very well."

She and Kit had decided to have the ceremony abroad so that his parents might attend—and so that her stepmother might not. After the revelations of the afternoon, Ellie preferred never to set eyes on that dreadful woman again.

"Then it's settled," the baroness said. "We set sail next Wednesday. In the meantime, I'll help you with opening bank accounts and the like. One doesn't want a sum that size sitting about in bills, after all."

"Very wise," the solicitor said. "We can meet tomorrow at the Royal Bank. Two o'clock?"

While her godmother settled the particulars, Ellie contented herself with imagining telling Kit the good news. With the investment from Lord Brumley, she had no doubt the tea plantation would thrive.

And with her inheritance, she had no doubt their family would, too. She closed her eyes a moment, conjuring up a vision—a house with a wide veranda tucked beside a prosperous tea plantation, she and Kit sitting outside, watching their children play. Two—no, three of them—a girl and two boys.

Henderson was there, and Mr. Atkins, who found the heat a blessing to his old bones. The Baroness visited every few years, bringing the children strange, exotic items from England. And surprisingly, Abby would visit as well, along with her ambassador husband, who altogether doted upon her.

Through it all—the year of drought, the monsoons that washed away a third of their crop, the blight five years after that—she and Kit persevered. And, at last, found financial prosperity.

But it was nothing compared to the wealth of love and companionship they would share together till the end of their days.

A *USA Today* bestselling author and two-time RITA nominee, **Anthea Lawson** was named "one of the new stars of historical romance" by *Booklist.* Her books have received starred reviews in *Library Journal* and *Publishers Weekly. A Lord's Chance* is the newest novella in her Passport to Romance collection.

Anthea lives with her husband and daughter in sunny Southern California, where they enjoy fresh oranges all winter long. In addition to writing historical romance, Anthea plays the Irish fiddle and pens bestselling, award-winning YA urban fantasy as Anthea Sharp.

Find out about all her books at anthealawson.com, and join her mailing list, tinyletter.com/AntheaLawson, for a FREE STORY, plus all the news about upcoming releases and reader perks!

For more sweet Victorian romance by Anthea, try the following novellas:

A Countess for Christmas
A Duke for Midwinter
A Prince for Yuletide
To Wed the Earl
A Lady's Choice

For more romantic adventure set abroad, the *spicy* full-length novel *Fortune's Flower* reveals Isabelle's past, as the Strathmore family adventures in Tunisia in search of a fabled bloom.

A LOVE TO CLAIM

Rebecca Connolly

Chapter 1

London, 1845

WAS THERE EVER ANYTHING more tedious than a ball? Crowds of people bustling here and there, jostling the unsuspecting guest and upsetting conversations and glasses of punch, and being forced into overpoliteness for fear of appearing uncouth by behaving in the reverse.

And that was only if the ball were hosted by the popular individuals.

God help the poor souls who hosted a ball that no one attended and at which the aforementioned occurrences could not occur due to lack of sufficient numbers to make the evening more hectic. There was no recovering from that sort of thing.

Not that Abigail Sterling cared one whit about popularity, balls, or recovering from a Society misstep. She did not.

Would not and could not.

She had enough to be getting on with in her own personal missteps and perceived follies.

Nearly three years, and she was still getting the occasional comment or remark from those who could not mind their own business or keep themselves informed on the current standings of various members of Society and the gossip that circulated among them. Well-meaning older women and impertinent younger women tended to let their interest in her resurface when there was nothing else to discuss, and it really was ridiculous.

Nothing had even happened! There had been no scandal, no broken engagements, and no jilting by either party! No one was ruined, and no one would be shunned by Society. Lives had certainly been changed, but only three of them, as far as she could count.

Nothing broken but her heart, and that had mended.

Mostly.

The cracks tended to reappear when the insensitive comments did.

She tried her utmost to keep herself aloof when such comments arose, and she could honestly say that she had no more emotional attachment to the situation beyond that of annoyance. No more broken heart, no more pining, and no more tears of any sort. The reminder of her past disappointment rankled but did not provide any sort of upset to her daily living, nor even to her sleep.

There was simply nothing else to talk about where she was concerned, so the gossips revisited it whenever they could.

She really ought to have spent more time away from London, but there was only so much good that avoidance could offer, and she had spent the lot.

"Don't look so disgruntled, Abigail. It's a ball, not a hanging."

She glared up at her brother, a high-and-mighty sort where his sisters were concerned, no matter how they could trounce him in nearly all of his gentlemanly pursuits. "It's all the same to me, Thomas, and you know it."

He grinned down at her, dark eyes flashing with mischief. "Any social occasion is a hanging for you. You'll never manage any sort of husband or friends if you don't change your tune."

Abigail scowled and looked away, wishing it would not cause comment to tread her brother's foot loudly and repeatedly in this particular environment. "I have friends enough."

"Mama's Spinster Chronicle friends, their husbands, and their offspring do not count," Thomas countered. "Particularly not Cousin Izzy's."

He had a point there. She was honest enough to say that much at least.

She made a small sound of complaint under her breath that made her brother chuckle. "How long must we stay?"

"It's been three quarters of an hour, Abs," Thomas pointed out without any semblance of sympathy. "And they've not even brought out the meal yet. Unless there is some great emergency preventing you from staying, you must wait that out, at least."

Abigail groaned without restraint. "But no one is asking me to dance, and so I stand here next to you, of all people, looking as though there is something wrong with me." She glanced down at her gown and put her hands on her sides, feeling the steady tension of her corset. "*Is* there something wrong with me? My skirts seem fine enough, and my bodice is in place. . . . My corset could go smaller, if my figure is an issue."

"I refuse to comment on your figure in a public place, Abigail Sterling," he retorted hotly, lowering his voice for the benefit of those in the nearest vicinity. "I am your brother, not your lady's maid, for God's sake."

That earned him a dark look. "Then ignore the figure aspect. Is my gown amiss?"

Thomas sighed the longsuffering sigh all brothers know well. "No, Abs. It is a very fine gown and suits you well. I'll even go so far as to say it makes your eyes stand out as greener than usual."

She made a face of polite consideration, and appeared a little impressed. That was a suitable compliment, especially from one's brother, who was more likely to tug her hair from its coiffure than praise anything about her.

Her hands flew to her hair, patting the aforementioned coiffure carefully. "And my hair? I was torn between ribbons or decorative pins, but the ribbons seemed more suited to the occasion."

The answer she received was a bewildered and indignant look.

She frowned. "I'm guessing you aren't going to comment on my hair either."

"You haven't got a single hair out of place," her brother assured her, still looking almost ill, "but I am gravely concerned that you seem to think I am one of your sisters. Are you feeling well? Have you a fever?"

He made a show of placing a hand against her brow, and she batted it away, smiling reluctantly. "Wretch. Ned would have taken me seriously, I'll have you know."

"I highly doubt that. Ned doesn't care about anything so tedious unless it comes dressed in a brilliantly scarlet officer's coat with glimmering gold buttons." Thomas widened his eyes meaningfully, his mouth forming a strained line that made Abigail laugh aloud.

"Aww," Abigail eventually replied. "Poor Ned. I'm sure he will make captain soon enough."

"Not soon enough for my taste," Thomas muttered, taking a glass from a passing footman and downing it in one ungentlemanly swig. "Our brother is obsessed with furthering his career, and I don't care."

Abigail smiled at her brother's statement, knowing he meant only part of what he said. Thomas and Ned were rather close, as it happened, and Ned and Abigail shared a close bond themselves, being just shy of a year apart in age. That had not stopped Ned from participating in whatever schemes Thomas concocted against the girls of the family, but when he was not a scamp, either at seven or seventeen, he was Abigail's favorite sibling.

"The point is," Thomas went on, his tone returning to normal, "that there is nothing in any sort of visible or obvious way as to detract from anyone's opinion of you."

"Meaning . . . ?"

"Some people are simply unintelligent, and there it is."

Abigail coughed a surprised laugh, as did someone near them. She didn't dare look to verify their eavesdropper's identity and kept her attention strictly on the dance. "Who told you that?" she hissed between restrained giggles.

"Papa did. Last week."

Now there was no way to control her laughter, and she turned her face into her brother's sleeve to muffle the sounds. He reached over with his far arm and patted her shoulder as though she were sobbing against him rather than snickering. "There, there, sister dear," he murmured with all the condescension of elder brothers. "Come, come, you mustn't make such a scene."

Abigail whacked at his shins with her slipper, and he grunted softly, much to her satisfaction.

"What's this?" a familiar voice inquired mildly. "Sterling siblings causing a scene? Unheard of and preposterous!"

"Uncle Hensh," Thomas greeted with a bow. "Do excuse Abigail. She's quite done for."

Another hand, heavier than Thomas's, patted her with a bit more force. "Dear girl, kindly stop your incessant giggling and spare your old uncle a dance."

Abigail gasped for air as she removed her face from the stiff sleeve of Thomas's eveningwear and faced the well-adored face of their father's closest friend. "How did you know I was not crying?" she asked, wiping any potential tears of mirth from her.

Uncle Hensh offered her a sardonic look and extended a hand. "Because I have known you since the day of your birth, Abigail Miranda, and I know very well you are far more likely to be laughing at something than crying at it."

She lifted a shoulder, placed her hand in his, and curtsied belatedly in greeting. "Oh Lord."

"Uncle Hensh will do just fine, thank you."

She turned away from him in the dance, shaking her head. He was getting worse, as he usually did, and any sign of encouragement would only accelerate matters. She had spent a lifetime perfecting a blank face specifically to prevent Uncle Hensh from worsening in his attempts at humor, and now was a perfect opportunity to utilize it.

When she faced him again in the dance, the mask was in place, and this time, it made Hensh laugh. "Oh dear, I've upset you. Is there no way to repent of my offense?" he teased, squeezing her hand.

Her lips quirked, breaking the cardinal rule of this particular mask. "Perhaps."

The pressure on her hand lessened at once. "Now I'm afraid. What would put me back in your good graces?"

"Taking me home the moment this dance is over?"

She felt Hensh laugh beside her, though he emitted no sounds of joviality. "Not at all likely, princess. I know better. Fond as I am of you, I am far more terrified of your mother, and I refuse to subject myself to her interrogation."

"Coward," she muttered with a scowl as she parted from him and joined the ladies in a line.

Uncle Hensh shook his head very firmly, still smiling. "Not at all. I simply have a healthy sense of self-preservation and the wisdom to know when to employ it."

There was no helping her smile at that point. He could irk her as well as her brothers could, but there was no denying that Uncle Hensh was the most excellent of men and possessed a remarkably resilient good humor. But then, he was her father's friend. He would have to be akin to a saint in order to endure that trial of a connection all these years.

Abigail didn't have a single friendship that had withstood to her present age, let alone an additional twenty-some-odd years beyond, unless one counted the friendships Thomas considered exempt from such a category. And those were more family friendships than personal ones. She could talk and visit with any of those people for ages on end at any given time, no matter the length of time apart, and feel quite herself throughout the whole.

But as far as her own friends, and not those she had been born into, there was not a single solitary soul remaining by her side.

What did that illustrate for a young woman of twenty-three?

She frowned at the thought.

"What's that for, Abby-girl?" Hensh asked, breaking into her cycle of self-deprecation with the name he alone had ever used for her.

She managed a smile that was fairly close to natural and hoped it would convince him. "Nothing at all. Thinking too much."

His raised brow indicated he had not been convinced by the smile. But he tutted audibly, shaking his head. "Thinking in the middle of the dance? I must be an abysmal partner indeed. Come, let's make this last pass the best one yet."

They proceeded up the rows of lines with an increased vigor in their steps, and Abigail found herself laughing in real delight by the time they reached the end. She had never been spry, and she doubted Henshaw had ever been either, but somehow they both managed it beautifully.

The dance ended, and they bowed and curtsied to each other. Then Hensh surprised her by taking her hand and looping it through his arm, leading her in the opposite direction of where she had Thomas had been standing.

She did not resist or protest, as she had no objection to being in his company, but she did give him a curious look.

He rubbed her hand and smiled with all the tender warmth in the world. "I can't stand you being a wallflower, Abigail. Even if you do not dance again this evening, now you will at least be more widely seen." His expression turned more teasing. "And in my company, you may be sure of garnering an increase in the good opinions of others."

"Ah," Abigail replied with a sly smile. "So this is all for my benefit, is it?"

"Naturally, naturally," he boasted, puffing his chest out as he nodded at some random person. "I am a slave to my own philanthropy, you know."

"I'm sure you are."

Abigail let her gaze run along the various faces around them, an easy smile on her lips, not particularly seeing anyone at all. A show of attention and consideration so as to appear warm and genteel, though she would never be able to tell anyone whom she had seen at this particular event, nor would she care to.

Then, suddenly, there was a face that did not belong, one that she somehow managed to see clearly, though she hadn't with any of the rest.

Don't look back. Don't look back.

Her eyes disobeyed with a flourish as she not only looked back, but dropped her smile as well.

He was gone, thankfully, and her heart, which had leaped

into her ears as she had turned, returned to its place within her chest.

"Someone you know?" Hensh asked softly.

Abigail shook her head with a swallow. "I thought so, but it appears I was mistaken."

Hensh made a noncommittal sound of acknowledgement, covering her hand with his again.

It was a comforting gesture, and she wondered if he suspected the identity of the person she had thought she'd seen. She hoped not, but it was a simple enough deduction to make.

Not many people on this earth would warrant a second look from her.

Not many at all.

"Abigail . . ."

Her heart veered sharply to her right, turning her body with it even as her lungs seized in distress while the rest of her protested wildly, knowing before she saw anything at all what she would see.

And there he was.

She hadn't imagined him, hadn't been wrong, hadn't . . .

He looked exactly as she remembered, though with neatly trimmed facial hair that made him look more a man than he had ever seemed in years past. The same eyes that were neither green nor brown, the barely contained dark hair kept at an almost fashionable length, and the same breadth of slender frame, though perhaps with an improvement.

And the exact same intensity in his gaze.

Matthew Weber-Grey.

Hensh said nothing beside her, but the tension radiating from him was palpable and his hold on her hand extremely tight, grounding her in an instant.

Abigail stared, swallowed, then blurted out, "What in the world are you doing here?"

Chapter 2

SAY SOMETHING, MAN. SAY anything.

Matthew Weber-Grey only stared stupidly at Abigail, wondering where his carefully laid plan had gone and frantically grappling for sense. He'd been thrown off course when he had seen her after so long, and now he couldn't remember a thing. She was exactly as he had recalled her ever being, yet somehow she was infinitely more. His heart swelled in a way he could not ever recall experiencing before, and he knew his course was right. Difficult, some might say impossible, but right. Belated, undoubtedly, but right.

What had she asked? What was he doing here? That, at least, he knew.

"I've returned to London," he heard himself say in a surprisingly polite voice, given the turmoil raging throughout him. "And we are old friends, are we not?"

Oh, that was a perfect thing to say, wasn't it? Abigail would love that after what he put her through.

As he suspected, her brow snapped down, and any of her hesitation and shock vanished in an instant. "Old friends," she repeated in a tone that made him wary. "Is that what you would call it?"

"Abigail," Henshaw murmured, completely devoid of emotion. He showed none of the warmth and joviality he was known for, and he eyed Matthew with all the severity he might his mortal enemy on the battlefield. Faintly, it occurred to Matthew to be grateful that no manner of weaponry was appropriate for social occasions.

At his word, Abigail fixed a smile on her face that raised his concern more than her tone had. "But of course we were, Mr. Weber-Grey. Those lovely summers as children at Hazelwood and Chisolm still live in memory. Very pleasant indeed, and I am glad to be reminded of them. Thank you for renewing such a fond acquaintance. I trust we shall see you about London often at the events of the Season." She inclined her head as regally as any monarch ever had, then let Henshaw sweep her away from him.

Formal, cold, and dismissive.

Well, it was better than hostile, murderous, and insulting, at any rate, so he must consider himself fortunate, he supposed.

Reputation was intact for them both. Glancing around, he could detect no hint of gossip from the surrounding guests, so there should be no complaints on that score—should Abigail actually speak to him again and do so long enough to complain about anything.

He blanched as he considered that now he had given her time to retire to house and catalog every single complaint from the last three years, likely starting and ending with that awful spring day.

He'd likely be pummeled repeatedly by Abigail herself during that particular conversation and ought to have a physician standing by at his home.

No matter what happened, he would deserve every single blow.

He hoped he would have a chance to tell Abigail that he knew that before she rendered him unconscious.

He knew what he had done to her, in every extreme and

in every facet. He knew the difficulty of managing each day for months on end after that day and the dull ache that never really went away.

You simply learned to ignore it and live with it.

He knew all of this.

Everything he had put her through, he himself had endured. He would never compare the extent of their suffering and would never presume to know if Abigail had found her way through. Where she undoubtedly would feel betrayed, he had felt guilt. Where she had likely felt humiliation, he had felt shame. Where she had potentially cried herself to sleep, he had paced for hours on end.

The experience and emotions were different. The pain was the same.

And he had been the cause of it.

Three years of torment was enough, and now he wanted to change things. Mend things. Renew things, if he was so fortunate.

Apologize if he was not.

But such things would take time and a significant amount of patience.

He had time, and he would learn patience.

Abigail was worth it. What they had had was worth it.

Redemption was worth it.

Belatedly, he recalled that he was at a ball, and if he were going to remain in Society for the length of time it would take for Abigail Sterling to forgive him, or at least accept him as something less than the greatest evil that walked the earth, he would need to actively participate in it.

Clearing his throat, he turned around and smiled pleasantly at the room around him. It had been years since he had been in London, spending his time in the countryside of Essex instead, though not at the family estate at Chisolm.

The barest hint of a chance that he could be near Abigail at all was enough to take him elsewhere, though his father refused to let him out of the county.

But now he was back in London, trying to recall the more rigid edicts of behavior in Society before he fouled up in a faux pas from which he could not recover. That would certainly put a marked hindrance into his plans, and he could not afford hindrance or delay. Not when he had so very far to go.

He smiled to himself as the rest of his plan unfolded in his mind, carefully constructed over months of plotting and strategizing. He obviously hadn't been able to perfectly predict how Abigail would respond to his appearance, let alone what he actually needed to tell her, but it wasn't much of a leap, either. The plan would work under a variety of reactions and scenarios, and he could adjust his course as needed to accommodate them.

Adjust his course. He sounded like a bloody navigator, and he'd been on a boat maybe twice in his entire life.

Still, the analogy was apt.

The smile on his face vanished in an instant as he caught sight of Thomas Sterling glaring with the power of seven thunderstorms in his direction. There were more threats in that look than he could count, and he swallowed the sudden rise of nerves with difficulty as Thomas led his sister out of the ballroom.

Right. He'd forgotten how close the Sterling siblings were, and that he would have to contend with the rest of the family as well as Abigail. It was entirely possible that the real challenge in all of this would not be Abigail, but the family behind and around her.

Her life had been changed by his actions.

Her family would be the ones to cry for vengeance.

That he should have thought about.

Hyde Park in the mornings seemed as close as Matthew would ever get to his daily walks in the countryside of his estate. There were still a great many more people than he had ever seen on his excursions in Essex, but he supposed he could not expect anything less in a place as bustling and popular as London, especially at this time of year.

Still, it was a respite from the frantic energy that seemed to emit from every corner of the rest of the city. Here, at least one could breathe freely and imagine themselves in a far more peaceful place. In the morning it was less crowded than in the afternoons or even the evenings, but it still had various members of Society flitting about its paths.

He rather liked this time of day wherever he was, and today was no exception. He had not seen nor heard from Abigail since the ball three nights ago, and part of him had clung to the sudden fear that she would leave London altogether. Still, he could not see her parents whisking her away just as the Season was beginning, particularly when Maren would only be in her first or second Season herself.

He would hinge everything upon her remaining, and once her saw her again and spoke more than three words of politeness, the plan could proceed.

"Matthew Weber-Grey."

He paused a step, his mind whirling about quickly to identify the familiar voice. Warily, he shifted to his left, afraid of what he might see.

Oh, damn. Lord Sterling, Abigail's powerful cousin.

Well, her father's cousin, at any rate.

A very close, more-like-a-brother, incredibly protective sort of cousin.

If he ran for it, would Lord Sterling catch him?

Lord Sterling tilted his head very slightly in a direct answer to the many questions Matthew was silently asking.

There would be no escape, then. Lovely.

Matthew strode forward, only three steps or so, and offered him a slight bow. "My Lord Sterling, a pleasure to see you again."

"Is it?" Lord Sterling asked without much of a question in the tone.

Not really, no, but he was not idiotic enough to admit that. He settled on a bland smile and a nod. "Yes, sir."

Lord Sterling clearly did not believe him, but Matthew hadn't exactly been convincing. "We haven't seen you in London for, what, three years at least?"

"Roughly, yes, my lord." There was no point in avoiding the awkwardness of the basic arithmetic of his being in London and the elapsed time since he had left Hazelwood for the final time.

"Why are you here now, then?" Lord Sterling was clearly following Matthew's thinking without any trouble whatsoever, his expression as mild as before.

Matthew clasped his hands behind his back, forcing himself to at least appear calm, if not actually manage the feeling itself. "I thought it high time that I come to London and participate in the Season, as I have yet to do so."

Lord Sterling raised a brow. "What, now that your wife is dead?"

Any and all air within Matthew's lungs evaporated in a painful heave. He stared at the barely gray-haired man in disbelief, wondering with horror if everyone in the family knew his current situation.

His hesitation made Lord Sterling roll his eyes a little. "She doesn't know, if that is your concern. None of them do, but I am not so disconnected from the world that it escaped my observation. So now that you are a free man, you've come to London to . . . what, find a new bride?"

The words were harsh, but the tone was anything but. Somehow Lord Sterling kept the whole thing purely conversational, as though they were discussing the morning air. Still, the effect was the same, and Matthew swallowed hard, driving back the burn of indignation before it could ignite his temper.

Remember the plan . . . Remember the plan . . .

"Not exactly, sir," Matthew informed the older man, lifting his chin just enough to remove any hint of appearing demure.

He may have imagined it, but he would swear Lord Sterling's mouth twitched into the slightest shadow of a smile for a moment. "Then what, pray tell, is your purpose, Matthew?"

There was a warmth underlying his words now, and it did not escape Matthew's notice that Lord Sterling had turned to informality in his address, though he refuse to dwell on it for the present.

He met Lord Sterling's gaze as squarely as he could. "I came for Abigail."

Lord Sterling raised a brow. "To claim her?"

Matthew nodded. "If she'll have me."

Now he knew he did not imagine the smile that flashed across Lord Sterling's face, and it stunned him into speechlessness.

"Good," Lord Sterling replied, either ignoring Matthew's shock or somehow unaware of it.

Good? How could anyone in the Sterling family, extended or immediate, find this to be a good thing?

Lord Sterling surprised him once more before he could react, nudging his head behind Matthew. "She'll come from that direction and should arrive at any time. Good luck." He turned and began to walk away, then turned back. "Feel free to call on me, Matthew, at any time. I'm willing to risk my neck for you on the chance you could make Abigail as happy as she deserves to be." He nodded, then continued on his way.

There was no explaining what had just happened, and no time to even attempt any sort of processing or hypothesizing. If Abigail was coming, and Lord Sterling thought he could speak with her . . .

To claim her, the man had asked. Yes, Matthew did want to claim her.

And he dearly wanted to be claimed himself.

By her.

Suddenly, there she was, completely unaware of his presence, walking down the head of the path at a pace too swift for leisure and too slow for haste.

How soon would she see him? Would she turn and go the other way? Would she march to him in all anger and let herself lash out at him?

He sucked in a breath and began to walk toward her slowly, averting his eyes until he drew closer.

She saw him before he returned his gaze to her, and he could see her stiffen. Yet she continued forward, nary a halting step in her tread, eyes spearing Matthew with all the efficacy of any skewer in the world.

Abigail stopped, folding her hands. "Did you know I was going to be here this morning? Is this part of some plan you've concocted?"

Matthew shook his head, praying he looked as earnest as he truly was. "No. I did not know you would be here this morning. I simply came out for a stroll. It reminds me of Chisolm, in a way, and the peace of the country."

She inhaled a breath, then released it in a rush, nodding.

"True enough, I suppose. This is the closest I come to Hazelwood, and it almost makes the longing go away."

He smiled with some hesitation. "You always did prefer Hazelwood to anywhere else."

"And that hasn't changed," she quipped, smiling herself. Then she seemed to recall that she did not want to smile in his presence, and her expression returned to the frigidity of before. "What are you doing here, Matthew? And I don't mean this park. I mean in London. You've never been here for the Season or any other social occasions, and I don't see any reason for you to start now."

Matthew nodded once, then cleared his throat. "I came to London to see you."

Abigail blinked unsteadily, the look on her face only mildly shifting in her surprise. "Why?" she asked in a flat voice.

He took a moment, taking great care with his words. "I wanted to explain. To apologize. To see if anything could be salvaged between us for the sake of the friendship we once shared."

Her lips mouthed the word *friendship*, twisting in derision, and she seemed to scoff without making a single sound. "What is there to explain, exactly? You chose Eliza over me. It was that simple."

"I know," he replied, ignoring the bitterness in her voice. "I betrayed you."

She lifted one shoulder in a shrug. "There was no formal understanding. Nothing was broken beyond repair, and no betrayal was committed, officially. My personal feelings have no relevance."

That he could not ignore. "They have all the relevance in the world! You have to know I never meant to hurt you."

"And yet you still chose a woman you barely knew over

one you shared an understanding with," she spat, the first signs of true pain appearing.

"And it was the greatest mistake of my life, I can assure you!" he admitted freely.

Abigail raised a silent brow, fuming where she stood.

Matthew took one step forward. "I have felt incomplete for the entire time I spent as her husband, and have thought of little else but you."

She laughed once. "And now you wish to be physically unfaithful as you have apparently been mentally and emotionally unfaithful? What a fine example of a husband you are."

"Eliza died, Abigail."

The lines of mockery on her beautiful face faded at once. "She what?"

"Died," he repeated. "Two years ago. In childbirth."

She had not been expecting that, he could tell, and she fumbled for words. "And the baby?"

He shook his head, a swell of pained emotion rising. "Lost with her. I have nothing, Abigail. Nothing to show for my life since betraying you. And while I rightly mourn the loss of my wife and my child, when I realized that I could make it all right, I felt hope as I have never hoped before."

Abigail frowned at that and cocked her head. "Hope for what?"

Matthew looked at her with all the love in the world, that which had never fully left him. "Understanding, Abigail. Understanding." He smiled, somehow finding encouragement here. "When you're ready, I'll tell you everything. Not to persuade you, not to plead my case, and not to make you pity me. Just because you deserve to know."

He bowed, touching the brim of his hat, and walked away, exhaling and smiling to himself, praying it would be enough.

Chapter 3

ABIGAIL RUSHED INTO THE London house her family owned, removing her bonnet and shaking her hair to rid it of stray drops of water. It hadn't been raining when she left the house, and nor had it rained overly much on her walk in Hyde Park.

But after she had seen Matthew today, yet again, the sky seemed determined to express what she could not and poured down upon her shamelessly.

How perfectly apt.

Not that she was especially wishing to cry excessively or rage at the heavens or anything that she might have been capable of three years ago, but every instance she saw Matthew dredged up all the despairingly gray memories of that time. Months upon months of dreary, rainy days, no matter what the weather was actually doing out of doors.

What was worse was that she found herself conflicted. Ever since that day she had seen him in Hyde Park over a week ago, she had seen him nearly every day. They had not spoken since, though he had clearly seen her walking as well. He would only smile with all politeness in her direction and tip his hat to her. No further attempts to gain her good opinion or to explain himself, or even to speak with her at all.

Simple, polite acquaintances. That was what they were at present, which was something they had never been to each other.

Despite her pain, despite everything he had put her through, this distance was awkward and strained. Every time she saw him, she was torn between heading in his direction, though not with any particular haste, and running headlong in the opposite direction with a great deal of haste.

And every time, she managed to keep her course exactly as it had been, and it never felt any less miraculous.

What was he playing at? He said he had wanted understanding, but understanding of what? What had happened? His situation? The way things stood now?

Curiosity ate at her, and thus far she had been able to prevent it from acting out. But for how much longer, she wondered.

When she was ready, he had said, he would tell her everything. But what could he possibly have to tell? This was not a particularly complicated issue, and surely any explanation was futile at this point.

And when would she possibly be ready to hear anything from him about what had happened?

Abigail had been friends with Matthew from childhood, and rather than spend his time with the Thayers, as the rest of his family did, he had elected to choose Abigail and the Sterlings. So it was only natural that they should have grown close, and somehow even more natural that a romance should have formed. Subtle and gradual it had been, but it had also been undeniable, particularly after one memorable night at the Queen's ball in Colchester. The Queen had not been in attendance, of course, but in honor of her birthday, a ball had been held nonetheless, and Abigail had taken it upon herself on that occasion to look her absolute best.

She had looked her best, and Matthew had never looked more striking to her than he had that night. They had caught eyes, and the air in the room had changed to something magical and wonderful. They had danced and talked and laughed, but everything had changed between them. Absolutely everything.

There had been an unspoken expectation nearly from that night on that the two would marry, and the Sterlings, at least, had speculated wildly about it among themselves. Which would surprise no one. Sterlings were notorious for their tendency toward speculation, for good or for ill.

Then he had shocked the lot of them by announcing his engagement to Eliza Thayer, and the marriage had followed nearly the moment the banns were completely read.

All very businesslike and straightforward, and rather than attend the nuptials to which she had almost callously been invited, Abigail had fled. Or rather, she had retreated to Dorset with her uncle Benedict, a well-respected physician who lived a rather quiet life with his wife and three children, the oldest just younger than Abigail herself. The peace and solitude of the life in Dorset had settled warmly upon her heart and deadened the pain of all she had endured.

And now she was expected to hear his side of the story? She wasn't at all sure she could bear to do any such thing without lashing out and letting her raw bitterness show.

But that was just it, wasn't it? She knew that was what he expected, but he hadn't made any sort of motion to bring any of it about.

So, what was it that he *did* expect and have planned for all this?

Groaning, Abigail craned her neck and jerked as one of the maids reached for her cloak, pulling it from her shoulders. "Thank you, Bess. Mind it doesn't soak your frock."

"Yes, Miss Abigail," she replied with a quick bob, scurrying away with it.

Abigail brushed back stray strands of hair with her hands

and sighed heavily, gripping her neck. All of this pressure that she was placing on herself, and there wasn't anything to do as yet. Apprehension was a terrible burden of its own, and she was accustomed to its weight.

"Pardon me, Miss Abigail," a formal voice intoned nearby. "A letter arrived for you."

She made a face and turned toward the butler. So, this was Matthew's plot. To send her messages in private and maintain distance when in public.

Conniving wretch of a man.

"When did it arrive, Tate?" Abigail asked the older man, not bothering to pretend at a polite tone even for appearances.

If the butler noticed, he gave no indication. "Perhaps a quarter of an hour ago, Miss Abigail. While you were out walking."

That made her frown, her fingers pausing just a breath above the note. A quarter of an hour ago she had still been in the park and had seen Matthew perhaps five minutes before that. This letter might actually not be from him after all.

But then what could it be?

She shook herself and plucked the letter up, nodding to herself and the butler. "Thank you, Tate."

He bowed and disappeared down the corridor, leaving Abigail to stare after him absently.

She glanced down at the letter, then moved into the nearest parlor and broke the seal, unfolding the paper and scanning it. There was nothing at all familiar in the handwriting, which was another sign Matthew could not have written it. She'd know his writing with one brief glance with all the notes they had sent each other over the years. And this was far too lengthy to be anything of his creation.

He had always preferred brevity to discourse.

She had tended to agree.

She forced herself to focus on the words before her, and to do so with an open and unbiased mind.

But nothing could have prepared her for what followed.

I pray you will forgive the anonymity of this letter, my dear Miss Sterling, but I could think of no other way to communicate to you the feelings I currently possess. It has been some time now that I have noticed you and have been unable to do anything else from that moment on. I pray this will not distress you, nor would I have you think that I am incapable of turning my thoughts to any other subject, though, arguably, none other could be so pleasant. I am not a man of many words, much as this letter might suggest otherwise, but I find I can prattle on remarkably well on the topic of yourself. But not to your person directly, for my nerves and more reserved nature prevent me from even approaching you. I will not make any bold declarations, nor will I sully your eyes with words of flattery and excesses, particularly when it would be untrue for the present. I would only express my admiration for you, Miss Sterling, and my hope that soon we may grow more acquainted in the future.

It was not signed, and nor did it give any indication in any place about who might have sent it. No particular descriptions of anything, no ardency expressed, and not even a hint of praise for her appearance or nature or being.

What a strange sort of missive to receive. Nothing threatening or frightening, and nothing at all that even made her uncomfortable.

A simple declaration of admiration and nothing more.

And yet it made her smile a little as she ventured out of the parlor and down the corridor. A man in London who admired her enough to send her a note about it but was reserved enough to not confess his identity. What a delightful mystery to suddenly have at hand!

"What are you smiling about?"

Abigail grinned in the direction of her younger sister, proceeding down the stairs without grace or care. Maren was a rather pretty girl, almost spritely in appearance, and in possession of a carefree spirit and manner that Abigail had always been envious of.

"My smile, my secrets," Abigail replied, her smile spreading. "What are you about today? Paying calls?"

Maren scoffed, her almost-blonde hair bouncing with her steps, one hand gripping the bannister and swinging around to Abigail. "Lord, no. It's too early in the Season for anyone to want me to call, and I'm not exactly keen on doing so anyway. I thought I might pretend to shop in Bond Street, see what the other ladies are up to and observe London Society in its natural habitat."

Abigail shook her head, amused by her sister, as always.

Maren suddenly tilted her head, her eyes taking on a wiser, knowing look. "Do you know what I think, Abs?"

"Not particularly."

"I think you ought to give Matthew a chance."

Abigail felt her body jerk in surprise and stared at her sister with wide eyes. "How did you know he was in London? I've said nothing."

Maren smiled her familiar rueful smile. "I noticed. But I'm a particularly capable eavesdropper, and when we were with Francis and Janet the other evening, I overheard him and Uncle Hensh talking. Matthew's appearance in London was discussed."

Oh, the horror . . . Uncle Hensh was one thing, but their cousin Francis? He was the most paternal extended relation she had and was likely closer to them than their true uncle

Benedict was. There was no telling what Francis and Uncle Hensh would do when working together for a common purpose.

She swallowed painfully. "Does Papa know?"

This time Maren shrugged in ignorance. "Difficult to say. He was not in the room during the discussion, but that is not to say that he was not informed of it later."

"Lord above . . ." Abigail breathed. She wet her lips. "Surely Papa would have said something if he knew."

"Most likely." Maren tossed her hair over a shoulder and folded her arms, fixing her focus on Abigail. "I mean it. You should give Matthew a chance."

Heart already racing, Abigail frowned at her. "A chance? After what he did?"

Her sister nodded twice, her jaw fixed. "Does marrying someone else three years ago mean he is now beyond forgiveness? Or friendship?"

Whatever pace her heart had been maintaining, it intensified at that, stealing breath as well as strength. "You cannot ask me . . ."

"I am not suggesting you love him again," Maren assured her with a gentle interruption. "And I doubt very much that was what he asked for when he spoke with you. Was it?"

Abigail was shaking her head before she knew what she was doing, and then she seemed to find difficulty ceasing the motion.

Maren waited a moment, no doubt to see if any verbal reply would be made, then prodded, "And? What does he want?"

"He said . . . He said he wanted understanding," Abigail told her simply, finally recovering some sense. "That's all he said."

"Understanding," Maren repeated thoughtfully. She

considered it, then smiled at Abigail. "Surely that is not so beyond you."

Abigail wasn't nearly so certain of that. Her hands were suddenly taken and tightly squeezed, causing her to look up at her sister, feeling suddenly unsteady.

Maren's mouth formed a tight line, her eyes soft. "I know you have the capability to listen, if not understand. For the sake of what you once shared, even before there was love . . ."

"Another chance, you said?" Abigail exhaled slowly. "I cannot risk my heart again, Maren. Not with him."

Maren's mouth curved to one side. "I don't remember him asking for that, nor did I suggest it. If you don't want to give your heart, then don't offer it. Don't put it up for consideration." She sobered and released Abigail's hands, clasping her own before her. "There was friendship long before hearts were involved, wasn't there? Surely that can be respected, at least."

It was odd, but what Maren was saying made a great deal of sense and appealed to Abigail's logical side, yet when she considered the application of it, the whole thing seemed entirely illogical and impossible.

There could be nothing perfectly comfortable about engaging with a man one had once loved, she supposed, no matter what capacity in which they would associate now.

But she had to try.

"All right," she conceded with another series of absent nods, though she wasn't sure if she was nodding to Maren or to the decision she had made. Or to Matthew in absentia.

Not that it mattered. Any of the three would have done just as well as the other.

Maren giggled and unlaced her hands, clasping them behind her back and rocking back and forth on her heels. "How does he look? Matthew, I mean."

She glared at Maren with darkness, though she did find

the antics of her sister amusing in a twisted sort of way. "Well. He looked very well, indeed."

Maren grinned, then let it vanish at once. "A well-looking man must always be appreciated."

"Sage counsel," Abigail retorted drily, shaking her head and moving down the corridor past her sister once more.

"Where are you going?" Maren called after her.

Abigail glanced over her shoulder but kept her course. "It seems I have a letter to write, if I am to begin this endeavor properly."

She didn't wait to see how her sister reacted and tuned out whatever she said in response. She couldn't bear any more, not when she was stepping out into the darkness she really ought to have avoided. She needed clarity and focus, particularly when reaching out to Matthew.

He mustn't think she was encouraging him, and she mustn't make it sound as though all was forgiven.

She was only taking one step.

Just one.

Abigail sat at the small writing desk in the front drawing room, extending her fingers in a faint stretching motion, exhaling slowly.

She could do this. She could.

Suddenly the weight of the letter still in her pocket seemed to weigh itself down and press rather comfortingly against her. Grounding her, in a way.

Her lips curved into a smile then. Her heart need not get involved in this muddle with Matthew, she reminded herself. Someone else had an interest in her.

And if he wrote again, she just might consider letting it take root.

She turned to the paper at hand, still smiling, and started the note.

Chapter 4

HE WASN'T SURE HE'D ever been more anxious in his entire life, and that was saying a very great deal.

But he was also eager, encouraged, pleased, and rather relieved.

The note from Abigail had taken him by surprise, but Matthew would be lying if he said this was not all perfectly part of his plan. He needed her to listen before anything else could happen, and he needed her to tolerate his company for longer than a few minutes.

This was the first step, and he wished most fervently that he wouldn't muck it up.

He'd arrived early, as was his way, and wandered the paths of the park without any real direction, breathing in the fresh morning air and taking its solace for his strength.

He was going to tell Abigail everything, and—if her note was to be believed—she would listen to him.

Whether she would let it truly reach her was another question entirely, and one he was not sure he knew the answer to.

He walked until he reached a stray stream from off the Serpentine, where, just as Abigail's note had said, there was a large, flat rock at its edge. It was big enough for two to be seated on, and he wondered faintly if that was what she had in mind or if she intended to place him on it and then shove him into the water.

It would not be beneath her, and there was nothing to indicate any particular tone in her note, so it could actually be entirely plausible.

"I wasn't sure if you would be here."

Matthew turned with a smile toward the sound of Abigail's voice, pleased to see her expression fairly open and easy. She was even smiling at him!

Well, sort of.

It wasn't a glower, and it wasn't a frown, so he would consider that a victory.

"You requested I be at this precise spot at this time, did you not?" he inquired mildly, sweeping his hands behind his back. "Why shouldn't I have been here?"

Abigail's lips quirked to one side. "I wasn't sure you'd find it."

He returned the almost-smile. "Your directions were very precise. It was no trouble to find it." He looked her over with a quick, polite glance, though his eyes noted every detail from the shade of the sky captured in her dress to the way the wind caught the tendrils of her dark hair in the front where her bonnet could not protect them. "You look well."

"Thank you." She inhaled deeply, then exhaled in a rush. "I don't know, Matthew, if I can promise understanding, but I can promise you that I will try."

That was everything, and he didn't bother hiding his relief, though he did take care to keep it checked. He swallowed quickly. "You are ready to hear it, then?"

Abigail laughed very softly and squinted toward the horizon. "I don't know that I, or anyone else, is ever fully ready or prepared to hear something of this nature. But neither can I avoid it. We were friends once, and out of respect for that friendship, I will hear what you feel you need to say."

He smiled with far more warmth than before. "That is more than enough. Please." He gestured to the large rock, and she nodded, coming past him to sit upon it. He waited a moment, then moved to sit on the other side, turning his legs somewhat away from her, mirroring her position.

"Let me be clear on something," Abigail murmured in a not-quite-steady voice. "I don't . . . I don't want to hear anything about how we were or what might have been felt or any proclamations of any sort of feelings. Understood?"

"Perfectly," he agreed with a firm nod. "I hadn't planned on doing anything of the sort, so you are quite safe there. If I venture into any tone or subject with which you are not comfortable, I give you full leave to stop me by whatever means you think necessary. Including shoving me into the stream."

Her perfect lips curved into a true smile, causing something wild to flutter in his chest, and she tilted her head. "I may have to consider that. Now, if you please, you may begin. Wherever you like."

Matthew sighed to himself and looked out across the stream to the green beyond. "I cannot say I know where to start, myself, but I suppose the beginning of it all will do well enough. In the weeks leading up to my engagement, my parents seemed to invite the Thayers over a great deal more often than usual. I felt as though I was on display the entire time. Our fathers would discuss the sort of partnership they could form if only they had the right circumstances to bring it about. If you remember, during all of that, I escaped from Chisolm quite often to see you. I'm sure you wondered why."

"I might have done."

He gnawed the inside of his lip for a moment, then released it on a rush of air. "I sensed what was happening, and I felt that you—that we—were slipping through my fingers."

"Matthew . . ."

"Apologies," he said with a shake of his head. "I'm not trying to be dramatic here, but it is a statement of fact. Anyway, finally my father sat me down and told me what the expectations were, and what the advantages were, and left me with no doubt that any other option would have put the family in danger, as well as diminished any future opportunities for my siblings."

Abigail shifted on the rock beside him. "How could that be? The Thayers were not especially wealthy, though well enough off. Nor were they of especially high standing."

Matthew glanced at her almost ruefully. "You forget the partnership they were planning. Individually, neither of our families were particularly impressive, but together?" He shook his head, returning his focus across the stream. "In any case, I did as I was bid, and both of our families succeeded in their aims. Both families became wealthier and more influential than before, and everyone was happy."

"Except you," Abigail stated without much emotion, though her tone was oddly comforting.

He swallowed once. "I wasn't miserable. The marriage wasn't an unhappy one. We both dedicated ourselves to it, working day in and day out to create a successful relationship. After all, we had years of friendship between our two families, so how difficult could it be?" He snorted and wrenched his gaze away from the distance and looked away from Abigail. "As it turns out, incredibly so."

"What happened?"

"Nothing." He half-heartedly shrugged. "Nothing specific, anyway. But it turned out that Eliza and I had almost nothing in common and did not agree on much at all. We never fought, but neither did we see eye to eye. It was a struggle for the first several months, right when we should have been our happiest."

Abigail didn't say anything to this, and he was grateful for it. This would have been the time to crow over him or tell him he deserved it, or something of the sort. The lack of such comments came as a small comfort.

"It was her idea," he went on, "to be friends rather than lovers, as we were forcing the whole thing, which only built resentment and strain. Only weeks later we discovered she was with child, and the direction of our lives shifted measurably."

He turned back to look at Abigail, his chest tightening with the memories of those days upon him. "I had always wanted children, you know this, and I thought that perhaps this could be what brought us together and made us more functional as a couple and as a family. Despite our arrangement, I was pleased with the news, and so was Eliza. It should have been a wonderful solution to our problem."

Abigail gave him a small nod of understanding but still said nothing.

"But it wasn't," he admitted, turning back to the stream once more. "Again, we disagreed on everything, including how we wanted to raise our child and how to order the house when the child was born. Eliza became more opinionated, more severe, more eager to turn disagreement into full argument. I knew the child must have been paining her, so I never took offense at what was said or how it was said. And it wasn't like that all the time. Eliza was a good soul, you must remember that, at least."

"I never had any complaint against her," Abigail agreed, her voice low. "She seemed to be almost perfection."

Matthew smiled to himself at her statement. "Almost." His smile faded, and he cleared his throat, rising to his feet and moving to the edge of the stream, the memories and discomfort getting to be too much. "At any rate, the child and her behavior put a new strain on our relationship that hadn't afflicted it before. She had a difficult labor, I was told, and Eliza insisted someone tell me how sorry she was, but she adamantly refused to let me up there with her."

He shook his head and looked down at the water, listening to its faint rippling against the banks and the rocks. "I paced in the drawing room below, hearing everything in a muted, distant way, and then suddenly there was nothing. No sound, no cries, and no footsteps. Not a single noise." His voice faded suddenly, and he cleared his throat, surprised by the emotion. "For some reason that nothing was louder and far clearer than any sound I have heard before or since. And I knew."

"And the child?"

"A daughter," he managed. "Dead before she was delivered. I had them buried together at Chisolm and gave the child the name Beatrix, which was what Eliza had wanted all along. She would be almost two years of age now."

Abigail shifted again on the rock, and he looked back at her, seeing that now she was turned fully toward him, expression pained and sympathetic. "I'm so sorry, Matthew."

He stared at her for a moment, then exhaled and returned to the rock, sitting beside her. "Do you know what the worst part of it was? More than my grief for Eliza, there was a strange sense of . . . not relief, exactly, but respite." He shook his head almost frantically, still unable to fully comprehend or express what he had felt. "I did not mourn her the way I should have, though I did mourn. I felt the loss of our child more than the loss of my wife. I've often wondered if I am to be damned for such feelings, which led me to guilt for putting Eliza through a marriage and ordeal that perhaps never should have been."

His words hung in the air between them for a long moment, the tension and emotion of them fading into the silence as if on a breeze.

"You think too much, Matthew," Abigail eventually told him.

He chuckled to himself. "Can you blame me?"

She pretended to consider that. "No, I suppose not. You always were lost in thought about something or other."

It was true, and he knew it well. But if Abigail knew just what topic had occupied his thoughts much of that time, she would have protested on the grounds of her one condition.

No matter.

A thought prodded at his mind, and he found himself speaking it before he could stop himself. "Abigail, how did you not know about Eliza's and my child? It is fairly well known about the county, and Chisolm is less than three miles from Hazelwood."

The first real sign of strain appeared in Abigail's features, but it also vanished on a rush of breath. "I haven't been at Hazelwood in three years."

That was a bewildering thought, and he stared at her with the full brunt of his surprise. "You haven't?"

She shook her head slowly, not meeting his eyes. "It was easier. I spent several months with my uncle Benedict at first."

"The physician?" he recollected from some vague recess in his mind. "In . . . Devon?"

"Dorset," she corrected. "He and my aunt were most accommodating, and I enjoyed time with my cousins and the lovely people in their village and the surrounding areas. Then I went to London for part of the Season, more for show than anything else, and when that ended, I spent the autumn and winter with Miranda."

"I'd wager you loved being with Miranda for so long," Matthew prodded, nudging Abigail's shoulder with his own.

Abigail scrunched up her nose, then nodded, snickering. "I did! Papa couldn't believe it, but I did enjoy it very much."

Then she seemed to recollect what they had originally been talking about, and her amusement faded. "So, no, I heard nothing of you, let alone that your wife had died. And no one in my family informed me of it either. I suppose they wanted to spare me any pain by the mentioning of it."

"Would it have pained you?" he inquired without any tact. "Just as the engagement had?"

She bit her lip, her brow furrowing. "I really couldn't say. I doubt it would have affected me the same way. I had resigned myself to it by then, so it may have simply been something to acknowledge. I'm sure I would have felt sad for you, as I do now, but pain me?" One shoulder lifted briefly. "Who knows?"

"Does it pain you to see me now?" The words escaped him before they had even formed coherent thought, and he immediately wished them back.

She didn't look at him, her eyes fixed across the stream. "I thought it would. But no, it doesn't. Not now. Not anymore."

Matthew winced, knowing now he had to proceed with penance, if nothing else. She deserved that much at the very least.

"Abigail," he began with his voice turning rough, "I am so very sorry for all the pain that I caused you. There are not words enough in any language to convey the pain I've felt over wounding you, and to now understand that my actions drove you away from your home and your family . . . I'm so sorry."

She had stiffened beside him, and he waited with bated breath for any sort of response, even a cold one. Then, miraculously, her shoulders relaxed on an exhale, and her hand slid over to cover his gently.

Lord, the touch of her, even like this . . .

"I know you are, Matthew," she murmured, her voice

distant. "I know you didn't set out to hurt me, and I know this wasn't any easier for you than for me. I'll be very honest, though . . ."

A cold jolt raced down his spine to his toes, and it was all he could to do stay upright in his apprehension.

She turned her eyes to him with a measure of wariness. "I don't think I'm able to fully forgive you yet. Not at this moment, anyway. I don't hate you for it, and I'm almost certain that time and consideration will settle forgiveness for you in my heart. But I would be very much false if I told you that all was well and forgotten, and you deserve the truth from me."

He didn't deserve anything from her, much less her forgiveness or any particular level of consideration or honesty. The fact that she thought so seemed monumental in his eyes, and his gratitude overwhelmed him.

He nodded at her words, hoping his smile didn't appear in any way forced. "I understand, and I accept it. More than that, I appreciate your generosity. I didn't even expect this much."

"Oh, come now," she scolded, her fingers drumming against his hand. "We were friends first, remember? Surely you can't forget the number of times you snuck into Hazelwood the way I'd taught you, showing up for our family dinners without any sort of invitation. I'd be grateful to recover some of that part of our past. I've little enough of friends in every other regard."

"No . . ."

Abigail threw a sardonic look in his direction, which was no less the perfection it had been when he had known her last. "Time away from London and Society without excuse, and you think the fickle females would remember me? I never took you for an idiot before this."

He barked a laugh, his thumb grazing the edge of her

hand on the rock. "Of course you did. You called me an idiot on a very regular basis. I could almost tell the days of the week from it."

"I did not!"

"You did."

"You can't contradict a lady!"

"It's not contradiction; it's correction."

"Because that is so much better," she scoffed. Then she paused, her eyes widening and looking down at their hands.

Damn.

She scurried from the rock quickly, pushing her loose tendrils of hair behind her ears. "Right. Well, that's enough conversing for one morning, I think. We don't want to give rise to comment. Thank you for meeting me and explaining. I shall keep your confidence. Good day."

She turned to go, cheeks flushing, steps quick.

Matthew smiled at the sight. "Abigail?"

She turned back, wary and rubbing her fingers together. "What?"

His smile deepened. "Do you think your family would hang me if I were to call at the house?"

Abigail immediately relaxed and tucked a smile against her still-flushed cheeks. "Not if I insist they don't."

"And would you?" he queried suspiciously.

An impish light appeared in her eyes and her smile. "Not today. But possibly tomorrow." She quirked her brows and dashed out of his sight.

His heart lurched with that smile, and he had to swallow hard.

Claimed.

He certainly was. And that would do well enough, wouldn't it?

Chapter 5

ABIGAIL RUSHED TO THE parlor with a wild, breathless grin, looking around before she entered to be sure that no parent or sibling was in the immediate vicinity. That would be the last thing she needed at this moment.

She dropped down on the divan and swung her legs up, grateful her laces were not especially tight this afternoon. Her fingers were nearly damp with an excited perspiration as they clenched the freshly delivered letter in their hold.

This was the third in a week, and the fifth total that she had received. Each one had intrigued her, and with each new writing, her attraction grew.

Yes, attraction, she freely admitted it. However simple and straightforward the first had been, the following ones had taken a more romantic turn until she had felt an intimacy in every line. Still no excesses in flattery and no overwhelming declarations, but a real, raw honesty and depth that had begun to steal her breath. This man, whoever he was, saw her for what she was, and his praise of her person and her mind and her behavior had become addicting.

For all his claims of reserve and not being a man of words, his prose was glorious. Thoughtful and pure, masterful regarding the English language, and poetic in its patterns, though without the sentimentality so prevalent in the actual poetry of the day. And he focused all of that talent and passion into words for her.

She'd never been a sighing and swooning sort of woman, but this man was pushing her very much in that direction.

The last letter still sat in the desk behind her, tucked behind an old journal that hadn't been written in for two years. She had read it over and over again until the words had begun to live in her memory.

The sound of your voice has become the music of my heart, and there surely has been no such heavenly singing in any angelic appearance in any scripture. The sweetness, the softness, the tender edges of every word from your incandescent lips pulls at my hearing, draws me in, clings to every fiber of me, and it sings brilliantly into the very blood of my body, vibrant and sustaining as life itself. I smile at hearing it, regardless of the content or context, yearning to catch every witty and intelligent word, straining for any hint of your feelings. Can you know me? Can you see me? I know not whether to hope or fear, my dear one, for both are rife within me concerning you.

She caught herself sighing then and cleared her throat, focusing on the new letter. She broke the nondescript seal and began to unfold it.

"What is that you have there?" Maren's voice suddenly asked from the door to the parlor. "A note from Matthew?"

Abigail leaped to her feet, clutching the letter tightly. "What? No, it's nothing. Nothing at all."

Her sister lifted a dubious brow. "Convincing, Abs. I didn't ask to see it, only what it was. So, is it from Matthew?"

The frantic pace of her heart began to slow, though her lungs still ached on every breath. "No. No, it's not from Matthew. You know him, he would write one line, perhaps two, and that would be the end of it."

"True. The man has no patience for the pen in his own hand." Maren scoffed, looking far too interested. "So, who is it from, then?"

A thousand different excuses and responses flashed through her mind, defenses suddenly rising, but nothing seemed quite good enough to express aloud. But how to properly define what exactly this was without seeming like a fool? "It's a surprise," she settled on. "And one that requires privacy, so…?"

Maren gave her a curious look but for once did not press further and left the room with a shrug.

Why in the world would she think it from Matthew?

It was a miracle that her family had accepted Matthew back with only slight trepidation the first night and none at all the second. They had all fallen back into their former rhythm of comfortable joviality with him, and as she had retreated to her bedchamber, it had occurred to her that the unimaginable had occurred.

She forgave him. She forgave Matthew. She hadn't forgotten it, not in the least, but she didn't resent him any longer. She could smile and joke with him without thinking about how he had hurt her.

They truly could be friends once more.

But nothing more.

Her heart could not take that again.

It wasn't even in danger of such things anyway. It had learned from experience, and it was hardened now.

And yet these letters . . .

This was madness. This was absolute madness to be letting herself get so tangled up in the contents of anonymous letters. It was also absolute madness for her siblings to stick their noses into her affairs, but they had always had trouble remembering the concept of the personal and private.

At least she knew that she could trust them not to tell their parents about all of this. They were far too intelligent to let Mama and Papa become involved, knowing the chaos that would bring about. Her mother would have some very strong opinions on the subject, and her father would immediately become suspicious of everyone and everything. She would not have a moment's peace ever again once that bridge was crossed.

But for the moment, she did not have to worry about any of that. She had a letter that she could read to escape from all of this for a time. A letter that would brighten her spirits and make her heart smile, if hearts could do such an impractical thing. It felt like her heart was smiling when she read his letters.

Then again, that could just be her newly discovered fanciful side overreacting.

She inhaled deeply, then exhaled in a slow, steady breath. Then she went to work on unfolding the letter once more, suddenly anxious for its contents.

"Someone is excited to read their post."

Abigail jerked up, refolding the letter once more, eyes wide. Then she relaxed and made a face of discontent. "Oh. It's you."

Matthew's brows rose and he put a hand to his chest. "I have never heard more disappointment about my presence in my entire life. I'm feeling quite insulted at the moment."

"I'm sure you will overcome the sensation." She swung her legs to the floor and waved him in with a disappointed sigh. "You might as well come on in. Everyone else has gotten in the way of this letter, why not one more?"

"I'm not sure I want to be lumped in with others that have ruined something for you," he commented even as he stepped in. "I've rather done that enough for one lifetime, no?"

She looked at him in surprise, stunned that he would reference it so carelessly. But then she found herself giving him a smile, the tension in her chest easing considerably. "Yes, as a matter of fact, you have. But at least you won't be annoyingly prying like my siblings, so it is not as ruinous to my plans as all that."

He bowed in acknowledgement, returning her smile, which, for some reason, made her take a second look at him. Despite what she had told Maren when she had first seen him again, he really was quite attractive. She had never truly preferred facial hair on any man, but it suited Matthew far more than she would have expected. He seemed less of a boy now, though he had hardly been one when they'd had their understanding, and in his place was a robust and striking man.

She might actually prefer him with facial hair, as far as looks were concerned.

Matthew indicated the seat next to her. "May I? Or would you prefer I take one of the chairs?"

Abigail shook herself out of the dangerous territory she'd unwittingly wandered into. "Oh, it makes no difference. Sit wherever you like."

As she suspected, he took the seat beside her, though he was far enough away that Maren could have come back in and sat between them comfortably. "Then I will sit here. Your mother always had the most comfortable divans, but I swear she let your military father select the chairs."

She snickered in response. "I wasn't aware that the furniture in public rooms was supposed to be comfortable for the guests seated in them. What would we do if someone dropped into a sleep when we were entertaining them?"

"I know this one," Matthew announced with an indicating finger as he leaned back against the rim of the divan. "Pluck a feather from whatever accommodating female is in the room and brush it against their skin and nose to see how they react, all while attempting not to wake them."

Abigail reached over and smacked him in the arm with a laugh. "Wretch! That is a perfectly horrid idea, and I sincerely hope you never entertain."

He grinned, the corners of his eyes crinkling. "Never do. But I've always wanted to try that."

"Ridiculous man. Are you a child?"

"Sometimes." Matthew was silent for a minute, then his eyes flicked down to the letter she held. "So, are you going to tell me what you are so keen to read, or must I perish from curiosity?"

The question wasn't exactly unexpected, given that he had come in just as she was relishing in the delight of having another letter to read, but of all people in the world, she was the least interested in letting Matthew Weber-Grey know about her private romantic dealings.

Still, the idea of informing him where things stood now might take away any ideas of rekindling a romance between them, which surely needed to be done.

So she fixed a friendly smile on her face and put the letter firmly in her lap. "You are not the only man in the world who has ever taken an interest in me. It just so happens that I have been receiving regular correspondence from a man with a particular interest in me."

"Have you indeed?" he returned, looking truly pleased. "I am glad to hear it. You should have suitors out the door for you to test out! So, come on and tell me about him. What is his name?"

Abigail shook her head, still smiling, though she was utterly bewildered by his response. "No, no, you don't get to know his identity. I must have some secrets, you know."

He nodded in agreement. "I should hope so. I think I

would hate to know everything about someone. Where would the surprise be?"

Where indeed.

"What does he say in his letters, Abigail?" Matthew teased, his tone blatantly suggestive.

She rolled her eyes with the dramatics he was employing. "He compliments my wit and intelligence and the sound of my voice and says he finds me to be the most fascinating woman he's ever known. And he seems very taken by my eyes."

Matthew's head bobbed in approval with each item. "Excellent choices, all. The eyes especially. The man has excellent taste. And you clearly like him in return."

"Why would you think so?" she asked, gaping a little.

He gave her a knowing look she remembered all too well. "You can't stop smiling. He excites you and invigorates you. Rather like I used to."

She stammered inaudibly, struggling for a response to such a statement.

"Abigail, I wasn't trying to dampen the moment," he told her gently. "I'm merely telling you something that only I could observe. I'm very happy for you, and it's a pleasure to see you look like this again."

He was *what*?

She blinked twice. "You're happy for me? You mean it?"

That seemed to surprise him. "Of course, I mean it. I still care about you, Abigail, and what I want above all else is for you to be happy." He shrugged helplessly and offered a hesitant smile. "That is what friends do, is it not?"

Abigail couldn't respond for a moment, incredulous and surprisingly touched. He actually meant it. He truly was pleased she had a man expressing interest and something that made her happy. Something that wasn't him.

"Yes," she finally replied, smiling back at him. "Yes, it is."

What man in his right mind would intentionally venture into the madness of shopping in London during the Season without a need to purchase anything? Particularly when he was going to be in the company of at least one female who will likely be mad for the whole venture and another who might be too distracted to be worth any sort of salt as far as conversation went?

But venture he would, and without a single complaint.

If this was how Abigail would allow him to associate with her, he would take it with all good graces and gratitude.

Audibly, at any rate.

He was filled with a very different sort of apprehension within himself, one that many a man had felt with such an excursion ahead of him. The only way that this would all diminish would be if Thomas Sterling were in attendance, and if he were as sensible as Matthew had always taken him to be, he would have fled from his sisters' request posthaste.

Provided he had been requested at all.

The Sterling siblings could be a bit fickle when it came to tolerating one another.

In short order, the hack had arrived at its destination, and Matthew disembarked with a reluctant groan.

The things he would endure for love.

Matthew had not walked for long when a familiar pair of sisters strolled out of the milliner's shop, one darker than the other, but sharing the same smile. The sight of it drew out his own smile, and he moved in their direction.

Unfortunately, he reached them just as they were entering a hosiery shop, and Matthew politely followed, hands behind his back, ready to engage in the act of perusing the shop. Men's hosiery wasn't nearly so exciting, but one must always be socked appropriately, so he could purchase a few things if need be.

At the moment, he couldn't recall what he already had in the hosiery department of his wardrobe, but neither did he particularly care.

"You're making a valiant effort."

He turned to look behind him, smiling at Abigail, who had followed him. "Of what?" he asked.

Her sardonic look made him chuckle.

"What? You don't think I have a genuine interest in hosiery?"

"No," Abigail retorted bluntly. "I don't believe you care at all."

Now he grinned outright. "You're right; I don't. But appearances must be kept up, so . . ." He resumed his slow meander, indicating that she follow.

She did so, and somehow she looked convincing in her faux shopping.

"Tell me something," Matthew murmured, pausing to examine a truly horrendous pair of socks. "Why did your mother agree to let me come on this errand?"

"She's curious about you," Abigail whispered back. "Mad with it, actually."

He nodded in thought, pleased that it wasn't just him, though he was fairly certain there had never been another man to truly consider where Abigail's future was concerned. "And what of your mystery suitor? Is she curious there?"

She looked over her shoulder quickly and picked up a pair of socks, pretending to examine them more closely. "She doesn't know. And she would not approve. I cannot pretend to be unmoved by the contents of his letters, nor that I am growing more so with each one."

Matthew paused again, this time to let another woman pass by. "You like him," he stated unnecessarily.

Abigail sighed, and the sound reminded him of days on the grass in the sun at Hazelwood. "Yes. Yes, I like him. I think I like him very much. Is that so very strange? I don't even know him. I have no idea who he is."

He looked at her with a smile, hopefully one that encouraged her. "I won't deny that it is strange, but that doesn't make it false. And let's consider this properly: what *do* you know about the man?"

She frowned and moved in front of him, now leading the way as they continued through the shop once more. "What, besides that he has taken an interest in me for some reason?"

"Yes, besides his excellent taste," Matthew quipped, winking though she would not see it. "You know that he is of your class, yes? Or else he could not possibly be seeing you at events."

Abigail's head tilted at that. "I suppose so. I also know that he is educated. He references Shakespeare and scholars on some occasions."

"Even better," Matthew praised. "Learned men must always be considered decent enough candidates, no?"

She stopped suddenly, then turned to finger a pair of wool stockings nearby. "He likes music as well."

Matthew drew up beside her, not bothering to pretend he was shopping anymore and leaning against the shelf next to him. "He said that?"

"No, but he describes it often enough. Refers to it. Particularly with regards to . . ." She trailed off, glancing in his direction without meeting his eyes.

It wasn't like Abigail to be shy, but he found it all the more endearing because of that. "To you," he finished. "He finds you musical."

"Which also shows his ignorance," she muttered as her face colored. "You know very well that I am not at all musical."

"Not in technical terms, no," Matthew admitted, keeping his eyes on her, waiting for her to meet his eyes again. "Not in abilities, no. But I've always thought your laugh somewhat musical. Not necessarily an aria . . ."

She giggled very softly, a smile playing at her cheeks. "Who laughs like an aria?"

"No one, I hope," he shot back with a shudder. Then he turned serious again. "I'd think anyone with a working set of ears could find you musical, Abigail. Not like an aria, but perhaps like a songbird on a spring morning." He shrugged as if it couldn't be helped, though in actuality he knew he had said too much and was trying to make light of it.

Abigail stared at him all the same, expression unreadable.

He made a quick face. "Too much?"

She shook her head slowly and without much certainty. "Not really, no. I just . . . I've never heard you say anything like that about it, and you've heard me laugh hundreds of times."

"Would you believe that it took me all these years to figure out what it sounded like?" he tried with a hopeful smile.

That broke the tension, and Abigail smirked, returning her attention to the stockings. "I would, actually. You never did have much of a way with words."

Silently breathing a sigh of relief, he turned to the safety of self-deprecation. "There's just so many words!" he whined plaintively. "I had my education, but I never told anyone just how I did in language and composition."

"Probably for the best," Abigail set as she laid the stockings back down. "We'd all think quite poorly of you if you'd received poor marks there. Your reputation would be quite ruined."

"I trust you to keep the secret safe." He hesitated a moment, watching as she turned away, then made his mind up. "Abigail?"

She turned back, still smiling, warmth radiating from her. "Yes?"

Matthew let himself return her smile, though perhaps more gently. "Whatever it is this man is praising in his letters, whatever he finds admirable in you, you ought to believe him. Someone should be acknowledging such an endless collection of incomparable things as what you possess, even if it cannot be me."

Her eyes widened, and her breath caught. He could see the return of tension in full, and he would swear he could see the fierceness with which her heart pounded within her. She said nothing, made no sound, and barely breathed.

Neither did he, for that matter.

But he cleared his throat all the same. "I thought you should know that," he murmured as he passed her again, his fingers accidentally brushing hers.

He wasn't sure if he gasped or she did, but it took several long moments for the burning sensation of that part of his hand to subside.

Chapter 6

"NO, I WILL *NOT* REACQUAINT you with Uncle Hensh tonight."

"Why not? What possible excuse could you have for refusing me?"

"Would you like me to produce a list for you? Or do you think you can remember on your own?"

Matthew did not appreciate her sarcasm, and Abigail knew it, but it did not follow that she cared all that much about his appreciation. His odd desire to regain a favorable reputation with every member of her family, whether extended or immediate, was no doubt admirable, but there really was no point to it.

And if this was his manner of attempting to procure an invitation to Uncle Hensh's card party this evening, he was seriously lacking in convincing arguments.

"You've already made yourself reacquainted with Francis," Abigail pointed out leaning slightly on her croquet mallet. "Enough that he included you on this picnic with the entire family."

Matthew raised a brow at her, pausing in his preparations to strike his green ball through a wicket. "Are you offended, jealous, or indignant?"

She stuck her tongue out at him, which made him snort and shake his head. "Hurry up, you perfectionist," she whined, cementing her current juvenile manner decisively. "We're going to miss the meal, and Janet has the best cook in London!"

"Patience is a virtue," Matthew reminded her in a calm, patient tone. He swung his mallet once, twice, then thumped the ball soundly, sending it through the wicket and rolling in a nearly perfect line toward the next one. He grinned outright and swung his mallet onto his shoulder. "And you do not have it."

That wasn't much of a surprise, was it? Anyone who knew Abigail knew full well that she was impulsive and impatient even on her best days, despite her better qualities, and it had been a frequent sort of mockery from her siblings over the years.

Abigail pushed past Matthew roughly, barely avoiding the impulse to sniff as she did so. "Well, if we are about to list all the areas in which we are in some way lacking . . ." She eyed the wicket and lined up the mallet for her yellow ball carefully, then exhaled slowly before whacking the ball through the wicket and sending it sailing beyond Matthew's until it rested just before the next wicket. She grinned tightly with exquisite satisfaction and looked over her shoulder at the openly gaping Matthew, "then we had best start with your failings in croquet."

He closed his mouth with an audible click of his teeth smacking against each other, his eyes narrowing. "You do know how to provoke a man, don't you?"

Abigail shrugged with a twirl of her mallet, feeling rather impish at the moment. "I don't set out with the intent of provocation. Can I help it if things naturally trend in that direction?"

"You steer it in that direction," Matthew corrected as he lowered his mallet to the ground and began to use it as a walking stick. "Navigate the ship toward the treacherous waters of provocation while keeping your crew blissfully unaware of the dangers ahead."

"Ahoy," Abigail replied in a dry tone.

He looked at her as he came to her side. "Fair winds and a following sea."

She placed a hand on her hip and cocked her head. "Are you sending me on an actual voyage, or do you simply not know when to end a joke?"

Again, his eyes narrowed, but he said nothing. Then, without warning, he poked her shoulder hard before racing off toward their balls. "First to the balls has full control!" he shouted over his shoulder.

"No!" Abigail screeched as she hiked up her unfortunately voluminous skirts and darted after him, her legs pumping hard, though her lungs were completely unable to match their efforts.

The fashions of the day were clearly doing nothing for feminine athleticism.

Matthew reached the balls first, as he had intended, and he took a moment to grin rather wickedly at Abigail, setting his mallet in place.

Abigail glared as she ran still. "Matthew Edward James Weber-Grey, if you so much as tap my ball . . ."

With a whoop, he swung at her ball hard, sending it careening off into the near patch of elms, its course interfering with birds, leaves, and, if her ears heard correctly, one or two trunks.

She stopped running, though her breath was as ragged as if she had run several miles, and she stared off into the trees with a sort of hopeless detachment. There was no recovering her score from all that, not when the next series of wickets were in the exact opposite direction, and she would have to backtrack to get through the one Matthew was currently tapping his own ball through with ease.

The sound of the mallet against the ball brought her attention back to him, and he watched her with a small grin, having completed what had to be the safest shot through a wicket ever made. "Well?" he prodded. "Are you going to retaliate, or have I won?"

The taunting only furthered her resolve, and she sneered at him as she went traipsing off after the ball in the woods. "If you prefer your victories by cheating, then by all means, call yourself the winner. I, however, will play by the rules."

"Since when?" he laughed as he jogged after her. "You've turned bending the rules into a form of artistic sculpture."

Abigail raised her chin, lifting her nose in the air superiorly. "I have matured, Matthew, unlike some other persons I know."

He reached her side and hummed in thought. "I wasn't aware maturity had a place in games and entertainment. What a fascinating discovery."

She nudged him hard, pressing him off her path, and he went, still chuckling to himself. "You are a horrible human being and a poor excuse for a gentleman."

Matthew straightened, his laughter only slightly fading. "Not so! I am escorting you into the woods so you might not be unaccompanied and intend to assist you in finding your ball, as it was my actions that sent it into such a place. And I will even let you have two strokes to make up for the misdeed."

Two strokes? She smirked a little, her mind spinning. Two strokes could get her out of the woods easily, if she was in position enough to accommodate it, and she just might be able to overtake him if all went well.

If, and that was a very large if, indeed.

"Well," she huffed, determined not to give anything away, "only time will tell if your actions truly amount to anything gentlemanly. It would be only too horrid if my ball would be stuck in a thorny bush, or . . ."

"In the middle of a rather large mud puddle?" Matthew suggested.

She opened her mouth to reply, only to see that her precious green ball was, in fact, swimming in a dark, muddy body of water right ahead of them.

A gentleman would fish it out for her. A gentleman would insist on getting dirty himself rather than her risk her skirts, let alone any other part of her. A gentleman would . . . Well, a gentleman would never have put her in this situation in the first place, but it was what it was.

And she refused to leave anything else to a gentleman simply because it ought to be done.

Abigail cleared her throat, then picked up her skirts just enough to be safe from the puddle, then marched herself to her ball.

"Abigail, you aren't serious," Matthew said with a faint note of alarm.

She ignored him, her mallet in one hand and her skirts in another, her boots sinking at once into the mud and water as she continued awkwardly on her way.

"How in the world are you going to hit the ball with your skirts occupying a hand?" he asked, amusement finding its way back into his voice.

Abigail eyed the ball, walking around it once to take in every aspect. Strategy would be crucial in this, and she would only get one opportunity. Her mother would likely scold her for soiling her boots, particularly when they were new, and there was no telling what she would have to say about whatever state her skirts ended up in. But her pride would be salvaged and her honor defended.

"Abigail . . ."

She looked up at him at last, quelling him with a cool glare of determination. She hefted her skirts over one arm, though she knew there was nothing to be done about her petticoat in the back, and did her best to handle the mallet with two hands without losing her hold on the skirts. She focused on the ball once more, held her breath, and swung her mallet with a firm *thwack*.

Mud splattered up at her, and she could feel the cool sludge hit her stockings above the level of her boots. She hissed, then looked down.

Her ball was gone.

Delighted and bewildered, she looked up and saw it rolling toward the head of the woods, apparently none the worse for wear. She laughed and looked at Matthew for his response.

He wasn't looking at the ball at all, but at her. His eyes were warm, and his smile was both impressed and proud. He wasn't laughing at whatever mud splatter she had created on herself or teasing her about the skirts lifted above propriety and slung over her arm.

This wasn't a look of friendship. It was so much more.

But rather than be upset about it, Abigail felt her skin warm and tingle, while her lungs seemed to constrict in the oddest fashion. She couldn't look away from him, couldn't find the strength and sense she had been so carefully maintaining. This was the Matthew she had known and loved. This look was more familiar than anything in recent memory, and she wanted to race across the mud and the green to fling herself into his arms, no matter the current state of her attire. She wanted his lips on hers, his arms around her, his hands cupping her face . . .

She wanted everything she had sworn never to give him. Never to feel for him. Never to experience with him.

Absolutely everything.

She ought to be horrified and embarrassed, ought to

avert her eyes and ignore her blushes, change the subject, and return to Francis's house without a word.

But she could not move. She was still breathing painfully, deep and almost frantic, and Matthew was echoing it.

Something needed to happen.

Something . . .

"Abigail! Matthew! Come and eat!"

Janet's voice broke through the impossible tension of their moment, and Abigail blinked with a ragged inhale that seemed to stretch her corset to new and agonizing extremes. But it did allow cool air and something almost resembling sense to flood back in, and she wrenched her eyes from Matthew, starting toward the edge of the pond. "We mustn't keep Janet waiting," she muttered aloud, hoping he would hear, as her voice had absolutely no strength. "She's been too kind to have us all here, and Maren will only leave us scraps."

"Your sister does have a voracious appetite," Matthew replied, his voice maddeningly calm.

Then his hand was on Abigail's, taking the mallet from her and looping her arm through his.

Abigail dropped her skirts to the ground and nodded, unable to meet his eyes. But his arm was delightfully warm against the sudden chill that seemed to be coursing through her, tingling her skin in an entirely different manner from what she had just been experiencing. She could only stare at her fingers on his arm, unnerved by how natural and comfortable it felt. How easy it was to do.

Three years. Three years since she had felt anything like this with him, and the fact that she *did* feel it seemed a peculiar puzzle. Was it too soon? Was it wrong? Was she an idiot for swaying in his direction though she knew she ought not?

"This isn't over," Matthew murmured to her.

Abigail jerked in his hold and looked up at him. What

wasn't? That moment? Her feelings? The sensation of dying for the touch of his lips? Or just the idea of them? All of that *had* to be over. It could not continue, not for an instant!

"Oh?" she managed weakly.

Matthew nodded once. "You think after a shot like that I would concede the match? You've just made things far more interesting, and I refuse to leave it unfinished."

The rush of her exhale was unexpected, and her lips parted into a relieved grin. "Naturally," she replied in a much stronger voice. "I am determined to win, despite the obstacles."

He laughed at that and pressed against her side with his elbow. "Don't tell my more competitive self, but I may be rooting for you."

Abigail echoed his laugh, an act that spilled over into giggles about the whole muddled mess of things. It was absolutely ridiculous, and the confusion and shock of it all suddenly struck her as being the height of hilarity and madness. She had no restraint and no resistance left. Matthew stared at her as though she had lost her mind, smiling the sort of patronizing smile one gives to those swimming in the sea of insanity.

No matter. Eventually, she would calm, and her walls would rebuild, and all would be well.

Or well enough, at least.

An evening without Matthew was a blessed relief, and mindless card playing with cousins and mere acquaintances had been the perfect respite for her frazzled mind.

What had she been thinking? Playing croquet with her friend was one thing, but hungering for him and finding his beard and his eyes and his form more appealing than anything else on this earth? It was horrifying, and she ought to have been far too hardened for such idiotic sentiments.

And there was her admirer to consider, after all. He had never betrayed her and wrote with a gentle honesty that pulled at her heart. He was a man she could trust, could turn to, and one she could wrap about her for protection, comfort, and adoration. Soon she would have to meet him in person and put an end to the mystery. They could not spend eternity in this one-sided correspondence, not if he felt for her as sincerely as he proposed, and not when she was beginning to feel something of the same.

And she *was* beginning to feel it.

His last two letters had been so tender, so captivating, and so perfect a gesture of courtship that she had begun to read them all before going to bed, desperate to bring some of the magic he spun into her dreams.

Dearest Miss Sterling,

I went for a stroll in the beauty of the park at St. James today and felt it would only be more perfect were you to have joined me . . .

Abigail snapped out of her pleasant reverie as she entered the house, stripping off the gloves and letting the maids take her cloak.

"Pardon me, miss," one of the girls said as she draped the cloak over an arm, "but this came for you just a short time ago." She produced a neatly folded missive from her apron pocket and handed it to her.

Abigail bit back a squeal and plucked it from her. "Thank you, Jeanie!" She looked ahead to ensure her family were not in view and rushed to the parlor, where the fire was still lit, to read her message.

The seal broke easily and she leaned closer to the fire to read the now-familiar tidy scrawl.

Dearest Miss Sterling,

Tonight, I saw you by the grace of chance, and it was all the more delightful for being unexpected. I don't know where you were going or by what mercy it was so close to my own residence, but I shall not complain of my ignorance under the circumstances. I am exceedingly grateful for any opportunity to be graced by your presence, even if you are unaware of mine. I could not follow you, though I longed to do so, and would not dare to infringe upon your evening or your person. The pleasure of seeing you in the evening light, so close to my home, brought me such joy and hope, though I had nothing to feel particularly hopeful for.

I could not tell the color of the dress or the shade of the ribbons in your lovely, dark hair—the distance was too great. But the image, such as it was, of you smiling and laughing with your family as day passed into night will be enough to sustain me for some time. You are magnificent, Miss Sterling, and are so many things. You are strong and passionate, warm and caring, intelligent, witty, and bright, and quick to smile or to laugh without being frivolous or flippant.

I have to wonder, Miss Sterling . . . could you, perhaps, be everything?

The time is drawing near, I believe, for you to know me for myself. I feel determined that we should meet, to see if what I feel could exist in truth, and to see if all that I feel might possibly be returned. I will find the opportunity and let you know when it shall be, if you are agreeable. Wait for me, if I may hope.

Yours most sincerely.

Abigail exhaled roughly, pressing a hand to her furiously pounding heart. This lovely, caring, perceptive man was growing dearer to her by the letter, and he, too, felt it would soon be time to meet. What a breathless, exhilarating thought!

Wait for him? If he were half as perfect as his letters made him seem, she would wait an eternity for him. No matter who else invaded her thoughts or her life.

Chapter 7

HOW MATTHEW HAD MANAGED an invitation to an informal ball at the home of some Sterling relative whose connection he couldn't recall, he would never know, but the Lambert family seemed pleasant enough. Even more incomprehensible than his invitation was how perfectly friendly they all were to him.

Still, he was grateful for the opportunity to attend any events in London, particularly when he knew that Abigail would be in attendance. He hadn't seen her yet, but he had only been here a quarter of an hour, and the collar of his dress shirt was beginning to chafe against his skin. Matthew barely restrained the irritable sigh known well to all reclusive individuals forced to integrate themselves with the social members of their society and did all in his power to avoid leaning back against the wall.

A sudden glimpse of brilliant white drew his attention across the room, and his throat seemed to plummet squarely into the center of his chest, pounding in synchrony with his heart and twice as painfully.

There was the woman he adored, smiling and glowing for all the world, entirely unaware of him.

Her gown was white, giving her more of an angelic look than she ordinarily bore, and the bodice was dotted with bits of blue embroidery that he couldn't make out from here. A ribbon of a similar shade wrapped around her waist, accentuating the remarkable figure she possessed, and the skirts flowed with a gauzy overlay dotted with blue over voluminous layers of white. Her shoulders were bare, the color of her skin a rosy ivory compared to the crisp white of her dress. At her throat, she wore pearls set off by a large blue jewel, which hung in the center, just below what had to be the most tempting dip of a throat he had ever seen on any living soul.

He had never seen her look thus, had never seen her hair so luxuriously curled and pinned, framing her face in a delicate halo. She had always been lovely to him, and certainly in their younger years she had been similarly dressed and coiffed, but this was entirely different. This was no slip of a girl he fancied and drew unto an understanding; this was a woman, all grace and poise and loveliness, that he adored with an undying fervor and could not imagine his life without.

This was how he always should have seen her, no matter how she was adorned.

He found his breath at last rushing out of him in a painful exhale that nearly had him swaying where he stood. How could someone he had known and loved for most of his life continue to affect him in ways he was entirely unprepared for?

Gathering what courage he had, he exhaled and moved toward them all, smiling with warm politeness. Something, and he wasn't entirely sure what, told him to go to Maren instead. She was dressed in a lovely shade of green that enhanced her natural looks to perfection, and the younger men would certainly be eying her for potential courtships soon, if not this very evening.

"My, my," Matthew praised gently as he approached her. "Here I was thinking little Maren was too young for such dances, but here I find a grown woman, all loveliness and elegance. I must atone for my error and misjudgment. If you would not object, Miss Maren, I should very much like my first dance of the evening to be with you."

Abigail heard him and turned to watch the exchange in a secret delight that only elder siblings can know.

Maren grinned without any sort of reserve, as was her natural way, and she nodded, sending the emerald earrings she wore dancing against her hair. "I would be most pleased, Mr. Weber-Grey."

"And for that," Mrs. Sterling chimed in from behind her children, smiling at him in a way he wasn't sure she had before, "you will get to dance with all the Sterling ladies, sir."

"For what crime?" Thomas protested with a crooked grin. "The man only asked for Maren, why should he . . . ?" He was cut off by someone, likely his father or his cousin Francis, pressing the back of one knee, making him buckle slightly.

Matthew moved Maren out to the dance before any other hijinks could occur.

"Thank you," Maren said quietly. "I was so worried no one would dance with me. Especially with how well Abigail looks this evening."

Matthew kept his expression perfectly blank. "Who?"

She beamed and nudged him in the ribs, her cheeks coloring. "Oh, you . . . You know perfectly well you are trying to dance with Abigail tonight in the only way that you know she won't refuse."

"I am not!" he coughed in mock surprise, knowing she could tell if he lied. "I find myself entirely devoted to this dance with you for your own merits and charms. Any other dances I may or may not engage in tonight will be entirely up to the same on those ladies in question."

Maren rolled her eyes, rapped his knuckles with her fan, and moved into the dance position. "Dance with Mama next. Then you can spend as long as you like with Abigail."

She winked at him, and he returned it with a smug smile. "You are a very fine ally, Maren Sterling. Now, no more talk of any other persons you may be related to. I am dancing with *you,* not the feminine Sterling collective."

Once he had danced with Abigail's mother as well, he had to wait for Abigail to finish her dance with Francis before he could have her. He instead spent the time chatting with Thomas Sterling, who, for the first time, did not seem in any way inclined to murder him, either on the spot or in the very near future. Matthew took that as a very great sign of some success, though he could not decide what to attribute the change to.

Their conversation, such as it was, stopped midsentence as Francis led Abigail over to them. Abigail was flushed and smiled brightly on her cousin's arm, and her brilliant eyes, still alight with laughter, rested on Matthew.

And did not change.

"Well?" Abigail asked as Francis released her arm with a knowing chuckle. "Is it finally my turn to dance with the man who is intent on gracing the dance floor with every female Sterling in attendance?"

Matthew bowed to her, still a bit breathless from what he saw in her expression, and scrambled for wit. "If Miss Sterling will allow me, I should dearly love to complete the set with her as the final partner."

There was no response, and he glanced up to find Abigail fighting a smile and pretending to consider the proposition. Then she sighed and tossed her head, sending her dark ringlets swaying against her fair skin. "Oh, why not?"

She held out her hand for him to take.

He snatched it as quickly as he could, squeezing tightly, relief shaking his knees in a way destined to make him a pathetic dance partner. He couldn't say another word and only smiled, dipping his head in what he prayed was smooth acknowledgement and not scattered desperation.

He must have been convincing, for Abigail laughed again and let him lead her into the dance. He cleared his throat just as they bowed to each other, and he smiled at his partner. "What has you in such a fine mood, Miss Sterling?"

Abigail still bore the coloring and smile of laughter as she passed about him. "It is a perfect evening, and my cousin is excessively diverting. And, if you will look to the end of the line, you will see my sister partnered with a most handsome young man who seems to be rather amiable."

Matthew did look, and just as Abigail had said, Maren was blushing and giggling while dancing with an almost gangly youth who could not look away from her. "That is rather promising, isn't it? Shall we send your Uncle Hensh or Cousin Francis to interrogate the lad?"

"No!" Abigail insisted with a bright laugh, gripping his arm tighter than she ought to have in the dance. "No, let her have whatever romance this may or may not be without interference for as long as she can! You and I both know that intervention is the enemy to progress in matters of the heart."

"It can be, sure enough," he allowed with a nod of consideration, his heart skittering momentarily on the slippery slope of their romantic past. "But this is Maren we are talking about. She defies expectation and restriction with flair."

Abigail raised a brow as Matthew now passed her. "And I did not?"

He exhaled quickly while momentarily out of her eyesight, then took a chance and let his expression change into one of raw emotion, something he had wanted to share with her ever since he had come to London. "You did everything with flair. You defied every expectation. And you haven't stopped."

He caught a flash of surprise in her eyes, her smile vanishing, and then they were forced to promenade down the lines with the others. He could feel her stiffening more and more beside him, and he couldn't bear that.

"You have to know that, Abigail," he murmured, his eyes fixed ahead. "You have to know that hasn't changed."

She inhaled shakily, and he heard it, felt himself echo the same. "You promised not to say things like this."

He slowly shook his head at her as they faced each other, dancing hand in hand around one side of the line. "I never said that. I said that I understood you and that you could stop me. By any means necessary. I'm willing to risk it tonight to tell you that I love you. More than ever. More than before."

"Matthew," she hissed, her tone heavy and her eyes filled with a light he couldn't interpret.

"Stop me then," he insisted without rancor. "Stop me from telling you that I've missed you more fiercely than I thought it possible for a man. That there could never be another woman in the world for me. That I would wait for your feelings for me to return until my last breath."

Abigail's eyes filled with tears, and her mouth pressed into a straight line. He passed her once more, as the dance required.

"Stop me," he whispered, her dark tresses grazing his lips as he did so.

Without warning, Abigail seized his hand and whirled out of the dance, barreling toward the nearest door, which happened to be close enough that their exit would barely be remarked upon. Abigail pulled him along, her grip tight, and neither of them said a word. Matthew, for his part, couldn't do so.

What was Abigail feeling? Was this move of hers in anger or in passion? Would she rage at him, or would his plan finally have its glorious resolution?

They moved down a corridor that no other guests inhabited, and then, to his surprise, she wrenched open a door and entered, hauling him in behind her, leaving the door ajar. It was a small room, a deep closet of sorts, though it was entirely empty for the present. Abigail released his hand as soon as they entered and began to pace as much as the small space would allow, her skirts slamming against Matthew's shins with every turn.

"Abigail . . ."

She held up a gloved hand that trembled slightly and shook her head. Then she bit the top of her middle finger and yanked the glove off, then did the same with the other, crinkling both her hands. She stopped suddenly and turned to face him, the tears in her eyes glinting in the faint light from the corridor. Her eyes rested below his, somewhere around the level of his chin, and it chilled him.

"You think," she began, her voice thick and rasping, "that you can drop yourself back into my life and I will fall into your arms without a second thought? You think that the suffering I endured day after day after what you chose to do has all been forgotten? You think that because I can now tolerate your company and smile at times and listen to your stories that it doesn't still pain me to see you smile?"

Matthew stared at her, mouth gaping, horrified. He had never imagined . . . well, he *had*, but he thought . . . He thought . . .

Abigail's hands became fists at her sides. "Did you think that I was sitting around just waiting for you to decide you wanted me after all? That you are the only measure by which I could possibly live my life? That all would be forgiven and forgotten because I understood the pressures you faced and pitied you for how it all turned out?"

He had, actually. He had thought that. Foolishly, stupidly, naively he had thought that.

"I gave you understanding," she raged as her voice rose and her cheeks flushed. "I listened, and I actually felt pain on your behalf! I began to forgive you, I won't deny that, and I thought there was a chance that my best friend could be back in my life. But never, not even once, did I think that you would put me through all of this just to confess things that I explicitly asked you not confess. Do you know why I asked that of you, Matthew?"

His mouth worked, but no sound came out. His legs shook, and his stomach clenched, his face slowly going numb with every word she spoke.

A pair of tears leaked from her eyes, one from each, and they began a slow, maddening path down her cheeks. "Because I couldn't bear it. Because day in and day out, I still live with the hurt that you caused me. I was the one who loved you, the one who wanted you for *you*, and you chose her. You chose *her*! You had a wife to divert you, though she failed to do so, and a life to live with her. You could forget all that we shared, though you failed to do so, and moved on with her. Do you know what I did?"

More tears fell, and with it his heart. "I ached. I burned. I woke up every morning knowing that the man I loved did not, and could not, love me the same way."

"No . . ." Matthew managed to force out, though it came without volume or force. "No, Abigail . . ."

She either did not hear him or chose to ignore him. "I had to live with the understanding that to the person I valued above all others, I was second best. I was found lacking. Wanting. For days on end, I was torn between wanting you and hating you, and then hating myself for somehow failing you."

Lord, he couldn't bear this. "Abigail . . ."

Finally, she looked at him again, another tear falling,

though her face seemed close to crumpling. "I have loved having you back in my life, Matthew. But every moment you are near reminds me of those days, and those feelings, and when you say all of the things you should have said then, I ache even worse than I did then. Because I want to believe you, and I don't know if I can."

He was to her in less than two steps and hauled her into his arms, pressing her trembling frame against his own as his arms clasped her tightly. One hand settled at her back, the other in her hair, and he kissed her hair with all the emotion he felt washing over him. "Oh, Abigail. Oh, my love."

To his surprise, she clung to him, and he felt his shirt dampening with waves of tears. "I tried to be enough for you," she whimpered, her hands gripping at his back. "Why, Matthew? Why?"

"I am so sorry, love," he murmured, pressing his lips to her hair again and again. "I am so very sorry."

She shuddered against him, her cries muffled, and, impossibly, she pulled herself closer. He let her do so, held her as tightly as she seemed to crave, yearning to give her the comfort she so desperately sought. Comfort he should have given her then.

Comfort he *had* to give her now.

"You *are* enough," he whispered. He shifted his mouth closer to her ear. "You always were enough. More than enough. More than I deserved. There is nothing lacking or wanting in you, and I never forgot you. Not for a day, not for a moment, and nothing in this world could ever make me forget you. Never."

Her nose brushed against his coat, and she sniffled once, then raised her head. Faint tracks left by her tears marred her cheeks, and her lips were swollen and full, parted now as she breathed through them. Her eyes were greener in this dim light, green and luminous and fixed on his with the same intensity with which she had just raged.

Remnants of her tears leaked from her eyes, and he brushed them away, gently stroking her skin with his fingers. "I never forgot you, Abby."

Abigail inhaled as his fingers passed over her lips, and a faint tremor rocked her frame, sending echoing waves into his own. "I never forgot you either," she breathed.

The words hung between them and rendered each breathless, their lips somehow hovering just out of reach of one another. Someone moved, though it was impossible to say who, and then their lips were melding, caressing and pressing, raising heat and sensation between them. Her lips pulled at his, insistent and demanding, reaching for something within him, drawing forth his very soul, which he was only too willing to give. Aching and need mingled together in the mad frenzy they were caught in the middle of, lips and teeth clashing together, scraping against skin, nothing gentle or tender in any of this.

Passion in its most honest and rare form surged between them. Matthew's fingers clenched in Abigail's hair, his other hand gripping the side of her face, keeping her right where he wanted her. Abigail's hands had moved to his neck, and she pulled him in with a constant strength that humbled him. She kissed him deeply, fiercely, holding nothing in reserve, just as she did with everything else in her life.

One hand moved and rubbed against his bearded jaw, her nails faintly scratching at the skin, drawing a ragged moan from his lips that echoed in the recesses of her perfect mouth. He broke from her lips and danced his lips across her cheeks and along her jaw, venturing down the slender column of her throat. She returned the favor as her mouth dusted against his brow, his ear, anywhere she could reach as she nuzzled against him.

Matthew kissed the base of her throat, and she released a raw, guttural sound that lit him on fire, and he moved back to her lips, seizing them with a renewed fervor, seeking answers and promises to questions he could not voice. Abigail matched him, her arm wrapping around his head like a vice, bringing her body flush with his, the contact searing every inch of them.

"I love you," he breathed as he caught her lower lip. "Abby . . ."

She gasped, arched her neck, then suddenly shoved him away.

Unprepared and unsettled, he stumbled, slamming into the wall of the closet. He stared at her, wide-eyed and panting, limbs and lips and skin still burning with the feeling of her. "What is it? What's wrong?"

Abigail had pressed herself against the opposite wall, staring through him rather than at him, her chest heaving every bit as much as his, hair and gown disheveled. She brought a shaky hand to her lips, then gasped very faintly as they touched.

"Abigail?"

She shook her head. "I can't do this, Matthew. We can't do this."

He braced his elbows on his knees, peering up at her through the haze of his receding desire. "Why not?"

He watched as her throat moved with a swallow that didn't seem to complete. "There's . . . there's someone else. Someone I am falling in love with. And I can't do to him what you did to me. Not if it's real." Her eyes focused once more on him, and he saw the steely determination he loved about her settle there and in her jaw. "No matter how much I may be tempted," she added as a soft afterthought.

He kept his gaze steady, heart ricocheting within him.

She couldn't do this to him . . . Couldn't drive him to this and then leave him for another.

The thought seemed to lodge itself in his throat, and he straightened very slowly.

Of course she could. It was precisely what he had done to her, only this time it happened in a condensed and accelerated manner.

Stunned and humbled, he dipped his chin just once. "I understand."

Abigail moved to the door, paused, and glanced at him. "I'm sorry."

"Don't be," he told her, struggling to swallow himself.

Then she was gone, and he was alone. He took a moment to collect himself, then straightened fully and pushed off of the wall, straightening his cravat and smoothing his hair. After tugging at his jacket once, he moved out of the closet with firm strides.

Only to see Francis, Lord Sterling, standing there leaning against a wall, smiling smugly, raising one suggestive brow.

Matthew scowled, his cheeks and neck heating at once. "How long have you been there?"

He gave nonchalant shrug. "Long enough to see my cousin come out of there disheveled and crying. And as to that, I have absolutely zero questions. Well done, lad."

Matthew's scowl grew into an all-out glower. "I failed, Francis. Everything failed."

Francis stepped closer, sliding his hands into his pockets. "Has it? Or is it the final push you need to win this war?" He gave him a look of reprimand, then strode back toward the ball.

Somehow, without explanation, a weak smile found its way onto Matthew's face. The final push . . . Yes, indeed, this was the final push.

And he fully intended to win this war after all.

Chapter 8

THIS WAS ALL AN absolute disaster. There was no other word for it. A massive disaster that she could not have foreseen.

She was in love with Matthew Weber-Grey again.

She was also in love with the mysterious writer of the letters.

Abigail Sterling loved two men and had told the one she was choosing the other. She had done to him exactly what he had done to her three years ago.

Yet Matthew had told her he understood. That she shouldn't be sorry. He had kissed her full near senseless, and she had returned the favor, and he hadn't said a word in anger, betrayal, or agony.

Impossibly, that had made her love him more.

How could she do this? How could she leave him, now that she'd found love, passion, friendship, and joy with him once more?

She didn't trust him enough. After what he had done, she couldn't. But why couldn't she? She had come to know him again and felt the same pull, the same attraction, the same need to be with him whenever she could. That had not changed, despite everything. And he was different now. Instead of the reckless, headstrong boy she had known, she had found in him a strong, steadfast, caring man.

So why had she backed away from the passionate haven he presented?

Abigail put her head into her hands. The plush fabric of the chair in the parlor seeming to scrape against her where it touched. Her head pounded furiously, just as it had been doing since that night at the Lamberts' two days ago. She had made a decision, but she wasn't clear on it. The poor thing waved to and fro like a willow in the breeze and made just as much noise.

The constant swaying in her mind was beginning to make her nauseated.

She rubbed her hands hard against her face, then stared into the fire in the grate.

She knew why she had done what she had. The man who was writing her letters had touched her soul in a way she had never felt before, not even in the days she and Matthew had been together. He seemed to understand her somehow and see everything in her that she wanted a man to see. Not ignorant of her flaws, but finding them to be just as much a part of her as any other feature.

She needed to know him. She needed to explore this love she felt for him and experience what he had to offer her. The depth of feeling he had stirred within her could not be ignored, not even for the temptation of a life with Matthew.

Matthew.

She closed her eyes on tears she hadn't known were welling. His image swam before her in her mind's eye, clear as he had been in that random closet she had tugged him into. His eyes held the same light of mischief she had always loved, and the deep dark of his facial hair gave him a new edge of mystery, even danger, that drew her to him. His mouth curved crookedly, the most attractive smile she had seen in her life, before or since.

Her best friend. Still, it would seem.

And she loved another enough to walk away from him.

Madness. Complete and utter madness.

She hadn't told Maren or Thomas and especially had not told her mother. She couldn't bring herself to do so for fear of what any of them might say. The irony and foolishness of her current situation, and even her choices, were not lost on her in the slightest. Hearing a confirmation of all that might be enough to dissuade her from her course, and she couldn't have that. She couldn't have proof of her errors, not now. She was too weak at the present, too keen for someone else to make the decision for her.

It would be so much easier if they would.

But this, unfortunately, was something she had to do on her own. And absolutely on her own, at that. Her own head and her own heart.

Neither of them were being particularly decisive or communicative.

"Miss Abigail?"

Sniffing quickly, Abigail turned to the open door, wiping at the tears on her cheeks. "Yes, Bess? What is it?"

The round-faced maid bobbed, smiling warmly. "You have another letter, miss."

For the first time since she had known what these letters contained, she wasn't sure she wanted to read it. Of course she wanted to know what he would tell her today, what insights he had gained, and to fall a little bit more in love with him, but in her current state, she feared it would only confuse matters more.

Still. It would not do at all to let Bess know that.

The maid handed Abigail the letter, then bobbed another quick curtsy before disappearing down the corridor.

Alone once more, Abigail stared down at the letter as

though it were something entirely foreign, the ambiguous seal on the back staring at her like some great, accusatory, critical eye.

She swallowed and snapped it, unfolding it hastily before her mind could change itself on the topic. Her heart swelled at the sight of the scrawl she had come to know and love so well, and her cheeks heated with guilt and shame. There was no possible way he could know what she had done with Matthew only days ago, she reminded herself, but the flaming in her cheeks wasn't aware of that fact.

Pushing all that aside, she focused on the letter.

Dearest Miss Sterling,

The time is upon us. I cannot wait longer for you to be made aware of who I am, and for your heart to, perhaps, open for me, as mine has been open for you. Open, aching, and waiting for any chance at all that you might step into its void. There can be no one there but you, and I would spend my entire life awaiting your arrival to that desolate location if there was a glimmer of hope.

I have loved you for so long that I could not know myself without you. Your smile, your impulsiveness, your towering strength, your ability to find wit and humor in any circumstance whatsoever, and even the maddening stubborn streak you cannot completely hide, all combine into a rare beauty equal to your physical loveliness, if not far above it, and I thank God Almighty that I have the eyes to see it, that I am graced with the eyes to behold you, to know you, to hope for you. Even now, in writing this, I am the most fortunate of men.

My love, I will never be worthy of you, and well I know it, but I cling to the hope that you might find the discrepancy not insurmountable. From the day I first learned which window of Hazelwood was yours and found the ability to perfectly aim pebbles at it, I wanted to spend every waking hour with you, and nearly did so, if your memory will serve. That night at the ball in Colchester to celebrate the Queen, I knew I was yours in every way conceivable. The friendship I so treasured deepened with every heartbeat until I could no longer fathom or describe it, and to this day my heart has never heard sweeter words than these: "Well, Matthew, I think I may have to lay claim to you the entire evening."

Beloved Abigail, lay claim to me this evening at the Queen's ball. Lay claim to me any day or night or hour that you wish. Lay claim to me for all the days of our lives. For I am and ever have been yours to claim.

Tears coursed freely and unchecked down her cheeks, falling onto the paper in a barrage of emotions, blurring the precious lines in places. It made no difference, as she would never be able to forget a single word of it. The entire letter would be emblazoned in her mind and in her heart, and the echoing burn radiated from limb to limb, roaring into more intensity in the center.

The very core of her screamed out in joyous relief and vigor.

Matthew.

Matthew all along, Matthew the entire time, Matthew both here and there . . . The answer to every question and every need was Matthew.

Part of her considered that she ought to have been peeved at the deception, at the onslaught he had set about in her life, but in this moment, all she could feel was unfettered joy.

This man knew her heart and soul and loved her as thoroughly as any man or woman has ever loved. Their past was behind them, barely in her recollection, and the forgiveness that had eluded her thus far filled her now. She felt light as a wisp of cloud, laughter bubbling up amid the symphony of every other emotion and sensation cascading through her being.

The Queen's ball. Tonight. Oh, but she had to see him, to tell him, to hold him, to run at him, if there were not too many easily scandalized ladies about. She wanted very much to apologize and make amends for refusing him . . . for him. He would undoubtedly find the whole thing rather amusing and tease her about it endlessly.

Horror suddenly washed over her in a frigid wave, gooseflesh rising on every inch of her skin.

Did he know that the man she had been talking about was the man in the letters? Had he puzzled it out that she had unwittingly fallen in love with him in writing? Or had her words the other night given him further reason to fear and doubt?

Lord, she had made a mess of everything!

Well, technically he had done so, but she was more than willing to accept part of the blame this time.

They would share it. Share everything. As they always should have done.

Abigail inhaled slowly and exhaled the same, calm and sense returning, only for a wild grin to dance across her face and send her heart ricocheting through her chest once more.

Matthew loved her, just had he had said, but with a completeness that stole her breath. And she loved him just as much.

And tonight, they would both know it.

The ball was an absolute crush. As it turned out, having a ball for the Queen when the Queen is actually in attendance tends to increase the number of guests who attend. And apparently all of them wished to stand in the middle of the room and block her view of absolutely everything.

It was a pity that she had not inherited the height that made her father so imposing.

Still, she was here, and Matthew would be here somewhere. She only had to find him.

"Steady, Abs," Thomas murmured, yet again escorting her about. "You've already been presented to the Queen ages ago. Surely being in her presence tonight isn't so bad."

Abigail shook her head, her tight ringlets twirling with it, one long, dark lock bouncing against her bare shoulder. "It isn't the Queen I'm worried about."

Thomas placed a hand over Abigail's, momentarily ceasing her attempt to mangle her fingers together. "He'll be here, Abs. He's not going anywhere."

She jerked her head around to look up at him. "What? How did you know?"

Her brother smiled ruefully. "You didn't think I knew? And even if I didn't, you're wearing the same gown from the last time you were anxious to see Matthew at a Queen's ball. The significance isn't lost on me."

"How did you know what I wore then?" she demanded after gaping for a long moment.

Thomas shrugged a shoulder. "Every now and then, I do pay attention to details."

Abigail returned her focus to the room in general, reeling from this revelation. Yes, she was wearing the same gown, which miraculously still fit without her having to sacrifice herself to the corset gods, but she had only expected Matthew to notice.

She was counting on Matthew to notice.

She knew she looked well; in this gown, how could she

not? It was a silk of the palest green with streaks of gold weaving in and out in lines that drew the eye to her bodice and waist. The neckline swept about her shoulders gracefully, gathering and dipping slightly at the center, where an intricate bow was tied. The skirts were of exactly the same pattern as the bodice, the lines dipping with each fold, and the gold details becoming more pronounced as they neared the hem. Her dark hair had been curled, pinned, and folded about, a sheer gold ribbon weaving in and out while small white flowers and pearls were scattered among the tresses. Pearl drop earrings and the same gold ribbon tied about her neck were the only other embellishments.

No less than three members of her family had told her how lovely she looked, but she could never trust familiar appraisals. Ages of time had been spent poring over her ensemble, desperate to be as close to perfection as she could get, and while she knew she did not look at all perfect, she hoped it was enough to strike Matthew speechless. For a moment or two, at least.

Abigail heard Thomas ask her permission to leave her so he could dance, and mutely she nodded, not caring in the slightest where he went or what he did. Her heart was pounding in her throat, and she had no energy to focus on anything other than finding Matthew.

"Oh, my sweet girl, what a vision you are!"

Abigail whirled, the voice as familiar and unexpected as anything else. Her grandmother stood there in resplendent blue, grinning without shame. "Miranda? What are you—?"

Miranda came to her and kissed her on both cheeks. "Beloved Abigail. You didn't think I'd miss the Queen's ball, did you? Especially when it will be so monumental for you."

Abigail blinked unsteadily. How in the world could Miranda possibly . . . know?

"I do hope you find Matthew soon," Miranda said with a wink. "He looks positively glorious. Come and find me later, won't you, dear? I want to hear everything."

Again, Abigail's cheeks were kissed, and Miranda swept away in a rustle of skirts, moving on to greet the other members of the Sterling family.

There wasn't time to properly consider what in God's name Miranda was doing here or how she knew or anything at all surrounding her, and Abigail forced herself to return her attention to the ballroom. To the people.

To Matthew.

Where was he?

The group in front of her moved then, and despite all her efforts, she found that she was the one without speech or breath.

Matthew stood in the new opening, hands clasped behind his back, dressed in the most perfect evening wear she had ever seen on anyone. And he was staring at her. Clearly had been doing so. He smiled at her, and in that smile she felt every ounce of love and affection she had ever craved in her life. Gentle and warm, reassuring, adoring, and perfectly Matthew.

His eyes stayed on her, waiting for her to take the first step. More than that, they stayed on her face, never once travelling down the length of her. Steady and direct, and filled with a power that sent her slippered feet moving.

Slowly, but moving all the same.

Every step came with a heartbeat, the pulse of which echoed loudly in her ears and at her wrists. Her throat constricted and her eyes burned, but she refused to swallow or to blink, for fear that something would change, that this magic would vanish.

Matthew exhaled when she reached him, his shoulders

nearly heaving with the motion. Then, and only then, did his eyes move across her, achingly slow and taking in every single aspect as though to commit all to memory. As they returned up the length of her, the skin they brushed over burned with pleasure, sending a shiver down her spine.

"I . . ." Matthew cleared his throat, then shook his head. "Abby . . ."

Speechless after all. Her heart swelled, and she reached a shaking hand out, which he immediately seized, the power in his grip stealing her breath. "Well, Matthew, I think I may have to lay claim to you the entire evening."

His smile returned in a flash, and with it a marked degree of heat. "Do you really?"

"Yes," she whispered. "I must."

"Why?" he replied as his fingers moved over the hand he held. "Why must you?"

Now the burning in her eyes intensified, and she tried to clear them with a shake of her head. Tears began to fall with a single blink, and he brought his free hand up to brush them away, cupping her cheek when he had done so. "Why, Abby?"

Abigail's jaw trembled, and her lips parted. "Because I love you, Matthew. I love you. And I want to claim you for the rest of my days."

His smile turned somehow tenderer, and his thumb stroked her cheek. "Oh my love, you already have. I'm yours for always, don't you know that?"

She turned her head and kissed his thumb, then the palm of his hand, holding it to her and closing her eyes on more tears. "Then claim me, Matthew. I want to be yours as well."

"Darling . . ." He pulled her to him, gathering her close and kissing her brow, then one cheek. "If you'll have me, I'll claim you until the end of time." Another soft kiss fell on her ear. "I meant every word I said and every word I wrote. I'm sorry for the deception, but I was so desperate to have you that I used whatever means necessary."

"I'm glad you did," she told him as she pulled back, hands at his chest. "Those letters meant more to me than anything I could think of. Then when I spent more time with you, I began to forget, and I wanted you. I've been tormented over choosing between you. I didn't even want to open the last letter for fear that I had made a mistake refusing you."

Matthew shook his head and stroked her cheek again. "Never. Never, Abby."

She smiled at his delusions. "And then it *was* you, and I cannot tell you the joy that it brought me. I love you. I've loved you all along."

And she was done with waiting. She slid her hands around his neck and pulled him to her for a long, slow, soul-searing kiss that sealed her fate with his. Claimed them both. Made them one.

He held her just as tightly, his hands clenching almost rhythmically against her, his lips molding to hers in a perfection that extended far beyond bliss. This even transcended exhilaration, of all things, and a gentle weight began to press against her heart.

This was right.

She sighed against his mouth with relief and satisfaction, and drew him closer for more.

"Have you no shame? The Queen is here, and you are in full sight of her!"

They broke apart, perhaps a bit reluctantly, and gave each other rather dazed smiles before turning toward the scandalized majordomo. He eyed them both with the same disgust one might a mangy dog in the gutters.

Matthew linked his fingers through Abigail's, and even through the gloves, she felt the heat of it. "Apologies, sir."

The majordomo sputtered. "Don't apologize to me. Apologize to the Queen!" He waved a dramatic hand in the direction of the far wall, where, sure enough, the small but mighty Queen Victoria and her tall, stately husband Prince Albert stood.

Abigail swallowed a laugh and proceeded forward with Matthew by her side. He bowed and she curtsied deeply when they neared the royal couple.

The majordomo moved in front of them. "I am told, Your Majesty, that these persons are Mr. Matthew Weber-Grey and Miss Abigail Sterling."

The Queen's lips quirked in a bemused smirk. "Charmed indeed."

Abigail opened her mouth to apologize but found a sharply raised hand before she could do so.

"No, my dear, I don't wish to hear a single word of apology." The Queen's smile spread just a little, tucking against her cheeks on a laugh. "Not from a couple so clearly in love. I'll not hear of it. What do you think, Albert?"

Prince Albert didn't look nearly as amused as his wife, but he wrapped an arm around his wife's waist and nodded once, which seemed something monumental.

The Queen covered her husband's hand with her own and winked at Abigail. "I am quite fond of all things love and romance, aren't you, Miss Sterling?"

Abigail bit her cheek as Matthew squeezed her hand. "I wasn't always, Your Majesty," she confessed, her face heating, "but I found I have recently come round to the notion."

Now the Prince seemed to be stifling a laugh, and the Queen beamed outright. "As you should. Well done, Mr. Weber-Grey. Well done, indeed."

Matthew bowed again. "Thank you, Ma'am."

"Have you proposed matrimony yet?" the Queen asked with a twinkle in her eye.

"Victoria . . ." Prince Albert murmured, still smiling.

"I was just getting to that, Ma'am," Matthew assured her, "but I have reason to be hopeful."

A soft giggle came from the Queen. "I should think so, and I dearly hope you will invite us to the wedding. Otherwise, I may not give the marriage my royal blessing."

"We would be delighted, Ma'am," Abigail told her eagerly.

"There now, Mr. Weber-Grey," the Queen said slyly. "I do believe you have your answer."

Matthew looked at Abigail with such adoration, she nearly wept again. "I can see that I have, Ma'am. And if you will forgive a moment's less-than-proper impulse under these circumstances . . ."

Without waiting for royal sanction, Matthew tugged Abigail back into his arms, and kissed her quite soundly.

And Abigail, not to be outdone, wrapped her arms about his neck and kissed him back.

Epilogue

AS IT HAPPENED, QUEEN Victoria and Prince Albert were invited to the wedding, actually came to the wedding, and requested, with all politeness, to come to the christening of their first child.

They were, of course, invited there as well.

And Victoria Georgiana Miranda Weber-Grey was the most delightfully spoiled girl ever born to parents so madly in love.

When she was old enough, her parents had walked her out to the boundary between Chisolm and Hazelwood very early on and instructed her as to the finer points of sneaking into her grandparents' estates undetected.

Which she eventually employed with great success.

Rebecca Connolly writes romances, both period and contemporary, because she absolutely loves a good love story. She has been creating stories since childhood, and there are home videos to prove it! She started writing them down in elementary school and has never looked back. She currently lives in Minnesota, spends every spare moment away from her day job absorbed in her writing, and is a hot cocoa addict.

Visit her online: RebeccaConnolly.com

Coming Home

Jennifer Moore

Chapter 1

Spring 1890
Isle of Wight, UK

GRANT MASON FROWNED, PULLING away as his mother's elbow poked into his arm.

"Do you hear that?" she hissed. "Right behind us."

The instant the hymn had begun, the unknown woman's voice sounded clearly among the others in the congregation. Of course he'd heard. It was impossible not to when she sat directly behind them, only a few pews back. Grant did not consider himself an expert on music by any stretch of the imagination, but even he could tell her singing was remarkable.

His mother continued to squirm. "Have you ever? That voice. Such perfect pitch." The feathers on her wide hat brushed his face as she turned her head for a better view. "Who is she?"

"Mother." Grant's whisper was rather loud, but he had no choice if he wanted to be heard with the congregation singing on all sides. "Turn around."

The woman's voice stopped, though the hymn continued.

Grant rolled his eyes. Obviously Mother's backward glances had not been discreet.

"She is sitting with the Wickershams," his mother whispered. "Do you suppose she is a relative?"

He shrugged, hoping his mother would imitate his silence. Her not-so-quiet whispers were drawing glances from other parishioners.

"I have never heard them speak of extended family, and surely they would have told me if a relative was coming for a visit," she continued.

"We can ask them after the service." Grant cocked his head, listening, but the woman's singing had not resumed.

"How long is she here, do you suppose?"

He touched his forefinger to his lips, then pointed down at his mother's hymnal, indicating for her to stop talking and sing.

"The choir festival—"

"I know, Mother." He put a hand on hers. "But we can do nothing about it until after the service."

She nodded and sat back, finding her place in the song just in time to sing the last words, and then closed the hymnal with a sigh.

Grant knew she must be disappointed. "It Is Well With My Soul" was one of her favorite hymns, but she had naught to blame but her own snooping for the missed opportunity. He wondered if the woman behind him felt the same regret. From the resounding sound of her voice, she must be a person who enjoyed singing. If only his mother's curiosity had not embarrassed her into silence.

Throughout the sermon, Grant's thoughts returned to the mystery singer. He had been enchanted by her voice and, though he'd not admit it to his mother, or anyone else for that matter, he was curious. His mother was right; he'd never known the Wickershams to have relatives visit. Their only son died years earlier, and none had come for the funeral. Grant assumed none existed, which was a pity indeed, because of any couple he knew, Walter and Deborah Wickersham possessed enough kindness and goodwill for an army of relatives. And he felt a tingle of suspicion at this newcomer, not liking the idea of a stranger among his people.

Truth be told, he was suspicious of all *overners*, or mainlanders. The island was a popular tourist destination, even more so since Queen Victoria had claimed it for her own vacation home, and in Grant's experience, tourists were full of criticism, condescension, and complaints.

There were plenty of other concerns to occupy his mind, and he pushed away thoughts of the stranger behind him, glancing around the congregation. The company of locals was scant, even for the off-season. Whooping cough had ravaged the parish this winter, leaving hardly a family untouched. Though the sickness had thankfully not resulted in many deaths, recovery had been slow, and Grant's tenants would need more help than ever with their spring planting. He'd already spent nearly the entire winter caring for animals whose owners were too weak to do much more than thank him.

But such was the way with *caulkheads*—island residents. They helped one another. When any challenge reared its head, the community rallied, caring for children, bringing meals, and assisting with chores. The people of Brading Parish were family, and though they had no choice but to welcome outsiders, they would always be just that—outsiders.

When the final hymn began, both Grant and his mother tilted their heads again to listen.

"Why isn't she singing?" his mother asked, twisting fully around.

He batted away the feathers with an irritated sweep of his hand. "Perhaps your attention has made her self-conscious."

She sat back against the bench, looking petulant. "She must be used to the attention." She thumbed through the hymnal until she reached the correct page. "With such a talent, of course people take notice."

The service concluded, and the congregation rose, moving to the aisles. Grant scanned the crowd, hoping to catch a view of the mystery singer, but only saw the back of her as she exited the church.

When they stepped outside, Grant's mother made a beeline for the Wickershams and their companion. The three were across the churchyard, talking with Mrs. Barlow, the vicar's new wife, and her friend Mrs. Pinkston, who held her youngest, Arthur, on her hip.

Grant followed at a more sedate pace, greeting neighbors and friends as he went. As he drew closer, he took the opportunity to study the unfamiliar woman. She wore a blue dress with a bustle and a high collar and upon her head a small hat set with a few silk flowers. Practical attire, he thought, yet upon her, it looked soft and feminine. Perhaps it was the thick, honey-colored curls just brushing her shoulders, or her pink cheeks. He concluded that she was young, not yet in her twentieth year. And she appeared very uncomfortable, shifting from one foot to the other, her shoulders tight. Was she wishing to be away from the company? He frowned.

A child darted through the crowd and dashed right in front of Grant, nearly causing him to lose his balance. Grant recognized his tenant's son, Barty Newbold. "Careful there."

"Beg your pardon, Mr. Mason. Didn't mean to trip you, sir."

"No harm done." He ruffled the boy's hair.

When Grant reached the group, his mother was, of course, speaking. He tipped his hat toward Mrs. Wickersham and the other women, winked at Mr. Wickersham, and tickled little Arthur beneath his chubby chin.

". . . loveliest parish in all of the island," Mother said to the newcomer with a flourish. She looked up at Grant and waved him closer. "And here is my son now, if I may introduce him, miss."

The young lady nodded.

"Grant Mason." Mother lifted a hand toward him, then spread it back in the other direction. "And Grant, it is my privilege to introduce Miss Clara Brightly."

She curtsied. "How do you do, sir?"

"A pleasure." Grant tipped his hat.

"Miss Brightly is my cousin," Mrs. Wickersham said, her face lighting with a smile that lifted her round cheeks and crinkled the skin around her eyes. "Come to live with us after the death of her father."

"My sympathies, Miss Brightly," Grant said.

"Thank you." She spoke in a soft voice and rubbed her arms.

Grant thought Miss Brightly seemed standoffish, and her indifference to the people around her raised his defenses.

"Mr. Mason and his mother reside at Haverstone Park." Walter Wickersham jabbed a thumb over his shoulder. "East of the town."

Miss Brightly glanced behind him. "I see."

Arthur Pinkston grabbed on to Mrs. Barlow's beads, sticking them into his toothless mouth.

"The Masons are our very good friends," Deborah Wickersham said in her gentle voice. She gave Grant and his mother a loving smile.

Grant smiled back and renewed his opinion that she was the kindest of women.

After a few moments of exchanging pleasantries, Walter cleared his throat and pushed his fingers into his waistcoat pockets. "Now that we've the formalities out of the way, Mrs. Mason, what was it you wished to speak with us about?"

"Actually, it is Miss Brightly whom I hoped to speak with." Grant's mother turned toward the young lady. "You see, I heard you singing during the service, and my dear, your voice is lovely. Isn't it lovely, Grant?"

"It is."

Miss Brightly gave a small smile. "Thank you."

"You are very accomplished," Mother continued. "I assume you've had professional instruction?"

Miss Brightly glanced between Grant and his mother. "I studied under a voice tutor," she said.

"I knew it." Mother's eyes widened, as did her smile, and she leaned toward Miss Brightly. "We need you."

The young lady's brows pulled together. "You need me?"

Another of the Pinkston children, Lucy, ran to her mother, tugging on her skirt. Mrs. Pinkston handed baby Arthur to Mrs. Wickersham and bent to tend to her daughter. The baby didn't release his hold on Mrs. Barlow's beads, so she moved closer to Mrs. Wickersham as if she were being pulled on a leash.

"Yes," Grant's mother continued to Miss Brightly. "You see, the May Day celebration in Wippingham is a long-standing tradition here on the island. Choirs from every parish perform at the festival." She gestured with her hands as she spoke. "Well, over the years, it has become something of a competition, and . . ." She trailed off, pulling her lips to the side as if unsure of her next words.

"And you wish me to join the choir?" Miss Brightly asked.

"Yes, well, what remains of the choir. Many of our parishioners have been ill this winter and are still recovering. Our very best tenor, Bentley Durham, is in Brighton with his daughter until summer. Gertrude Nuttal, our lead soprano, broke her ankle." Mother wrung her hands, and Grant recognized the look of anxiety that talk of the festival had caused over the past months. "And with the Ladies' Charity Society sponsoring a booth at the festival, I've simply had no time to dedicate to the choir, and neither have most of the parish women."

"We know, Mrs. Mason," Mrs. Barlow said as she pried the beads from the baby's fat fingers. "You have been so busy."

Mrs. Pinkston and Mrs. Wickersham nodded their agreement.

"I'm not sure how I can be of help," Miss Brightly said.

"Well, I'd very nearly made up my mind to give up on the choir altogether this year, since we are already quite into April, but when I heard you sing . . ." Grant's mother placed a hand on her breast and sighed. "It was as if the Lord himself sent you to Brading as an answer to prayer."

Mrs. Pinkston and Mrs. Barlow exchanged a glance, Walter grinned, and Grant rubbed his brow. Mother was laying it on rather thick.

Miss Brightly's cheeks turned pink. "What exactly do you need me to do?"

"Well, everything, dear." Mother spread her hands to the side. "We must recruit new members, as our choir is so dwindled that I think only a few will come to rehearsal. And of course you must choose a song to sing, one that will not suffer for lack of a crowd, and then teach it to the choir."

Miss Brightly's eyes were round, and Grant did not blame her for being overwhelmed. May Day was less than three weeks away. He had half a mind to whisk his mother away and save the young lady. But doing so would only postpone the conversation.

"I do not know if I am the person for the job, Mrs. Mason." Miss Brightly rubbed her arms again. "I only just arrived and—"

"Oh, but you must." Mother linked her elbow with Miss Brightly's, turning her to face the churchyard and spread her arm toward the parishioners. "It cannot be a coincidence that you arrived at Brading just as I had given up hope of a choir. And we can't disappoint everybody."

Miss Brightly looked around the churchyard for a long moment, then removed her arm gently from his mother's grasp. "May I have a moment to consider?"

"Yes, of course, dear." His mother took young Lucy's hand and moved toward the other women. "Take your time. We have plenty to discuss."

"The Ladies' Charity Society will be making its rounds this week." Mrs. Barlow held her beads away from the baby. "I thought beef stew or possibly lamb . . ."

Miss Brightly leaned closer to Walter. "Do you mind if we move to stand in the sun?"

"Certainly." Walter offered his arm and led her out of the church's shadow to a sunny spot on the grass.

Not wanting to listen to a discussion about stew, Grant followed. "I hope my mother did not overwhelm you, Miss Brightly." He clasped his hands behind his back. "She can be, ah . . ."

"Earnest," Walter said. His grin spread his thick mustache.

Grant smiled. "I was going to say aggressive."

"Nonsense." Walter clapped a hand on Grant's shoulder. "Her heart is in the right place, but when she gets an idea in her head . . ."

"Then we should all beware," Grant finished with a grimace.

Walter smiled his agreement, then turned to the young lady. "And Clara, you do not have to do anything you don't wish to do. Mrs. Mason will understand if you choose not to lead the choir."

"Eventually," Grant muttered.

The men laughed, and Miss Brightly smiled, though her brow remained furrowed as if she were still contemplating.

"However, my dear," Walter said, "it might be just the thing. A fine way to meet people. I think it very important to be involved in a cause."

"I agree," said a voice behind them.

The three spun at the sound and greeted Harrison Barlow, the vicar and Grant's closest friend, who'd approached without their notice.

"From the sound of it, Mrs. Mason has been recruiting a new choir director," Harry said.

"She has." Grant gave a knowing look to his old friend.

Harry's lips twitched. He knew firsthand how Grant's mother operated. "And what are your thoughts on the matter, Miss Brightly?"

"I am . . ." She glanced between the men, then to where the ladies were still, no doubt, discussing the benefits of beef versus lamb stew. "I am thinking it over."

Barty Newbold darted past again, running to join a group of children sitting in a ring on the grass. One of the older girls led them in a chant, and the others followed in a clapping game.

Grant remembered playing on the same patch of grass after Sunday service as a child. Most likely, he'd been waiting for his mother to finish her church business, he thought. Some things never changed.

The women joined them. Mrs. Barlow slipped her hand into her husband's elbow, giving him a warm smile. The couple had been married less than a year and were very affectionate. Emmeline Barlow was from Shorwell, just fifteen miles away. The entire parish was quite taken with the vicar's wife, and Grant was pleased to see his friend happy. Walter smiled at his wife, then patted Lucy's head and tickled baby Arthur's chin.

"Mr. Barlow, Mrs. Mason, have you ever considered a children's choir?" Miss Brightly said, her gaze still on the game.

The vicar blinked.

Grant's mother frowned, then tipped her head to the side. "Oh, well, I don't know . . ." She turned with the others and watched the children at play.

"In India, parents sent home their school-age children to England," Miss Brightly said. "I am not used to so many in church, and I noticed their voices among the congregation." She faced the vicar, her expression relaxing into a gentle smile. "There is something very special about hearing children's voices, especially when they sing about Jesus."

"Witness of truth borne by innocents has the power to soften hearts." Walter nodded and scratched his neck. "The idea is unexpected." He looked at his wife, then back to the young lady.

"Delightful," Mrs. Barlow said.

"It would certainly be unique," Grant's mother said.

"A children's choir." Mrs. Pinkston shifted the baby on her hip and glanced down at Lucy, smiling.

"A wonderful idea, dear." Mrs. Wickersham nodded.

"I think I like it." Grant's mother's face lit in a grin. "Perhaps it is just the advantage Brading Parish needs at the festival."

Walter patted Miss Brightly's shoulder, giving a crooked smile. "By Jove, but it might just win the competition."

"How fortunate that you've come to us, Miss Brightly," Mr. Barlow said. "A fresh idea and a talented musician to carry it out."

"You will, of course, lead the choir," Grant's mother said.

She glanced between them. "I can assist, certainly, but not lead."

Grant pursed his lips, not liking her reaction—as if coming up with a brilliant idea were all the contribution she cared to give and the implementation of it was beneath her.

Miss Brightly folded her arms. "I do not have much—any—experience with children, and I wouldn't even know where to begin."

"Nonsense." Mrs. Pinkston shifted the baby to her other hip. "It is easy as you please."

Grant was becoming tired of the fickle Miss Brightly. She seemed extremely arrogant. If she did not wish to lead the choir, so be it. His mother could certainly find a person better suited for the job, and one who did not require the entire parish to beg her.

Miss Brightly met his gaze and looked away quickly, no doubt startled by the displeasure in his expression.

The vicar patted her arm. "It is a daunting task, Miss Brightly, and we certainly do not expect you to do it all alone." He raised a finger as if an idea had just occurred to him. "Grant will assist you."

He must not have heard correctly. "Pardon?"

Walter and the vicar grinned, and the ladies all chattered their agreement.

Grant's stomach sank. "I can't . . . Harry, you're aware of how busy I am this time of year."

His mother linked her arm through his. "You know all the children, dear. And like Mr. Barlow said, we can hardly expect Miss Brightly to undertake the entire project alone."

The vicar continued to grin. He clasped Miss Brightly's fingers in one hand, and Grant's in the other. "It looks as if we have a plan. A choir-directing team. I will announce the first rehearsal shall take place directly after the children's Bible Study meeting on Wednesday."

Mother grinned and clapped her hands. "Oh, it has all come together, hasn't it, Grant?"

"Indeed." He spoke the word through clenched teeth.

The Barlows made their farewells, and the others chatted excitedly about the festival and the children's choir. Grant's mind scrambled to think of a way out of the situation, but with each passing second, he grew more resigned to his fate. He looked at Miss Brightly, who was rubbing her arms and watching the children.

As if she could feel his gaze on her, she glanced toward him.

He gave a cool stare, then looked away. Miss Brightly may have a beautiful voice and a pretty face, but she was still an overner—one who thought herself above the simple people of the island. He tightened his jaw. He would work with her for the sake of his parish, but that didn't mean he would trust her.

Chapter 2

AN INVITATION FROM THE Queen changes nothing. I am still leaving. Clara Brightly tucked the heavy parchment card back into its envelope, fingering the royal seal for a moment before handing it across the carriage to Deborah.

Deborah took it with a smile and slipped the invitation back out, reading over it with Walter for what Clara thought must have been the hundredth time.

She and the Wickershams were headed to Brading. As it turned out, the Ladies' Charity Society met at the vicar's cottage on Wednesday evenings during the children's Bible Study. Clara's fingers tingled with nervousness as she thought of leading the choir. In addition to the shyness she already fought against, she had no idea how one went about teaching children, and based on her impressions of Grant Mason, her partner wasn't going to offer any help. She didn't think it possible for a person to look less pleased about the prospect of working with her. The memory of his unhappy expression made her stomach burn.

Deborah clasped her hands together, bending the fancy paper. "To be invited to a ball at Osborne House is such an honor. You know, Walter and I went to London for Queen Victoria's Golden Jubilee celebration. Absolutely marvelous." She shook her head fondly, the colorful plumes on her hat blowing in either direction, then turned back to Clara. "Isn't it gracious of the arrangement committee to extend the invitation to include you as well?"

"It is indeed," Clara said. Though she was becoming tired of the topic, she was glad for the interruption of her thoughts. She would much rather think of . . . well, anything other than Mr. Grant Mason's rude behavior.

"Such a benevolent ruler, our Queen Victoria." Deborah pressed the letter to her bosom.

Walter sat up taller in the seat next to his wife and raised a finger toward the ceiling. "And I shall be accompanied by the two most beautiful women on the island." He grinned, his crooked incisor poking out beneath his furry top lip at a curious angle. "Won't the other gentlemen be jealous?" He chuckled, and his wife joined in, her giggles sounding like they belonged to a young girl.

Clara couldn't help but smile at the merry pair. Deborah and Walter were both plump, their cheeks, chins, and tummies bouncing with every bump of the carriage wheels, and in the week since her arrival, they'd been nothing but cheerful. In their presence, Clara's shyness and the horrible anxiety that came with speaking to strangers was nearly forgotten.

Deborah was a distant cousin of her mother's and among the few living relatives the London solicitor, Mr. Poppy, had been able to locate. Clara felt a mixture of gratitude for the couple's kindness, as well as guilt for the imposition. Taking in an unknown relation could not have been a desirable situation for the two. But the Wickershams assured her again and again that her arrival was an unexpected ray of light in their dull lives.

As pleasant as Clara found life with the Wickershams, Wardleigh Manor wasn't home, and her heart ached to return to India. She was determined to do so as soon as the opportunity presented itself, which was another reason she'd been reluctant to lead the choir. Committing to something she may have to abandon before its time felt like a betrayal, and if there was one thing Colonel Brightly had taught his daughter, it was to be true to her word.

As she thought of her father, the ache grew into a pain she could never get used to, squeezing her heart and compressing her throat. She looked through the window, blinking away tears. What had begun as a marvelous adventure eight months earlier—a steamship journey to England by way of Cairo, Athens, Rome, Venice, and Paris—had turned into a series of misfortunes. The foremost being her father's sudden death in Egypt.

Clara shivered, remembering the months of uncertainty in Cairo, the journey to England with strangers, and the long, cold winter she'd spent with her father's great-aunt (twice removed) and her family in London. She'd been told how very different British society was in England compared to the close relationships of expatriates, and her firsthand experience only convinced her that she did not care for the community one bit. She missed her friends at the residency compound.

Deborah reached across the carriage, tapping Clara's hand, and pulling her from the dismal memories. "Here we are." She pointed to the other window.

The carriage crested the top of the hill, and the town of Brading spread out before them, looking like a page from a fairy tale book. The town was filled with blossoming trees and surrounded by rolling hills and acres of freshly planted fields, dotted here and there with farmhouses and an occasional manor. White buildings with pointed roofs and wooden trim clustered around a stone church.

"Glorious!" Walter sighed. "One never gets tired of such a sight."

"And just wait, Clara," Deborah said. "In a few weeks, spring will be in full bloom, and there is nowhere lovelier. Many claim the Isle is the Lord's personal garden."

Clara forced a smile and wiped her wet eyes with the tips of her gloved fingers. She hoped, at the very least, that the Lord's personal garden would produce some sunshine. She hadn't been warm in months. The streets of the town were quiet, so different than the crowded bustle of Calcutta with its colorful markets and noisy chaos.

When they reached the churchyard, Walter helped the ladies from the carriage, then bid them farewell as he left to spend an hour with other husbands of the Ladies' Charity Society members at a local tap house.

Deborah left to her meeting at the Barlows' cottage, and Clara entered the church. She waved at the vicar, who read to the children seated on the front pews. Mr. Barlow acknowledged her with a nod and continued with his lesson.

Clara shivered inside the cool building, pulling her shawl tighter around her shoulders. For a few days after she'd arrived in London, she'd thought it fascinating how her breath turned into a white cloud in the cold, but the novelty of the phenomenon had worn off quickly. Being cold all the time was exhausting.

She counted the children, and her nerves tensed as the number grew. Nineteen in all. *How shall I ever do this?* She started toward a pew to wait, but seeing Grant Mason, she changed direction, joining him where he stood on the side of the nave.

His arms were crossed, and he leaned on one shoulder against the stone wall. He dipped his head to her but did not extend a greeting.

Clara tried not to let his coolness bother her. She had business to discuss. "I-I wondered if I might speak with you for a moment, Mr. Mason." Why couldn't her voice sound more self-assured?

He straightened, turning fully toward her, and Clara hadn't realized until she faced him in the candlelit shadows how very imposing he was. Mr. Mason was tall and broad-shouldered with an athletic build. He wore a dark blue coat and a black necktie. As even in the dim light, his tanned skin stood out against the white of his shirt collar. His hair was cut short and side whiskers grew on his jaw. But it was his blue eyes that captured her attention. The light color gave the impression that he was looking at something far away or, more disconcerting, directly through her.

She forced herself not to duck away. "Sir, I did not want to say as much in front of the Wickershams and the others on Sunday, but since this affects you as a fellow choir director . . ."

His expression gave no encouragement, and the cool way he stared made her lose her train of thought. Her father would tell her to "stop rambling and come out with it." She cleared her throat. "Mr. Mason, I was reluctant to accept the task of choir leader because I intend to l-leave the island, and I did not want to . . ."

He continued to watch her, and her nervousness was joined by irritation. "I am informing you out of respect, sir. I did not wish to abandon you without warning to conduct the choir alone."

His expression did not change. "When do you depart?"

Clara glanced toward the Bible class, wishing for some interruption. Mr. Mason was making her quite uncomfortable. She tightened her shawl. "Well, I am not certain. But I intend to return to India as soon as an opportunity presents itself."

"So you are leaving, but you have no plan in place to do so."

Perhaps it was a trick of the candlelight, but she thought she saw a smirk. Clara lifted her chin. "Not yet, but I *will* leave."

"You have family there," he said.

"No, I . . ." She clasped her hands together, hating to have to explain herself, especially when it was none of this man's business. "I have no family there."

"Ah." Mr. Mason's brow ticked upward. "A suitor?"

Clara shook her head. "India is my home. I . . ." She swallowed at the tightness in her throat. "I belong there." She looked away from his piercing gaze, embarrassed that her emotions were getting the better of her. "You wouldn't understand. People here are not like . . ." She shook her head, frustrated at her inability to finish a sentence. "You do not know how it is to live so far away from your homeland and have to rely on the people around you. They become closer than family."

He furrowed his brow. "You're right, Miss Brightly. I do not understand. But I do see that you are keeping this from the Wickershams, and you do so to protect your own feelings, not theirs."

Her cheeks heated. "I do not see how that is any of your concern."

His eyes tightened, and his expression grew, if possible, more disapproving "The residents of Brading Parish are my people—*my* family, though we are not related by blood. We look out for one another." He folded his arms. "Perhaps I understand better than you realize, miss."

Clara was tempted to wither under his gaze, but she stood firm, though she had to hold her hands tightly to keep them from shaking. "I do not mean to hurt anyone. I simply want to go home. And I do not deserve your censure, nor do I particularly care for your thoughts on the matter. I m-meant only to inform you because it affects my leadership of the choir. And so I have. Excuse me."

She hurried away to wait at the other side of the church. Her entire body shook. She breathed to calm herself and didn't glance toward him again, though she could feel him watching her. It was only her imagination, but Mr. Mason's icy stare seemed to make the temperature drop even lower.

Half an hour later, Mr. Barlow closed the Bible and motioned for the choir-directing team to join him.

"Children, this is Miss Brightly. She and Mr. Mason are going to teach you a song for the May Day festival. Please give them your attention and sing your very best."

Mr. Barlow patted Clara's arm as he passed, nodded at Mr. Mason, then departed through the church doors.

A small girl with dark curls followed behind the vicar, and Clara wondered if she was his daughter, or perhaps she needed to get home to bed. Curiosity about the little girl vanished when Clara saw all the children staring at her. Suddenly, her skin felt extremely heated, and she started to sweat. Her breath even felt hot and difficult to draw into her lungs. She removed her shawl and laid it on the front pew.

"H-Hello." She formed her mouth into what she hoped was a convincing smile. "As the vicar said, I am Miss Brightly." She took a calming breath, knowing that if she became too nervous, her stammer would grow worse. She looked toward Mr. Mason, but he had taken a seat on a pew across the aisle, apparently not planning to participate.

"Is it true you've come from India?" an older boy with curly blond hair asked.

Clara turned back to the children. She nodded, discreetly wiping her damp palms on her skirt. "Yes, that is true. Now before we sing, I'd like to speak to you for a moment about chorale performance. The goal of a choir is to sound like one voice. Each vocalist matches his or her—"

"Did you ever see a tiger?" another boy asked.

"And a snake charmer?" a girl asked.

Clara halted the speech she'd prepared, feeling a drip of sweat slip down her back and reminded herself to breathe in and out steadily. "Yes. I saw snake charmers quite frequently in the Calcutta marketplace, and I did see a tiger once. He was in a c-cage."

The children spoke among themselves, and she clapped her hands to quiet them and hopefully recapture their attention. "Now, children, we have only a short time to rehearse, and—"

"Have you ridden an elephant?" the curly haired boy asked.

She held up her hand to forestall any other interruptions. "If you would please save your questions until—"

"Elephants live in Africa, not India." A smaller boy with freckles leaned forward over the pew, whispering loudly to the blond boy.

"They live in both," the first boy replied in an equally loud whisper.

"As I was saying . . ." Clara tried to ignore the boys' conversation, but their distraction derailed her train of thought. "I . . ." She swallowed. "The festival is very soon, so I thought we should sing a hymn you already—"

"Africa." The freckled boy punched the other on the shoulder.

"They live in both." The blond boy reached back to return the punch.

"B-Boys, please . . ." Clara's voice caught, and she clenched her hands into tight fists to keep calm.

Perhaps they should just sing, and she'd speak to them later about their vowels and sound. "The song I've chosen is 'Gentle Jesus, Meek and Mild.'" She purposely avoided looking at the two boys arguing about elephant habitats, though they were very distracting. "Before we sing, I'd like you all to stand and move to the choir seats. Arrange yourselves by size, taller in the back."

As if she'd opened a box of puppies, the children tumbled out of the pews. Boys wrestled, pushing one another, and girls squealed, jumping out of their way when the shoving got too close. The argument about elephants drew other participants, and before long, pandemonium had taken over the choir rehearsal.

Clara guided a crying girl to one of the choir seats, then turned back, pulling a boy down from the pew and pointing out where he should sit. "Everyone m-move to your correct—" She broke off her words when she realized none of them were listening. Tears stung the backs of her eyes. Her breathing became difficult, her hands tingled, and she feared another attack of nerves would take over if she did not calm herself and the unruly children down.

"That is enough." Mr. Mason's voice cut through the turmoil. The tone was not loud, nor was it angry, but it caused everyone to listen. "Take your places."

He stepped through the crowd and laid a hand on the freckled boy's and the curly haired boy's shoulders, leading them to the choir seats. The other children followed, moving quietly to their spots. Mr. Mason sat behind them.

Clara's stomach was hard with embarrassment, and her thoughts muddied. She blinked rapidly, praying no tears would betray her utter humiliation. She drew in a deep breath and let it out slowly. "Stand please," she said. "And let us begin." She hummed a note, raised her hands, and led the children through the song.

They sang, and she sang along automatically, but her mind wouldn't stay with the task. What was she doing? She wasn't cut out to lead a choir. Just speaking to people was difficult enough. And there was Mr. Mason, sitting smugly in the back row, happy to show her and everyone else that she wasn't up to the task.

When the song ended, she forced a smile. "Very nice. Thank you. That is all for tonight." She turned and hurried down the aisle and outside. All the while, her throat grew tighter. The instant the church doors closed behind her, the tears she'd held back all evening overcame her defenses and burst out in a torrent. She wanted her *ayah*, she wanted her friends, she wanted to go home. But more than anything, she wanted her father.

Chapter 3

THE MORNING FOLLOWING CHOIR practice, Grant dismounted in front of the Wickershams' house. He gave the horse's reins to the stable boy, then stepped up the front stairs of Wardleigh Manor, but paused before knocking. He fingered the soft wool of the shawl Miss Brightly had left behind at the church and considered for the hundredth time exactly what to say.

He rubbed the back of his neck, feeling extremely ashamed for his treatment of the young lady and for his narrow-minded assumptions. He'd assumed her haughty and had attended the rehearsal hoping to see her fail, thinking Miss Clara Brightly needed a dose of humility. But as he'd watched her speak to the children, it became increasingly clear that her temperament was not so much conceited as it was nervous. Though she'd tried to hide it, her hands shook as well as her voice. She had been completely terrified.

He knocked, berating himself for his ungentlemanly behavior. He should have stepped in earlier when he could clearly see her dismay.

The housekeeper opened the door and, upon Grant's inquiry, informed him that Miss Brightly was away with Mrs. Wickersham, making visits with the Ladies' Charity Society, but Mr. Wickersham was at home if he would please follow her to the library.

Walter rose from his chair, grinning when Grant entered and sent for tea. "A visit from Grant Mason, how fortunate for me." He shook Grant's hand, clapping him on the shoulder. "How are you this fine day, sir?"

Grant grinned in return. It was nearly impossible not to do so. The man exuded cheerfulness. "I am well. I'd hoped to find Miss Brightly at home." Seeing the knowing twinkle in Walter's eye, he hurried to explain. "She left her shawl at the church last night."

Walter glanced down at the folded cloth in Grant's hand. "I see. Very good of you to return it. She will be happy to have it back. Poor dear is always cold. Used to jungle climates, I suppose."

The housekeeper arrived with a tea service.

Grant accepted a cup and poured in a spoonful of sugar, taking a grateful sip.

Walter stirred his tea, then set the spoon onto the saucer. "And how goes the children's choir?"

"Rehearsal went . . . well," Grant said, fully aware that his words were a lie. "Miss Brightly is quite a competent musician." That, at least, was the truth.

"Oh, I am glad." Walter's shoulders relaxed. "I admit I was rather worried. Clara didn't speak much on the way home from town last night." He sipped his tea. "But that is nothing new. She doesn't speak much at all. Very shy, you know."

The bitter taste of shame rose in Grant's throat. "I see."

"Young lady's been through difficult times." Walter set his cup onto the low table in front of him, then leaned back, knitting his fingers together over his ample belly. "From what I've been able to piece together, her father's passing was quite tragic. He died suddenly on a tour in Egypt. Poor Clara was stranded for months without family or friends as the consul general sorted things out." Walter shook his head. "He finally made contact with a relative and sent Clara to London to live with a distant relation she didn't know, and from what I gather, the situation was . . . difficult."

"How so?" Grant set his cup onto the table and rested an ankle on his knee.

Walter wrinkled his nose and tapped one of his fingers on the others. "Well, she didn't say as much. She is a private person, you know. But when Mr. Poppy, the London solicitor, came to us, inquiring about taking her in, he mentioned that she'd sought him out. We understood, though he didn't say in so many words, that she was unhappy with her situation, lonely. She'd actually inquired about returning to India, but of course he couldn't send a young lady not yet of age halfway round the world alone."

"Obviously not," Grant agreed. "And so instead of sending her back to India, the solicitor located you."

Walter's face lit in a grin. "We're so very pleased he did. We adore Clara. Deborah thinks of her quite as her own daughter, and I think she is a delight." The light in his eyes dimmed. "I know she'd rather be in India, but if any place can mend an aching heart, it is our beloved Isle. I hope she can find happiness here."

Grant smiled at his old friend. Clara Brightly was lucky to have landed here with the Wickershams. "Do you know where the Charity Society is today? Mother mentioned visiting Mrs. Nutall."

"Yes, and Deborah planned to visit Philip Herd as well."

Grant nodded. A blind widower, Philip Herd was a regular beneficiary of the Society's visits. He lived on a farm with his son Marcus, one of Grant's tenants. He imagined if the ladies paid Mr. Herd a visit, it wouldn't last long. The man was notoriously ill-tempered and had been ever since Grant could remember.

"I thank you for the tea and for the company." Grant rose. "But I must be getting on."

"You're welcome anytime." Walter shook Grant's hand with both of his own. "And thank you for your friendship to Clara."

Grant departed and rode back toward the town. His heart was heavy as he contemplated what Walter had said. He remembered the devastation of his own father's death, but he hadn't been alone. He'd had his mother and the entire town for support during those dark weeks and months. Clara had been alone. No wonder she wished to leave, to return to a place where she felt loved. It was what anyone would want. He didn't blame her at all.

An unfamiliar feeling moved through him, and he analyzed it. A hope—or perhaps a desire? When he considered it further, it surprised him. He wanted Clara to stay. Though he examined it from all angles, he couldn't quite grasp where the feeling had come from, nor could he understand the reasoning behind it. Perhaps it was pride. He hoped she would come to realize the Isle was a true treasure. Maybe he felt guilt for his earlier actions and sought to make things right. Or he may just feel compassion for the young lady and what she'd endured.

He considered further, but neither of these explanations felt . . . complete. He may just be taking to heart Walter's hope that Clara could discover what she sought here in Brading. She could find friendships and feel cared for. But that didn't feel complete either.

He rode toward Haverstone Park but turned up a side lane when he saw through the trees that his mother's carriage was still at the Herds' cottage. As he rode closer, he heard a piano playing and the unmistakable sound of Clara Brightly's singing. He dismounted and stopped, listening closely to another voice that joined Clara's—a man's voice he didn't recognize. It couldn't be . . .

Marcus came around the side of the house and waved when he saw Grant.

Grant dismounted and motioned toward the house with his chin. "Is that . . . ?"

Marcus shrugged. "Couldn't believe it myself when I came in from checking the herd. The pair've been at it for an hour." His smile was wistful. "My father hasn't sung a note since I can remember. Forgot how he used to love it." He took the horse's reins and, when he heard Grant was looking for the ladies of the Charity Society, offered to water the animal while Grant went inside.

Grant stopped in the doorway of the drawing room, even more surprised to see that Philip Herd was not only sitting beside Clara on the bench of the old upright piano, singing a duet of "Lavender's Blue," but that he was the one accompanying them. He had a vague memory of his mother telling him that Philip had been very fond of music, but he'd never seen the man play, nor had he any idea the man possessed such a rich-sounding voice.

Clara glanced up, and their gazes met for a brief instant. Her eyes widened and she blushed, but her singing did not falter. She looked back toward the sheet music that sat on the shelf, turning a page, even though the blind pianist obviously did not require it.

When the song ended, Philip smiled. "We make a good pair, young lady. Now what—" He cocked his head, turning his unseeing eyes toward the doorway. "Who's there?"

"Grant Mason, sir. How do you do this morning?" How the man was able to detect him was a mystery that had long been a source of speculation among the parishioners in Brading. Some attributed it to a supernatural ability, but Dr.

Hurst claimed that when a person lost one of their senses, the others became stronger. Grant wondered if it was the old man's sense of smell that had detected him—the smell of his horse, of course.

"Well, come in, then. Don't particularly care for folks lurking in doorways." He scowled. "Suppose you're here for your ma." He jerked his head to the side. "In the kitchen with the others, arguing about lamb stew or some such nonsense."

This attitude was much more in line with the Philip Herd that Grant knew. "Thank you, sir. But I've actually come to see Miss Brightly."

Her cheeks went, if possible, even darker.

"You left your shawl at choir practice, miss."

She moved her gaze to the shawl, not meeting his. "Thank you."

"Set it on the sofa." Mr. Herd motioned with a wave of his hand, then set his fingers back on to the piano keys. His features softened into something that very nearly resembled a smile. He played the first chords of a familiar seafaring melody.

"You're a sailor. I should have known." Clara spoke in a teasing tone that made Philip's clouded eyes light up and his face beam.

"I'll wager you aren't familiar with a rowdy sea shanty, miss."

"*What shall we do with a drunken sailor?*" Clara sang the words to the tune he'd played. "I hope you don't worry about offending my delicate sensibilities, Mr. Herd. I was raised in the army. My father hosted naval officers quite often." She giggled and bumped him with her shoulder. "*I'll* wager I know more verses than you do. And some might just make you blush."

"A wager I'll gladly take!" Philip's smile spread into a grin that showed his missing teeth.

Grant gaped. The old saying about music's ability to tame the savage beast came into his thoughts, making him shake his head in amazement. Removing his hat and gloves, he sat on the sofa. He couldn't wait to report every detail of this marvel to Harry Barlow.

Philip played again, and he and Clara sang the shanty, taking turns answering the age-old question of what to do with a drunken sailor "ear-lay" in the morning. Grant could only stare in amazement at the transformation. It was as if the years fell away and the crotchety old man became a merry young sailor singing with his shipmates. His voice was robust, his face alight; he even sat straighter.

Miss Brightly sang just as loudly, though her voice could not be described as anything less than exquisite, proving that any song could sound beautiful with the right singer.

After a few rounds, Grant couldn't remain seated. He crossed the room and joined in. The lyrics weren't difficult to follow, and the others seemed happy to have him. The song continued with each verse becoming sillier, some downright bawdy. Both men burst out in laughter when Clara's verse about the drunken sailor suggested they "shave his belly with a rusty razor."

"What on earth is going on in here?" Grant's mother came in from the kitchen, putting her hands on her hips.

Philip laughed so hard that he had to stop playing to wipe his eyes.

Deborah Wickersham entered behind her. "You are supposed to be resting, Mr. Herd."

"Resting won't bring back my sight." He waved his hand as if to banish the idea. "Singing with Miss Brightly today has improved my constitution more than any stew ever did."

Clara smiled.

Deborah nodded proudly.

"I am very pleased to hear it." His mother's gaze met Grant's. She raised her brows but didn't ask aloud why he'd come. "We've others to visit today, Miss Brightly. It's time to leave."

"One more song before you go?" Philip asked.

Clara looked back and forth between the ladies who were clearly ready to leave and the elderly man who looked as if his heart would break if she went with them. "I . . ."

"I'll see Miss Brightly safely home," Grant offered. "If that is acceptable to you, miss."

"Thank you." Miss Brightly's gaze darted to him, then away quickly, and Grant felt the familiar sinking feeling. He definitely needed to apologize.

Grant accompanied his mother and Mrs. Wickersham to their carriage, helping them inside, promising to take good care of Miss Brightly and not allow her to remain too long.

When he reentered the house, Philip turned toward him. "Mr. Mason, do you have a request?"

Clara watched him expectantly.

"'Greensleeves,'" Grant said, sitting on the sofa. "It's my favorite."

Philip nodded. "Always a good choice." He played a short introduction and opened his mouth as if he'd start to sing, but when Clara began, he didn't join in.

Grant understood his restraint perfectly. Any addition to the sound would diminish the effect. Clara's voice was emotive, the beautiful words clear and unbearably lovely, touching a place so deep inside that it pulled at his emotions as no music ever had before. He had heard the song often, but when Clara Brightly sang it, it stirred his very soul. He closed his eyes, sat back, and let the music carry him away.

The song ended, the last notes hanging in the air, and Grant sat, frozen. He'd experienced something unexplainable through the music, something moving and very tender, and wanted the moment to stretch on as long as possible.

After a bit, Clara rose. She patted Philip's hand. "I enjoyed myself very much today, Mr. Herd."

He caught up her hand in both of his, turning his knees toward her. "Thank you." He swallowed. "Miss, I can't remember the last time I've felt so . . . so happy. Please say you'll come again."

"How could I not?" She bent down and kissed his cheek.

They bid Philip farewell and stepped outside.

Grant placed the shawl over Clara's shoulders. "I spoke without thinking, offering to see you home. I don't have a carriage. The walk isn't far, but if you'd rather, I can borrow a horse or ride to my house for a carriage."

"I don't mind walking," she said, raising her chin and starting in the direction of the village.

Grant considered offering his arm but thought her present feelings toward him would not incline her to accept. He stepped quickly to catch up, then matched her pace. "Miss Brightly, I owe you an apology."

"It is not necessary, sir." She pulled the shawl tighter, and he could see by the tension in her shoulders that she was uncomfortable.

"I disagree. At the choir practice, I should have helped you instead of allowing—"

"I told your mother and the vicar, I do n-not know how to teach children." Her hands were fisted inside the shawl.

He winced at her nervous stammer. "Yes, you did." He blew out a breath. "I didn't realize . . . I thought you simply didn't want to, not that you . . ."

"That I'm ridiculously bashful," she finished in a soft voice.

"I was going to say, I didn't realize that you actually

needed assistance." He cleared his throat. "Miss Brightly, my assumption was a shameless misjudgment, and for it, I apologize."

She glanced at him. "You thought I was being arrogant."

"I'm sorry."

"Do not let it trouble you anymore." She tugged at the shawl. "I know I can seem very aloof, especially to strangers."

"Perhaps that is our problem. I do not think the children's choir-directing team should be strangers. We should get to know one another."

She darted a cautious look at him, as if to ascertain his intention.

"To make the team stronger." He rubbed his chin and nodded thoughtfully, but winked, hoping to cheer her or at least set her at ease.

Clara gave a shy smile. "Very well."

Grant took her assent as an invitation to begin the conversation and considered what topic might be appropriate when developing an acquaintance. With some surprise, he realized he'd rarely met new people. He'd known the vast majority—in fact, all—of his friends his entire life. Everyone he interacted with, aside from the occasional tourist, had always lived on the island. Very few people left, and fewer moved here. The thought brought him up short. How exactly did one go about making a new friend? And what should he say that wouldn't cause further offense?

"Ah, how is it you have no experience with children, Miss Brightly?" Not the most suave beginning, but it could have been much worse.

She shrugged. "I was rarely involved or even acquainted with any. British children are sent home to England for school." She glanced at him. "*Most* children."

"Not you," he guessed.

Clara shook her head. "I was an exception." She grimaced. "When the time came, I was so . . ."

"Timid," he said.

She nodded. "And frightened. We had no close family in England. I begged my father not to make me go, and he allowed me to remain in India and be instructed by a tutor."

"But you stayed this winter with family in London, did you not?"

She squinted, as if trying to remember whether she'd told him as much.

"Mr. Wickersham mentioned you had remained there during your mourning."

"I did." Her face cleared, accepting the explanation. "I lived in a townhouse in Grosvenor Square with my father's great-aunt and her children." Clara's lips pressed tightly together.

"You didn't enjoy London?"

She rubbed her arms beneath the shawl, and her demeanor became decidedly less cheerful. "London was cold, and my father was dead." Her voice was nearly a whisper. "I was not familiar with the conventions and complexities of English society. I'm afraid I was not the best company."

A young lady alone in a strange country, mourning her only family . . . Grant felt a swell of pity as he imagined bashful Clara trying to hold her own with London's high society.

"Tell me about Mr. Herd," she said, changing the subject. "He is such a pleasant man, not at all how Mrs. Wickersham and your mother described him."

Grant clasped his hands behind his back. "Philip Herd was, as you deduced, a sailor. Fought in the Crimea."

"And is that where he lost his sight?" Clara asked.

He gave a sharp nod. "Head injury."

"How sad."

"From what my mother and others of the older generation have said, the explosion took more than his sight. It changed him from a cheerful person to one who is bitter and resentful. Truthfully, I've known Philip Herd my entire life, and today was the first time I've seen the man smile."

"Music is powerful," Clara said. "It can change people."

"I believe the credit goes to the musician," Grant said. "I am by no means an expert, but your voice . . . it is special. You have a unique gift, and it touches hearts."

From the side of his eye, he saw her cheeks turn pink. The personal nature of his declaration made his own ears heat up.

"I don't feel shy when I'm singing," Clara said.

The pair walked through the town, shifting to the side of the lane to make way for wagons and horses on High Street. Walking beside Miss Brightly, Grant saw Brading through fresh eyes and noticed details he normally took for granted. Laundry flapping on clotheslines, stained glass in the church windows, storefronts with their hanging signs all seemed to him charming, but did Clara find them so? He felt such pride and love for his home and wondered how it appeared to someone seeing it for the first time. Did she notice the blossoming cherry trees or the cracks in the church wall?

Leaving the town behind, Grant led Clara off the road, taking her in a more direct route through the countryside. They came to a field of tall grass, and Clara stopped, pulling back.

Reflexively, he put a hand behind her back. "Is something the matter?"

Clara looked up at him, then toward the field. "An old habit." She gave a small smile. "Cobras hide in tall grass."

"Ah." He offered his arm. "Well, you probably don't miss that aspect of India, do you?"

Clara's smile dropped away. She slipped her hand into

his offered arm. "I miss all of it," she said as they started through the field. "Everything here is so different, so quiet. When I wake, I hear sweet little birds chirping instead of loud squawks or wild dogs barking. The bushes don't buzz with insects; the trees aren't filled with monkeys. The very air smells wrong, food tastes different." She sighed, glancing toward him. "I'm sorry to complain."

"It's not the worst place to find oneself," he grumbled.

"Yes, I've heard it is Lord's personal garden." The corners of her mouth curled in a halfhearted smile.

"That sounds like one of Deborah's sayings."

Clara nodded and her smile grew wider, though the expression remained sad.

"The Isle is beautiful in a different way. Much less . . . poisonous." He grinned. "Just wait until the hawthorns bloom—white blossoms on dark green hedges set against the background of the sea. Nothing is lovelier. And caulkheads are the best people in the world." Grant patted her hand. "I can only imagine how it is to be away from home and to feel alone, but you're not alone, Miss Brightly." Their gazes met, and the feeling he'd felt before returned. He wanted her to love it here, to see the beauty, to feel at home, to . . . stay. "You have not seen much of the island, have you?"

"Just from the window of the train to Brading."

He stepped over a fallen log, then held her hand to keep her steady as she followed. "There is your problem. You missed some of the very best parts."

Clara smirked, and a twinkle lit her eyes. "Brading—the Lord's personal garden—isn't the best part?"

Grant smiled. "Of course it is, but there are others almost as glorious—the castle at Carisbrooke, Shanklin Chine, the Needles Lighthouse. Have you even been to the seaside?"

"No."

He shook his head, making a tsking noise. “Such an oversight must be remedied immediately.”

Certainly if Clara Brightly gave it a chance, the Isle of Wight would work its magic.

Chapter 4

THE FOLLOWING SUNDAY AS Clara exited the church, she forced her gaze straight ahead instead of searching for Grant Mason. The man was confusing and unpredictable, and her feelings about him were the same. At the choir practice, he'd been arrogant to the point of rudeness. But his apology the next day seemed genuine, and though Clara reminded herself to be cautious, her instinct told her that he was a person to be trusted. After the visit with Mr. Herd, Grant had been outright friendly. She'd wanted to confide in him and enjoyed his company, but his invitation to see more of the island put her on guard. It seemed too much too fast. Why would he extend such an offer? Did he have an ulterior motive? They were only co-directors of a small choir, not *friends* precisely. Would Grant revert back to his earlier rudeness the next time she saw him? Was he irritated that she'd spent their entire walk complaining about being on the island? And why was it necessary to employ every bit of her self-control to keep from looking for him?

A motion caught the edge of her gaze, and Clara glanced up. The girl with the dark curls who'd left the church before choir practice stood on the grass with a group of children. When she caught Clara's gaze, she waved shyly.

Clara hesitated for a moment, wondering if the girl were indeed waving at her. She glanced around but saw nobody nearby looking in the girl's direction, so she crossed the churchyard toward her. When she arrived, Clara felt silly, not knowing what to say.

The girl smiled up at her, then looked down at the ground.

"Hello," Clara said. "I think I saw you at Bible Study Wednesday evening."

The girl nodded.

"My n-name is Clara Brightly. What's yours?" Clara almost whirled and ran when she saw the other children watching. She was making a fool of herself. What must they be thinking? A fully grown woman stood before them, stammering like a nervous schoolgirl.

"Annie Warner." She curtsied, tugging on her skirts.

"How do you do, Annie?" Clara smiled at her bouncing curls and rosy cheeks. "You left before choir practice began, didn't you?"

Annie nodded, tucking her chin against her chest. "I don't want to sing."

Her voice was so quiet that Clara had to turn her head to hear. The girl's shy words touched her heart. She knew exactly how it was to be that girl, too shy to join in with the others. She crouched down to the Annie's level, catching the girl's gaze and smiling. "You know, a choir has other jobs besides just singers. I was hoping to find a helper who will hold signs to remind the choir of the correct verse."

Annie studied her for a moment. "Isn't Mr. Mason your helper?"

Clara kept her face serious, though she wanted to grin at the bluntness of the question. "He is, but—"

"But he will be busy making certain you are all behaving," Grant said from behind Clara.

She and Annie looked up.

"How do you do, Mr. Mason?" Annie curtseyed again.

Grant reached out a hand and lifted Clara to her feet. "What an excellent choice for an assistant, Miss Brightly," he said. "Annie is just the person we need."

His words sent an unfamiliar wiggling feeling through Clara's middle. She smiled at Annie's beaming face but for some reason couldn't meet Grant's gaze. She pulled away her hand. "We'll see you at rehearsal on Wednesday, Annie?" Clara felt her insides squirm again. It felt strange to speak for herself and Grant, as if they were a couple.

Annie nodded.

Clara bid her farewell and walked toward where the Wickershams were speaking with Mrs. Mason. Grant fell into step beside her. She snuck a glance at him, but based on his calm expression, he didn't appear to think it unusual to follow her around the churchyard.

"The weather is nice today, isn't it?" he said, clasping his hands behind his back. "Warmer."

Clara wore her shawl, and though there was a slight breeze, she wasn't excessively uncomfortable, a rare occurrence over the past months. "It is very pleasant," she agreed.

Grant smiled, closed his eyes, and tilted back his head, drawing in a deep breath. He peeked at her from one eye. "An ideal day to visit Carisbrooke Castle, if you would care to join me?"

Clara twisted at her fingers. Her confusing feelings regarding Mr. Mason left her both panicked and extremely bashful. She walked faster. "You told the vicar you are very b-busy this time of year," she said.

Clara stopped beside Deborah, wishing she were fifteen years younger so she could hide behind the woman's skirts. Her heart was racing.

"One is never too busy to take a Sunday afternoon ride to Carisbrooke in the springtime."

"What a lovely idea," Mrs. Mason said.

Deborah nodded in agreement. "Oh, yes."

"For propriety's sake and to prevent either of us from having an opportunity to speak, I will, of course, bring my mother." Grant winked and put an arm around his mother's shoulders with a squeeze.

Mrs. Mason swatted him with her fan. "Grant, Miss Brightly will think you've no manners at all." But her smile revealed that she didn't mind the teasing.

"Would you join us, Mr. and Mrs. Wickersham?" Grant asked.

"We would indeed, wouldn't we, my dear?" Walter turned to his wife.

Deborah was studying Clara's face, her brows raised as if making certain the plan was agreeable.

Clara nodded, feeling much more comfortable about the outing now that the party was expanded. She turned to Grant, fighting against a threatening blush. "A castle visit sounds delightful."

Two hours later, after Sunday luncheon, the group set off in Mr. Mason's landau. Due to the pleasant weather, both the front and back of the hood had been retracted to give a full view of the landscape.

The men sat facing the rear, and Clara watched the scenery pass from her seat between Mrs. Mason and Deborah. The unfamiliar trees bursting with blossoms, the fields of wildflowers, and the hedgerows were all beautiful, but it was a different beauty than she was used to. England was proper and manicured, whereas India was wild and unkempt. The birds sounded sweet; the little squirrels chattered. Taking an excursion without sepoy escorts to protect from bandits and tigers felt strange. But although England seemed tame, Clara didn't feel secure. She was still a stranger, no matter how gracious her companions were. She still didn't belong, and she still missed her home.

Mrs. Mason nudged her out of her ponderings with a bump of her elbow. "See that lane there?" She pointed off to the left. "It leads to Alverstone, where I grew up."

Clara leaned forward and looked in the direction she indicated. "Oh, and how far away is Alverstone?"

"A mile or so. Not far. My family attended church in Brading before the church in Sandown was built."

"Does your family still live there?" Clara asked.

Mrs. Mason nodded. "My brother's son and his wife occupy the house now."

While Deborah and Mrs. Mason chatted about the Mason's extended family and the Sandown Parish, Clara looked back at the farmland, wondering what would grow in the newly plowed fields. As she watched the landscape pass, she felt rather than saw Mr. Mason's gaze on her.

Her nerves buzzed, and she folded her hands together, attempting to look calm and ignoring the sensation. After a long, uncomfortable moment, she glanced toward him and saw he was indeed watching her. The icy-blue color of his eyes always made his gaze seem intense, and she looked away quickly. His expression felt expectant, and she wasn't certain how to react. Clara shifted, pulling her shawl tighter around her shoulders.

When she finally got up the nerve to glance his way again, he was looking in the other direction. Allowing her gaze to linger a bit longer, she saw a white line around the base of his hairline, as if his hair had been recently cut. Against the white of his shirt, the skin of his face and neck were very tan. She wondered how anyone could possibly get tanned in a place with no sun.

Clara wondered what occupied Grant Mason's days. He had mentioned being busy this time of year. Was he a member of a sporting club? Judging by his broad shoulders and lean body, she could imagine him playing cricket or perhaps polo. He certainly would cut a striking figure on horseback.

Grant glanced toward her, and she turned her gaze downward, realizing he'd caught her staring. A blush burst on her face at the thought that her expression may have given away her contemplations.

"How do you find the view, Miss Brightly?" Grant asked.

"Very beautiful," she said.

"There is nowhere on earth more lovely than Brading Down in spring." Deborah held up her palm toward the vista beyond.

"Hear hear," Walter agreed.

"And just wait until the hawthorns bloom." Mrs. Mason pressed her hands over her heart and sighed. "You'll think yourself in paradise."

Clara smiled at their enthusiasm. "So I've heard."

Mrs. Mason elbowed Clara again. "You see that tree there—that grand sycamore?" She pointed forward along the road to an enormous tree with limbs that stretched wide from the trunk. "You remember that tree, don't you, Grant?"

He shifted in the backward-facing seat, craning his neck to look ahead of the carriage, then turned back around. His expression had changed. Darkened. His brows were furrowed and eyes pensive. He appeared . . . sad. "I remember."

Walter turned to get a view as well. "A majestic tree, to be sure."

"Do tell us the story," Deborah said.

Mrs. Mason's gaze remained on the tree, and her expression was thoughtful. She smiled wistfully as if remembering something both pleasant and sorrowful. "Grant was very young, perhaps five or six. I do not quite remember his age exactly, but small enough that he fit between Bernard and myself in our little victoria carriage." She leaned toward Clara. "Bernard was my late husband."

Clara nodded her understanding.

Grant's gaze flicked to his mother, then he turned back to watch the tree as the carriage approached.

"We were driving on a warm summer afternoon to Carisbrooke," Mrs. Mason continued. "Your father did so love to visit the castle, didn't he, Grant?"

Grant moved his head in a very slight nod.

"Just a bit farther ahead down the road, a wheel hit a loose stone, slid into a ditch, and cracked the axle in two."

"Oh my," Deborah said.

"You must have had quite a fright," Walter said.

"Yes, well luckily, none of us were hurt, and neither were the horses."

"Thank heavens," Deborah muttered.

"We spread out a blanket in the shade to wait while the coachman went for help, and that little mishap led to one of the most pleasant days in memory." She smiled, her eyes unfocused as if they were watching something far away. "We ate the picnic we'd prepared for the castle lawn, then Bernard and Grant climbed up into that tree like a pair of squirrels."

"Or monkeys," Clara said, imagining the young father and his boy laughing as they scampered up into the branches.

Mrs. Mason raised a finger. "Exactly like monkeys. Bless me, I thought my heart would beat clear out of my chest when I saw my darling little boy sitting up on a limb fifteen feet above the ground."

"Bernard was a fine man," Walter said. "And an excellent father."

Grant turned back to face the group. He swallowed and cleared his throat. "He was at that."

The choking in his voice brought tears to Clara's eyes, and she blinked them away. In all this time, she'd been so occupied with her own grief that she hadn't even considered the others had all lost family as well.

They rode in silence for a long while, and Clara wondered if the memories of her father would bring her pain or comfort when she returned home to India. She knew thoughts of him would be all around in the places they'd gone together, and she would miss him. But at the same time, she longed to be where he'd been, to remember. She felt very far away from him here.

At last, the castle came into view. Set high upon a hill, Carisbrooke was a medieval stone structure with a surrounding wall. The coachman stopped before the gatehouse, and Grant assisted the ladies from the carriage. The group walked up the pathway and stopped before the enormous stone entrance.

Clara looked up at the turrets on either side and the battlements above and was immediately reminded of the Red Fort in Delhi. This castle was much less ornate, and older—built for defense instead of beauty.

"Impressive, isn't it?" Walter said, coming up beside her.

"It looks like a castle from a fairy tale," she said. "I half expect to find a sleeping princess inside or a medieval jousting tournament."

She took Walter's offered arm, and they walked through the archway, beneath the portcullis, and into the fortress.

"Now, my dear." Walter motioned around them with his walking stick. "This site has been a refuge from invading armies for almost two thousand years, protecting island residents from the Vikings, Normans, Spanish, and most recently, the French. You can see the different building styles used over time—some medieval, some much older, and the chapel over there was built in the last century." He led her around, pointing out various architectural differences. "And did you know this is where Charles I was imprisoned to await his execution?"

"I did not know," Clara said. She'd, of course, studied European history but struggled to remember exactly who Charles I was and what he had done to deserve his fate.

As if hearing her thoughts, Walter launched into an explanation of the House of Stuart and the English Civil War.

"Walter, come now." Deborah joined them, interrupting his discourse. "Clara doesn't want to hear all that. We've come to enjoy ourselves, not listen to a lecture." She took his arm and gave him a warm smile to soften her reprimand. "Join us on the lawn, dearest." She led her husband away, turning back to give Clara a wink.

Clara smiled in return and followed across the courtyard to where the ladies had spread a blanket. Mrs. Mason sat beneath her parasol, taking out parcels of wrapped refreshments from a basket. Deborah joined her, tucking her skirts around her legs. Walter set down his walking stick and eased down next to his wife, unwrapping a bundle and biting into a finger sandwich.

Clara moved to join them, but a hand on her elbow stopped her.

"Perhaps you'd care to explore a bit more." Grant raised his brows and smiled.

She wondered if he was just being polite or if he truly wished to walk about with her. "I'd like that." She returned the smile and took his offered arm.

"She's not seen the Norman keep." Walter pointed across the castle lawn with his sandwich. "Or the gardens."

Grant led Clara away from the others.

"Make sure you point out the rooms where Charles I attempted to escape." Walter's voice came from behind them.

Clara couldn't help but smile at the man's passion for the castle history, and she felt rather than heard Grant give a soft chuckle. They walked across the lawn, following along an ancient foundation that was now only a line of stones on the ground.

She glanced up and saw Grant watching her, then fumbled for something to say to alleviate the fluttering feeling in her middle. "Your father brought you here often?"

Grant pressed his lips together and nodded. "He loved this castle." A smile tugged at one side of his mouth. "And everything else about the island."

"You miss him," Clara said, her heart swelling with compassion, remembering the story his mother had told.

Grant raised his gaze to the top of the high walls. "That's the strange thing about grief. The pain eases, sometimes you hardly feel it, but there are other times, when you don't expect it, the intensity overwhelms you."

His voice was low with a tightness that made Clara's heart ache. She missed her own father so badly that there were times she didn't think she'd survive the pain. "How old were you when he died?"

"Fifteen," Grant said. He let out a breath, then turned toward her. "But I had my mother, of course. And men like Walter to act as father figures. I cannot imagine how it must have been for you to endure your father's death alone."

Clara's throat clogged, and she tried to push away the tears stinging her eyes. But it was no use. She took Grant's offered handkerchief and wiped her eyes.

"I'm sorry." He stopped beside the remains of a crumbling old wall. "It wasn't my intention to upset you."

She shook her head, not trusting her voice. Her heart hurt. She thought of her father, of their friends back home, and she longed for India. Her ayah, Pari, had been more than a nursemaid; she was as close to a mother as Clara had known. Did Pari miss her? Had she gone on to care for a new family?

She pushed away the painful memories, knowing that indulging them would only make them grow, and her weeping would become unmanageable. "I—" She choked and cleared her voice, forcing herself to speak calmly. "I don't mean to ruin our outing."

Grant tapped beneath her chin, lifting her face. "Do not apologize."

Her heart jumped at his touch. Swallowing hard, Clara closed her eyes and pushed out a calming breath. *No more tears.* She slipped her hand into the bend of Grant's elbow and gave a little tug, forcing a smile. "Now then, where is the Norman keep?"

He watched her face for a moment, then turned to walk beside her. "Directly ahead." He waved his hand toward what appeared to be the very oldest part of the castle. Stone steps led up to a roofless structure, and ivy grew over the old walls.

"Shall we climb up?" she asked in a cheerful voice, hoping he would forget about her weeping.

"Carefully," Grant said. "The steps may be loose."

They climbed up into the keep, then once inside, climbed the steps along the wall leading to the very top of the ramparts. Grant kept a strong hand on Clara's arm, and when she leaned forward to look over the edge of the battlements, his grip became tighter.

"I'm not going to fall." She considered his furrowed brows and tight jaw. "Are you afraid of heights?"

"Not heights." He glanced toward the edge. "Falling. Or more specifically, *you* falling."

"Don't worry. It's strong." She moved closer and gave the edge of the wall a push to demonstrate.

Grant sucked in a breath through his teeth.

His worry sent heat radiating from Clara's chest, making her feel soft and very safe. She wondered if this was how Grant had felt climbing in the tree with his father. Had he felt secure, knowing someone strong was watching over him?

She moved away from the edge, content to enjoy the view from the center of the walkway. Grant loosened his tight hold on her arm, sliding his hand down to take hold of hers.

"What is it that you do, Mr. Mason?" she asked as they strolled around the top of the keep's battlements. "Why is it that you told the vicar you are busy this time of year?"

"Spring is always busy in farm country," he said. "Crops to plant, animals being born. And so many of my tenants were ill this winter."

"It is kind of you to help them," she said.

"Healthy livestock and a productive crop benefits all of us," he said.

She could tell he was downplaying his generosity. "I don't think many landowners participate in the physical aspects of their tenants' labors," she said. "But perhaps I'm mistaken."

He shrugged. "Perhaps not. But I enjoy the work."

"And you care about them." She smiled when he turned to her. "I've seen how kind you are to the children."

"Landowners, tenants, children, choir directors." He smirked and winked as he said the last example. "We're all caulkheads, and all neighbors. That's how it is on the island. We look out for one another."

They continued along the narrow walkway, and she thought of the Ladies' Charity Society and their weekly visits to the members of the parish who needed assistance or, in Mr. Herd's case, a friend. "I've noticed it," she said. "You are fortunate to be part of such a community." The homesickness returned—the loneliness and feeling of not belonging. When she glanced up, she saw he was watching her again, holding her gaze as if he were waiting.

She blinked. "Are you . . . I mean, what am I doing wrong?"

Grant squinted. "I'm just waiting."

"Waiting for what? Am I expected to do something?"

He raised a brow. "I'm waiting for you to fall in love with the island, to say you never wish to leave." He gave a teasing smile. "I don't know what's taking so long."

Clara laughed at his joking manner. "I didn't realize it was required."

"Not required. It is inevitable. One cannot help oneself." He led her down the steps, turning to assist her once he reached the bottom. He held both of her hands as she took the last steps. "But you are an unusual case. I've never seen it take so long."

She smirked in return, then her expression spread into a genuine smile. "The island is beautiful, truly. And the people are warm and kind. But—"

"But you still intend to return to India."

Did she see hurt in his eyes or was it imagined? She hadn't meant to cause offense. She released his hands. "I must, Mr. Mason. I must go home."

His chin tipped upward the slightest bit as he studied her. "Very well." He blinked, and the seriousness was gone. He offered his arm and led her from the keep and down into the castle courtyard. "Now, if you don't mind, I think it's high time the children's choir-directing team conducted an official meeting."

Taken aback by the sudden change of topic, Clara didn't know how to respond.

"First order of business." He tipped his hat to an older couple as they passed. "I propose that when alone, the choir directors call one another by their Christian names . . . to make things simpler."

Clara's heart thumped, and her cheeks went hot. She didn't dare look at him and instead kept her gaze on the groups of picnickers. "Very well." She pushed the words through a dry mouth.

"Good." He patted her hand that rested on his arm. "Now that the formalities are out of the way, Clara, let us form an action plan."

Hearing him say her name felt like an electrical jolt through her chest. Heat spread from her cheeks down her neck and burned her ears.

Grant turned toward her, apparently having no idea of the intensity of her reaction. "First of all, our newest team member . . ."

"Oh, Annie." Clara was relieved to have a neutral topic. "I should have consulted with you before extending the invitation. She just seemed so . . ." She considered exactly what it was about the girl that had affected her. She looked up. "She needs this."

"I could not agree more." Grant studied her, his expression seeming much too thoughtful for the subject, and Clara got the impression he was thinking more about her perception of Annie than of the girl herself. "You have a particular way of seeing people, Clara, perceiving those who tend to go unnoticed." He continued to hold her gaze.

Clara's skin felt hot and her insides jittery at the compliment. "I suppose that is what every person wants," she said in a quiet voice. "To be noticed, to feel valued."

He opened his mouth as if he'd answer but closed it. He scratched his chin and nodded, his brows furrowing. "I suppose it is."

They walked in silence back to the crumbling wall, and Grant leaned against it, crossing his arms. "Now then, Clara, what does our choir need? And how can I help?"

"They know the song, but they need to sing louder." Clara held up a finger. "And breathe together." She held up another. "Oh, and they must stand up straight and smile." Her third finger joined the others.

Grant raised his eyebrows. "Is that all?"

She wrinkled her nose, thinking of all the elements lacking in the small choir. "If we had more time, I would help them to match their vowels and perhaps teach some of the girls a descant. But we only have two more rehearsals, and so we will focus on sound and presentation."

"And behavior," Grant said.

Clara tensed, remembering the last rehearsal, and her chest became tight. "Grant, I honestly do not know . . ."

He grinned, sending a flare of anger through Clara. She scowled, furious that he'd make light of something that had been so upsetting to her. "I find no humor in this."

His expression fell, and worry took its place, wrinkling his forehead. "You misunderstand me. I'm not laughing. Simply pleased to hear you calling me by my name."

She rubbed her arms, feeling foolish for so easily taking offense.

Grant stepped closer. "We are a team, Clara. Neither of us can do it alone. I am not able to teach music, but I have a very capable partner. I will do what you cannot." He took her hands in his, squeezing so that she felt the heat of his skin through her gloves. "I left you alone last time, but I promise I will not do it again. Can you trust me?"

Clara nodded, her throat tight. Although she'd only known him for a short time, she found it surprisingly easy to put her faith in Grant Mason.

Chapter 5

GRANT DISMOUNTED AND TIED the horse's reins to a post outside the churchyard. He had come to town ahead of his mother, hoping for some time alone to speak with Harry Barlow before the children's Bible Study. As boys, the two had been inseparable, even managing to remain close when they went away to university. But the duties of a landowner and a married vicar over the past year hadn't led to their paths crossing as often as they previously had. And though he was happy for the Barlows, Grant missed his friend. The vicar was cheerful and optimistic, but level-headed, and it was the latter quality Grant was depending on. He needed advice.

He started toward the vicar's cottage behind the church, but the sound of upset voices and a child crying made him change direction. He followed the source of the noise along the church wall, past the cemetery, and down a side street until he found it.

Mrs. Pinkston was crouched down, helping her son William to stand. The boy had fallen in a mud puddle and was quite distressed. Another of the Pinkston's children, Lucy, stood close by, the sound of her brother's tears making her cry as well. The baby, Arthur, was thankfully asleep in his pram.

Mrs. Pinkston balanced at an odd angle with her skirts bunched up in her lap to keep them out of the mud. She held out a hand to keep Lucy from coming too close to the puddle as she wiped at William's muddy clothing with her lacy handkerchief, which obviously did no good. She looked up when Grant approached. "Oh, thank goodness you're here, Mr. Mason."

Grant stepped around the pram, taking Lucy's hand and leading her to where she could see her mother but wouldn't be in danger of falling into the mud herself. "Is William hurt?"

"Only his pride, I fear." Using the back of her wrist, Mrs. Pinkston pushed a lock of hair from her forehead. "And he's quite torn his stockings."

Hearing this, William started to cry again.

Grant glanced toward the pram, worried the noise would wake the baby. "How can I help?" He handed Mrs. Pinkston his handkerchief. "Shall I take William home?"

Lucy's crying intensified along with her brother's.

Mrs. Pinkston left off wiping William's clothes. She rose and picked up the girl, soothing her. Grasping beneath his arms, Grant lifted William out of the mud and set him onto the dry road, brushing at his dirty knees.

"He'll need to change his clothes before Bible Study," Mrs. Pinkston said. "And I'll have to wash off his shoes." She rubbed the boy's back, comforting her two weeping children. She wiped her forehead again, looking utterly exhausted. "Mr. Mason, will you be in town for a bit?"

"I'm just heading in to see the vicar," Grant said.

"Would you mind watching baby Arthur—just for a moment? I'll take the children home and hurry back in time for the children's meeting." She looked into the pram. "He should remain asleep, but Emmeline Barlow will know what to do if he wakes."

Grant prayed that the vicar's wife would be home. "Certainly." He smiled and put a hand on the pram's handle.

Reassuring Mrs. Pinkston once again that the baby was

no trouble, he bid the woman farewell and pushed the pram toward the church—something he'd never done in the entirety of his life. Each bump in the road made him catch his breath as he worried it would wake the baby. He steered carefully around the rocks in the churchyard, his muscles tense as he avoided the stones of the path entirely. By the time he reached the vicar's front door, his shoulders ached, and he felt every bit as worn out as Mrs. Pinkston had looked.

Harry opened the door before Grant even knocked. "Grant, what on earth?" His wide-eyed expression turned into a grin as he looked down at the pram. "This is a good look for you."

"William Pinkston had a small accident. I told his mother I'd bring the baby to—"

As if he just now realized his mother was gone, Arthur Pinkston woke and began to wail.

The men stared at the baby, then at each other.

"You better pick him up," Harry said.

Grant felt a twinge of panic. "Isn't your wife home?"

"Sadly, no." Harry grinned again. "I'm afraid nursemaid duties fall to you."

Grant looked into the pram. "The task seems more befitting a member of the clergy," he grumbled but lifted the baby, holding him at arms' length.

Harry pulled a wooden rattle from the pram and offered it. The baby snatched it away, sticking the toy into his mouth.

Stepping back, Harry opened the door wide. "Won't you gentlemen come inside?"

Grant tucked the baby against him, holding him in the bend of his arm as he would a rugby ball, and followed Harry into his office.

Harry sat behind the desk, straightening the already straight stack of papers. "Shall I order tea?"

"Not necessary." Grant sat, placing Arthur onto his lap and wincing at the string of drool that dripped from the baby's mouth onto his trousers.

"How goes the children's choir?" Harry asked in a cheerful voice. "You and Miss Brightly left so quickly last week, I didn't have a chance to inquire."

For Clara's sake, Grant was glad the vicar hadn't heard about the rehearsal. "It went well enough. And we've plans to make it more productive tonight."

Harry nodded, steepling his fingers on his desk and leaning forward. "And how do you find Miss Brightly?"

"Initially, she is quite timid, but she"—Grant searched for the words—"is actually the reason I've come to speak with you."

"Oh?" Harry raised his brows.

"You may or may not know that she intends to return to India."

"I did not know." Harry tapped his pointer fingers against his lips. "A pity. She will be missed."

"It is more than that," Grant said. "Of course I will *miss* her, but there is more—"

Harry's smile grew into a smirk. "I meant by the Wickershams."

The baby reached for an inkwell on the desk, and Grant moved him to his other leg. When he reached again, Grant stood and paced across the floor of the small office, holding Arthur against his shoulder. "I think Miss Brightly should stay. Brading is good for her. She can heal here, be happy." He shifted the fussing baby around, fitting him into the bend of his elbow and handing him the rattle. "And she is good for the town. Do you know she befriended Annie Warner? Asked her to help with practices, to hold signs, and told her she wasn't required to sing."

“Mrs. Warner mentioned something about it,” Harry said.

Grant paced quicker, frustrated that Clara still wanted to leave when Brading was clearly the place for her.

“And I’m sure you’ve heard about Philip Herd,” Grant said. “Brading needs Miss Brightly, and she needs this town.” He stopped pacing and bounced the baby in his arms. “I hoped to convince her. I took her to the castle, thinking she could not help but fall in love with the island after seeing the downs in spring, but it wasn’t enough.” He shifted the baby into his other arm. “This is why I need your advice, Harry. Maybe the seashore? Or do you think a visit to Shanklin Chine would do it?”

Harry shook his head, the infuriating smile remaining. “Grant, you don’t wish Miss Brightly to fall in love with the island.”

“How else do I convince her—?”

“You want her to fall in love with *you*.”

Hearing the words, Grant’s impulse was to argue, but he froze, staring at his friend. Could Harry be right? Unable to think of a response, he closed his mouth and looked through the window toward the churchyard. Was he in love with Clara? He hadn’t even considered the possibility. “How? I barely know her.”

“It hardly signifies.”

“But—”

Harry held up a hand, stopping his words. “Grant, aside from the three months after my birth, I’ve known you my entire life, and all of yours. I think in this, I can draw a reasonable conclusion.” He leaned back in the chair, rubbing his palms on the armrests. “I’ve rarely known you to feel this distressed about anything, let alone an overner wishing to leave.”

"Dearest, it's almost time for Bible Study." Emmeline Barlow poked her head into the office. "Oh, I beg your pardon, Mr. Mason, I didn't see you there." She blinked. "And with Arthur?"

Harry rounded the desk and kissed his wife's cheek. "Welcome home, darling. Little Arthur is just waiting for his mother." He winked at Grant. "And Grant would be very pleased if the child could wait with you."

"Of course." She reached out her hands.

Grant felt a tug at his neck as Emmeline took the baby from him, and looking down, he saw his necktie had replaced the rattle in Arthur's mouth. He grimaced and reached into his pocket, then remembered he'd given his handkerchief to Mrs. Pinkston. "Thank you," he said to the vicar's wife, holding his soaked necktie away from his shirt.

Emmeline and Arthur left the room, and Harry walked toward the door. "Remain as long as you'd like, Grant." He motioned to the office. "I imagine you've some thinking to do."

Grant wasn't certain how to define the mess of emotions churning inside him or the spinning thoughts in his head. One overshadowed the others, and it filled him with an anxious dread. Clara was leaving, and he was powerless to stop her. "Harry, what do I do?"

Harry turned from the doorway. His smile was genuine and full of concern. "Ask her to stay."

Grant sank into a chair, rubbing his brow. The solution was hardly that simple.

When Grant entered the church, Clara was already seated in a pew near the back. He sat beside her, setting his hat in his lap. "Good evening," he whispered. Grant's recent revelation left him feeling self-conscious, and he wondered if he should have said something different.

Clara smiled and returned the greeting. "I brought all our supplies." She pointed at the satchel at her feet.

"I anticipate a successful rehearsal," he said. "Thanks to your planning."

"*Our* planning." She smiled again, and he noticed a dimple in her left cheek. He wondered if he'd simply not noticed it before or if her previous smiles had been guarded. Either way, she was lovely this evening. Her eyes were bright, twinkling in the candlelight, her hair shone softly, curling over her shoulders, and her demeanor appeared relaxed, which was the best indicator that she was not feeling anxious. He felt very pleased that her bashfulness around him had eased.

"I saw Mr. Herd today," she whispered.

"And how did you find him?"

"Happy," Clara said. "He insisted on singing 'The Coasts of Old Barbary.'"

Grant removed his gloves, put them into his hat, then set it on the pew beside him. "He is fortunate to have your visits."

"I enjoy singing with him." She tipped her head to the side, looking up at him. "I enjoyed singing with you as well." She looked down at her hands. "You have a pleasant voice."

"Perhaps I will accompany you next time?"

"I would like that." She ran her fingernail over a pleat in her skirt, watching the fabric as her cheeks colored. "And Mr. Herd would too, I'm sure."

Grant doubted it. He had seen the way the older man's face shone when Clara kissed him farewell and expected Philip would consider an addition to their merry singing party to be an intrusion. But he did not care one whit for what the old man thought. Clara's invitation and her compliment lit something warm inside him, and he savored the sensation.

Once Bible Stüdy ended and Harry left them alone with the children, Clara's easy manner changed. Her face paled, and she held her shoulders tight. She instructed the children to take their places in the choir pews, and Grant ushered them to their seats, climbing up onto the row behind the older boys.

Clara opened her satchel, removed the prepared signs, then crouched down, giving instructions to Annie. When she stood and faced the choir, she held her hands together tightly. "I'm so happy to see all of you at rehearsal." Clara's smile looked more forced than natural. "Since we do not need to learn the words to the song, we will work on singing together. The goal is to sound like one voice. So, as you sing, you should always hear the voice of the people beside you."

In the row ahead of Grant, Freddy Pinkston whispered something to Barty Newbold. Barty responded with a jab of his elbow. Before Freddy could get in a jab of his own, Grant leaned forward and patted each boy's shoulder. They quieted immediately.

Clara gave Grant a grateful smile. "Tonight, we'll practice breathing all at the same time throughout the song. But this means you need to watch me. When it is time to take a breath, I will make a motion like this." She raised her hands in front of her and at the same time lifted her chest as if she were breathing in. "If you forget the words, you can glance to the cards Annie is holding, but keep your eyes on me to know when to breathe. I'll demonstrate with the first lines."

Clara sang the first verse of "Gentle Jesus, Meek and Mild," drawing in an exaggerated breath between the phrases. She chewed on her lip, her brows furrowed as she looked at the choir. "Now, let's do it all together."

She raised her hands, and the children sang along with her. When they finished, she nodded. "Very good."

"You didn't breathe." Barty pushed Freddy.

"I did!" Freddy slapped his hand away.

Grant cleared his throat, and the argument stopped.

Clara motioned to Annie to switch signs. "Now, the second verse."

Once they sang the entire song and the children seemed to have mastered their breathing, Clara told them to sit.

"I am very pleased with your progress." She smiled, looking less nervous and revealing her delightful dimple. "In only a short time, you've begun to sound like an accomplished choir."

She motioned for Grant to join her. "Next week, we will work on presentation—how to walk to your places, how to stand, that sort of thing—but there is one last skill we need to practice today."

She turned toward Grant.

He nodded. "Yes, and this is where I come in. Our choir sounds beautiful here in the church, but the festival is out of doors, and you all need to sing much louder if you are to be heard." He reached into Miss Brightly's satchel and drew out a stuffed toy tiger the size of a small cat.

The children's eyes went wide. Some whispered and others gasped.

He cleared his throat and made a show of petting the toy while waiting for the children to quiet. "This tiger has come to us directly from India," he said, using the narrative he and Clara had come up with at the castle. "What is his name, Miss Brightly?"

"*Her* name is Sita."

He nodded, seeing he had the children's undivided attention. "Sita is going to help me today as we practice singing loudly."

"Singing in a loud voice isn't the same as yelling," Clara said, holding up a finger. "You must still sing as a choir, without anyone louder than the others."

"Sita goes higher when she hears a choir singing loudly, breathing together, and sounding as one voice," Grant said. He lifted the tiger high above his head. "But when Sita hears one voice louder than the others or thinks the choir is too soft . . ." He lowered the tiger and frowned, shaking his head as if it were a true pity to disappoint the toy tiger.

"Shall we see how high we can get Sita?" Clara said.

The children smiled, some whispered to one another, but all looked excited to see whether Sita would go up or down. Grant had thought the idea silly when Clara first proposed it, but seeing their eager expressions changed his mind. This simple game was precisely the thing to encourage them.

"Everyone stand, please," Clara said. She glanced at Annie, then at Grant. She raised her hands to begin.

As the children sang, Grant raised and lowered the tiger with their volume. He'd never have believed something as simple as a stuffed toy lifting up a few inches would have the effect it did. All the children sang in strong voices that rang out through the church.

He walked backward along the aisle, holding one hand behind his ear, and with the other, he lifted up the toy tiger, moving her a little higher as the voices grew. When he reached the back of the church, the choir started the last verse of the song. Their sound swelled, and he held up Sita as high as he could reach, then stepped onto a pew to hold the toy even higher. The choir's sound was enormous as the children sang with all their hearts.

The song ended, and the last note resonated.

The children's cheeks were rosy, their faces glowing with pride. Clara clasped her hands together, looking back at Grant as if he were a hero who had just slain a dragon instead of a choir director who had waved a stuffed toy above his head.

The church doors opened, and the vicar entered,

followed by the Ladies' Charity Society. And though he heard the applause and felt the cool air, Grant didn't look away from Miss Brightly. Her smile was full and her eyes shone, and in that moment, Grant knew Harry Barlow was right. He was in love with Clara Brightly. He only had to tell her, to ask her to stay, and he resolved to do so, but the moment must be perfect.

He smiled when the idea came to him. The perfect moment was just under a week away. He would declare his feelings at the Queen's ball.

Chapter 6

CLARA LOOKED THROUGH THE window of the East Cowes hotel suite, watching boats sail in and out of the River Medina. Gazing toward the Solent, she could see the battleship guarding the port as it did when the Queen was in residence. Earlier that day, Walter had pointed out the Queen's yacht—not that it needed pointing out. It would have been impossible to miss the enormous steamship with its royal pennants flapping on the masts. She let her gaze travel back to the street below. Night was falling, and gas lamps were coming to life. They would leave for the ball soon.

She and the Wickershams had arrived by train the evening before and taken rooms in a town close to the Queen's summer home at Osborne House. The trip had been very different from her lone journey a few weeks earlier. Traveling with the Wickershams—*being* with the Wickershams—was a delight. The pair were happy, and their conversation always uplifting. Clara could not imagine anyone loving their home as much as the Wickershams loved this island.

She centered the pendant on her necklace, her fingers brushing the filigree gold and dangling pearls. The ornate necklace was a gift from her father. Her throat tightened as she remembered her first ball at the Government House in Calcutta. Papa had looked so regal in his dress regimentals, his boots shined, and his medals sparkling in the light. He'd claimed her first waltz and kept a close eye on the younger officers who asked for a dance as the night went on. She swallowed hard, pushing down the tears that would leave her eyes puffy and cause her companions concern.

Hearing a knock, she crossed the room and opened the door.

Deborah entered in a flurry of feathers and lavender ruffles. When she saw Clara, she gasped. "Oh, don't you look lovely?" She took Clara's hands and held them as she stepped back to admire her. Her gaze traveled from the top of Clara's head to the tips of her shoes. "And Emily arranged your hair beautifully." She gave a satisfied nod. "Not that much work was needed."

"She did a lovely job." Clara turned back to study the hairstyle in the dressing table mirror. She was pleased with the style. The servant had pulled her tresses back into a complicated braided arrangement, leaving curls to fall over her shoulders and cheeks. A simple white orchid completed the presentation.

"And your dress . . ." Deborah let out a theatrical sigh. "Utterly splendid."

"Thank you." Clara adored the white gown with its lace-trimmed sleeves and full skirts. And Deborah's attention reminded her so much of her ayah that she couldn't help but smile. "You look very beautiful yourself."

Deborah flounced the ruffles on her skirt. "It is not every day one gets to attend a royal ball." She craned her neck to see the back of her dress in the mirror. "I've heard the Queen's residence has undergone some renovations since we were last invited. I am very curious to see what has been done." She adjusted a sparkling bracelet.

"I didn't realize you'd been to Osborne House before." A quiver moved through Clara's insides as it always did when she faced the unfamiliar.

Deborah turned back, but when she saw Clara, her grin died away. She shook her head and made a tsking sound. "You're nervous."

Clara grimaced. "I am, a bit. I shan't know anyone at the ball."

"Do not worry yourself." Deborah wagged her finger. "Walter and I won't leave you alone for an instant. And of course Grant Mason will be there. And his mother."

Clara's cheeks heated, and she kept her face turned down as she pulled on her gloves. Knowing Grant would be in attendance gave her both comfort and apprehension. Over the past weeks, she'd grown easy in his presence, feeling safe when Grant was near. But tonight was different, and she couldn't pinpoint exactly why. Instead of feeling calm, nervous shivers moved over her skin. What would Grant think of her gown? Would he ask her to dance?

One moment, she hoped he would, and the next, the very idea made her heartbeat race in panic. She pushed away the confusing combination. She was being silly. She'd seen Grant only five days earlier at choir practice. There was no reason to feel anxious. Grant was her friend, and she would be happy to see him. In spite of her self-encouragement, the nervousness returned, making her stomach feel even more constricted than when Emily had pulled tight her corset strings.

"The ball will be an intimate affair. The house has a small gathering area, not an enormous ballroom like you'd find in a palace," Deborah said. "I think you will discover it is quite magical." She came near and fluffed Clara's sleeves. "You know, Walter and I danced our first time at Osborne House." Her brows bounced, and her smile grew mischievous. "The setting is very romantic."

Clara fought a giggle, turning it into a smile. "I am glad to hear it. You found your true love at the Queen's ball. Just like in a novel."

Deborah sighed and clasped her hands. "My dear Wally really is charming, isn't he? And such a graceful dancer."

"Ladies, it is time." Walter's voice came from the passageway outside Clara's bedchamber exactly on cue. When Deborah opened the door, he kissed her cheek. "My dearest, you are a vision."

"Thank you, darling." Deborah fluttered her lashes.

Clara couldn't help but feel warm, seeing the two so happily in love.

Walter looked past his wife and smiled when he saw Clara, his crooked tooth making its appearance beneath his mustache. "Beautiful, my dear. I do believe you shall turn quite a few heads tonight."

The party rode the short distance to Osborne House in a hired carriage. They turned down a tree-lined road and emerged into a courtyard with a garden in the center. The carriage lane encircled a raised planter filled with purple bushes Deborah identified as heather. When they stopped before the grand house, Clara took Walter's hand and stepped down out of the carriage.

The house itself was made from yellowish brick and arranged with smooth columns, balconies, and a flat roof in a style Clara recognized as Italian. A tall tower rose from one corner, reminding her of a mosque. Dark mahogany wood surrounded the windows, and an arch held up by columns crowned the main door. Beautiful, but hardly imposing, she thought, a bit disappointed.

"The backside is much more impressive," Deborah said, as if reading her thoughts.

Footmen in regalia held open the doors, and the trio entered into a wide corridor. Elaborate tile designs covered the floor, paintings in carved frames decorated the walls between colored trim, and marble sculptures added life and dimension. They walked slowly, and Clara studied the artwork as they passed. Royal guards in their red coats with polished brass buttons stood at intervals along the passageway.

Walter left Clara and Deborah at the door to the ladies' dressing room. When they entered, all the ladies turned. Clara's muscles tightened and her nerves hummed with anxiety when she saw so many gazes looking in her direction.

Deborah began chatting immediately, introducing Clara as she went.

Clara searched the crowd for a familiar face and sighed in relief when she saw Mrs. Mason. The woman approached, having to elbow and squeeze all her bustles, feathers, and petticoats through gaps in the crowded room.

"I am so delighted to see you." She clasped Clara's hand, waving a feathered fan with the other. "Very warm tonight, isn't it?"

Clara nodded. The small room was stifling.

"Grant will be happy to see you as well," Mrs. Mason said. "Made me promise not to tell—" Her eyes went wide, and she closed her mouth so quickly that Clara heard her teeth click together. Her brows furrowed, and she looked to the side. "I . . . well . . . you'll enjoy the ball, Miss Brightly. I am sure of it."

If the room had been hot before, that was nothing to the heat spreading over Clara's neck and chest. What was Mrs. Mason not permitted to tell her? Did Grant intend to ask her for a dance? Why would he keep such a thing secret?

The air in the room buzzed with excitement. Seamstresses and maids tended to tears in skirts and unpinned curls, and ladies inspected their presentation in the mirrors. Clara attempted to concentrate on the conversations around her but only managed to give an occasional answer when asked a question directly. Her thoughts tumbled, and her insides trembled. Mrs. Mason's words had sent her already tensed nerves into a nearly manic state. She fisted her hands together tightly, knowing that leaving was not an option. It was, of course, an insult to the Queen, and it would also ruin the Wickershams' enjoyment of the evening.

She could do this. But what had Mrs. Mason meant? What did Grant ask his mother not to tell her?

The floor manager entered, calling for everyone's attention and informing the ladies that the procession was to begin.

Clara straightened her shoulders, following the crowd to the outer passage where they'd meet the men and enter all together into the ballroom. She gave Walter a smile when she took his arm, but inside, her heart pommeled.

He patted her hand where it rested on his arm. "No need to worry, my dear."

Deborah took his other arm, and they walked the remainder of the passageway to a pair of double doors that led outside onto a terrace. A rush of cool night air went over Clara's heated skin. The crowd thinned, spreading over the area, and she got a better look at her surroundings.

Lights illuminated the planters and balustrades, showing Italian fountains, statues, and gardens stretching off into the darkness.

"I told you," Deborah said. "The terraced gardens are utterly stunning."

"And farther down the path is the Swiss Chalet." Walter motioned with his chin off into the darkness toward the sea. "A charming playhouse built by Prince Albert for the royal children."

Some of the guests, Clara was happy to see, wore regimental uniforms, but most of the men were in dark coats and top hats. The ladies' dresses were a rainbow of colors, some with trains and head veils. The ball attendees clustered in groups on the far side of the courtyard near a door leading to another wing to the right of where they exited.

"This is the newer section of Osborne House." Deborah leaned forward around her husband to speak to Clara.

Clara nodded, scanning the crowd, hoping for a glimpse of Grant, but between the crush of people and the uneven lighting, she was unable to distinguish between all of the similarly dressed men. Trumpets sounded, and the crowd organized itself into a line. The doors were flung open, and the procession began.

Aside from the people directly in front of her, Clara couldn't see much as they made their way through the door and along a passageway. They emerged into a ballroom, joining the crowd to await the Queen's arrival, and she continued to scan between the other guests, searching for Grant. How could such a tall man blend so completely?

She'd been inside the ballroom for a full thirty seconds before she noticed her surroundings. And when she did look up, she froze. The room was an exact replica of a Sikh palace.

The walls and ceiling were stark white, every inch detailed in intricate plasterwork. The floor was a dark wood, matching the trim of the doors and the rails of the upper galley. Gold fixtures shone in the lamplight. Turning around, she saw a carving of Ganesh on the wall above the entrance, and over the enormous fireplace was an elaborately carved white peacock.

The emotions Clara had tried to push down came in a rush. India with all its ornate beauty surrounded her, and she felt overwhelmed, missing her father and her home all over again. The trumpets sounded, and the entire company turned toward the upper gallery. A herald called out, "Her Royal Majesty, Queen Victoria."

He stepped aside to reveal a small, wide woman. Even though Clara had only seen drawings, there was no mistaking Queen Victoria. The woman held herself with a regal bearing. She wore a black dress with wide petticoats, and a black lace veil covered gray hair beneath her jeweled crown. Diamonds hung at her neck and dangled from her ears.

Queen Victoria raised a hand, and the silent company lowered in bows and curtsies.

“We would like to welcome you all to Osborne House and the Durbar Room,” the Queen said. In spite of her size, her voice was strong, carrying easily through the space. “Do enjoy yourselves.” Queen Victoria held out her hands, then with an assistant, stepped away from the railing, settling into a chair where she could watch the dancing. At the Queen’s nod, an orchestra began to play.

“Shall we, then?” Walter tugged on Clara’s arm to lead her and Deborah from the dance floor.

Clara found it difficult to pull her gaze from the Queen. Victoria was at the same time the most beloved and most hated ruler in the world. How could one small woman possibly carry such a heavy charge? Clara decided in an instant that if anyone could, it was Queen Victoria. Power and strength radiated from her, though she hardly appeared physically strong.

The Queen’s blue eyes moved over the gathering, and for just an instant, her gaze locked with Clara’s.

Clara looked away immediately, thinking that staring at the Queen must be against some rule or another. She followed Walter to the side of the room, and before she could properly study the carvings, Grant Mason stepped into her path. At the sight of him, Clara’s breath caught.

“Miss Brightly.” Grant took her hand. He held her gaze, placing a kiss on her fingers. “You look very beautiful.”

Something about the way Grant spoke tonight was different. He seemed to study her closer than usual. Warmth spread from the spot his lips touched, and Clara's insides shivered. "Thank y-you." Her voice came out in a whisper.

Walter clapped Grant on the shoulder. "Mr. Mason. A pleasure to see you, sir."

Clara blinked, and a blush heated her face as she remembered there were others in the room. She took a step back.

Grant shook Walter's hand. "I'm always happy to see my old friend." He took Deborah's hand and bowed over it. "And Mrs. Wickersham, you are stunning this evening."

"Oh, do go on." Deborah swatted at him but smiled, her cheeks reddening.

"How do you like the room, Miss Brightly?" Grant asked.

Seeing his penetrating glance again, Clara was glad for an excuse to look up at the carved ceiling. "Utterly exquisite."

Grant looked up as well. "I'd hoped to see your face when you first entered. You were surprised?"

She turned fully toward him and waved a hand toward the room. "Is this what your mother promised not to tell me?"

He widened his eyes but nodded.

"I *was* surprised. And delighted. I . . . I feel like I am in a Sikh palace." She looked across the room at the peacock carving. "*Durbar* means both a formal reception and the place where such an event is held. I've only been in one other—at an assembly in Lucknow."

"Then shall we see it all?" He offered his arm, and when she took it, he led her around the edges of the chamber, moving among other guests who were making the same circuit. They gazed into glass caskets that held ivory work, copper vases, and a model of an Indian palace, studied gold vases and a display of Indian armor.

"I'd heard Her Majesty wished for a room to represent

her sovereignty in India"—Grant spoke in a raised voice to be heard over the orchestra—"but I had no idea. This is much more spectacular than I pictured."

Clara nodded but didn't answer. Seeing these reminders of India and, by extension, her father brought her emotions very close to the surface. They stopped before the entrance, looking up at the elephant-headed god.

"Ganesh," Clara said, glancing at her companion. "The god of good fortune and luck."

"I could use some of that," he muttered.

Clara studied him for a moment, waiting for him to clarify. "For the choir competition?"

He turned his head and looked at her. Seeing his brow wrinkle, Clara got the distinct impression he'd not meant his words to be overheard. "Among other endeavors."

"Such as?"

Grant glanced behind her, and she heard the music change. "Such as hoping you will agree to a waltz."

The jittery feeling returned, but it held less fear and more anticipation. "I would love to."

He led her to the floor, taking her hand and placing the other at her waist. Clara set her fingertips on his shoulder. She had noticed the broadness of his shoulders the first time they'd met, but seeing him in a formal coat, his carriage straight as he bowed, made her heart skip. Surely all the other ladies could not help but stare as well. He really was handsome.

Grant pulled her into the rhythm of the dance. "Tell me about your necklace."

"My father gave it to me when I turned eighteen." She didn't have to speak very loud at all for him to hear. "It's beautiful, isn't it?"

"I admit I hardly noticed it until now. The wearer's beauty far surpasses the ornamentation."

Clara drew a quick breath. She glanced up, but Grant's gaze was so intense that she stared instead at his necktie. What had he meant by such a compliment? And why had it completely scrambled her thoughts?

"Last time Mother was at Osborne House, she changed the entire color scheme of our home," Grant said. His lips twitched. "I wouldn't be surprised if she changes it all again—this time with an Indian theme."

"I hope she does," Clara said.

"You prefer that style?" he asked.

Clara nodded. "I quite like it. But of course, it holds sentimentality for me."

Grant regarded her, and again she got the feeling he had something on his mind tonight. Something had changed, and it felt significant.

"I have never seen your house." Clara spoke in a cheerful voice, hoping to lighten the mood. "In fact, I am not quite certain where it is. East of Brading, I know, and I assume near Mr. Herd's, since he is a tenant of yours."

"How rude of me. I will repair the oversight as soon as possible. Perhaps you'd come to dinner soon?"

"I didn't mean to solicit an invitation." She felt flustered, not only by the conversation, but the way he studied her gave the impression he was searching for an answer or expecting her to do or say something. "I was simply curious." Her arm grew tired, and she rested her hand more fully onto his shoulder.

"We would . . . *I* especially would love to have you. I believe . . . I *hope* you'll approve of it." For the first time since she'd known Grant Mason, he seemed uncertain.

"I will most definitely approve of the company," she said.

His hand tightened around her waist, pulling her closer.

The song ended and following Grant's suggestion, the

pair exited onto the terrace. The night was cool but refreshing after the confines of the ballroom. And while she was with Grant, Clara realized, she had hardly noticed the temperature. Grant fetched punch, and they stood near the balustrade beneath a gas lamp. Waves sounded in the darkness, muting the noise of other conversations, and the scent of roses perfumed the air. The evening was as close to perfect as Clara could conceive. She closed her eyes breathing in the sea air.

"Clara?"

Grant's voice held that same note of uncertainty she'd heard earlier, but it sounded husky as well. Clara's breath felt thick in her lungs, and her pulse was erratic. She turned toward him, and the sight of his deep gaze sent tingles over her skin.

He took the drink from her, set it on the railing beside his, and grasped her hand. "There is something I wish to tell you." He touched her cheek, and heat burst across her face. "I know we have only known one another a short time." Grant slid his hand to her shoulder. Clara's heartbeat was so loud in her ears that she feared she'd not be able to hear him. He breathed in and out, then leaned closer, his thumb rubbing over her collarbone. "Clara, I—"

"Miss Brightly, is that you?" a familiar woman's voice called from across the terrace.

The interruption shook Clara from the trance of Grant's eyes. She blinked, disoriented as she looked around for the speaker.

Grant stepped back.

"It is! It *is* her! It's Clara Brightly." The woman hurried toward them, pulling her red-coated companion into the circle of light.

Clara gasped, pressing her fingers over her mouth as her throat choked with tears. "Mrs. Henry. Major Henry." She hadn't seen her old friends since they'd left for England years earlier on military sabbatical.

Mrs. Henry pulled her into an embrace. "We were so sorry to hear about your father, my dear. Such a tragedy."

"Thank you." Clara wiped at her tears, accepting the major's offered handkerchief. "Please excuse my emotions. Seeing you was a bit of a shock."

"I understand." Mrs. Henry shook her head sympathetically.

"We were surprised to see you as well," Major Henry said. "I never heard the colonel mention having family on the Isle of Wight."

"I was sent here to stay with a distant cousin," Clara explained. "Oh, where are my manners?" She turned, holding a hand toward Grant. "Allow me to introduce my friend, Mr. Grant Mason. Mr. Mason, these are my dear friends from the residency compound in Calcutta, Major and Mrs. Henry."

There was no sign of Grant's former smile. His expression was reserved, and the warmth in his eyes replaced by suspicion. Clara was reminded of how distant he'd acted the first time they'd met.

"A pleasure." Grant inclined his head, exchanging greetings with the Henrys. "And what brings you to the Isle?"

"We are here on official business," Major Henry said. "Her Majesty brought in quite a few craftsmen to build the Durbar Room, and now that it is finished, we are to return them back to India."

Clara's mouth went dry, and she squeezed the handkerchief. "You are to escort a group? When do you depart?"

"The day after tomorrow." Mrs. Henry looked at the major, then back to Clara. "We'd be happy for you to join us, my dear."

"I have been hoping to return." Clara was finding it

difficult to breathe. At last, she'd found a solution to her dilemma. "I have missed India and my friends, but I do not wish to be a burden."

"Well, of course you shall come with us, then," Mrs. Henry said. She put an arm around Clara's shoulders. "And your company will be a pleasure—not a burden in the least."

"I will need to make some arrangements," Clara said. She didn't like the prickly feeling in her stomach. The final choir practice was in two days, and the day after was the festival. She'd come to love the Wickershams, and leaving them would be difficult. And Grant . . .

How would he react to her plan? But when Clara turned to find him, her heart sank.

Grant Mason was gone.

Chapter 7

GRANT SET THE LAST pile of quilts onto the Ladies' Charity Society's table. He inspected the ropes holding up the canvas tent and, after ensuring his mother and the other ladies didn't need anything further, he left to join the choir at the center pavilion. He'd cancelled the last rehearsal the evening before but had arranged to meet the children before the competition to show them their places on the stage and where they'd enter—perhaps ease some of their anxiety.

Grant rubbed his eyes. He had no idea what he was doing. If only . . . But he pushed away the thought. He'd spent three days analyzing every second of their interactions. What could he have said or done to change things? How could he have convinced her to stay? He'd hoped the ball would have been a turning point. The Durbar Room seemed the perfect place for Clara to leave behind her old life and begin a new one with—

He shook his head, clearing his throat against the tightness. Clara was gone, and he needed to accept it. He wanted to be angry with her for leaving him to direct the choir alone, but he couldn't manage the emotion. The only thing he felt was an ache, and if he allowed himself to dwell on it, to consider what might have been, to wish for "if only," then the ache grew, swallowing everything else. Today wasn't for feeling sorry for himself. The children, their parents, and his town depended on him.

He glanced at his pocket watch. An hour until the competition began. Did Annie remember the signs? Perhaps he would have the children practice the song one more—

His thought cut off as the sound of singing reached him. Grant froze as the music stirred his memory. It was "Greensleeves." That voice—it couldn't be.

He followed the music toward the pavilion, his heart pounding as the familiar voice moved over and through him. He stepped inside and allowed his eyes to adjust.

Clara stood alone on the stage, her eyes traveling throughout the crowd as she sang. When she saw him, her gaze locked on his, and she smiled, her eyes sparkling and her voice growing louder. The beauty of the song surrounded him like a warm quilt.

Grant's heart stretched until he thought it would burst.

She was singing for him.

The flood of sensations he'd felt when she sang at Philip Herd's house were nothing to the maelstrom that seeing her released. His insides shook. His heart beating against his ribs was nearly painful. Did he dare allow himself to hope?

When the song finished, Grant met Clara at the steps, taking her hand as she descended from the stage. "You came back."

Clara looked up at him. "I couldn't do it. I couldn't go."

He took her other hand, feeling her shaking.

"When the time came to step onto the ferry, my feet just wouldn't move."

He searched her face. "I thought you wanted to go home."

She nodded slowly and winced. "I realized India isn't my home." Her bottom lip shook, and her eyes shone with tears. "I thought it was. I ached for it. But it was the memories I missed. Without my father . . ." She swallowed, then took a calming breath. "Home isn't just a place. It's where I'm loved and with the people I love."

Grant tipped his head. "Oh? And who might those people be?"

She flicked her gaze to his, then looked back down, apparently fascinated with his necktie. "Well, of course the Wickershams."

"Of course." Grant moved closer.

"And Mr. Herd and Annie Warner."

"Yes." He released her hands and slid his arms around her waist. "Anyone else?"

"The choir," Clara whispered the words, her mouth nearly touching his lapels.

Grant tapped beneath her chin, lifting her face. "And the choir director?"

A blush flowed over her cheeks. "I suppose I do rather love him."

Grant didn't waste another moment. He touched his lips to hers, and when she responded by putting her arms around him, he pulled her against him. Her mouth was warm and soft, and Grant lost himself in the kiss, thinking how something he'd resented as much as directing a children's choir had brought him the greatest miracle of his life. Clara, the shy, lost young woman, had found a place here, had found a community, a family, a home. And she'd found him.

He drew back, resting his forehead against hers. "I love you, Clara Brightly."

Clara opened her mouth to respond, but applause sounded, and her eyes went round as she pulled back. Grant kept his arm tightly around her, not allowing her to flee, even though he knew she wished to run away and hide.

The children's choir, their parents, and practically the entire town of Brading filled the benches, clapping and cheering for the couple, calling out well wishes. Some of the older boys made faces, as if what they'd witnessed had caused them to become physically ill.

The Wickershams stood beside the stage; Walter wiped at his eyes, and Deborah pressed her hands to her heart, her face shining. Harry Barlow grinned, giving an approving nod while his wife wiped a tear. Even Philip Herd smiled.

"Oh, Grant." Mother hurried toward them. "And lovely Clara. Just imagine it. A summer wedding."

"The hawthorns will be blooming," Mrs. Pinkston said.

"I'm afraid life in Brading Parish does not allow for much privacy, Clara," Grant said in a low voice.

"I w-wonder if we should give an encore?" Clara said. Her voice sounded timid, but a teasing smile tugged at her lips.

Grant twirled her around, pulling her into his embrace and kissing her soundly. She'd make a fine caulkhead after all.

Jennifer Moore is a passionate reader and writer of all things romance due to the need to balance the rest of her world that includes a perpetually traveling husband and four active sons, who create heaps of laundry that is anything but romantic. She suffers from an unhealthy addiction to 18th- and 19th- century military history and literature. Jennifer has a B.A. in linguistics from the University of Utah and is a Guitar Hero champion. She lives in northern Utah with her family, but most of the time wishes she was on board a frigate during the Age of Sail.

You can learn more about her at: Authorjmoore.com

Made in United States
Orlando, FL
27 September 2023

37330286R00146